THE DARK LADY

Once again Jamie Stuart, the swashbuckling hero of *The Stuart Legacy* and *The Black Pearls,* finds himself on a collision course with danger. In this new adventure Jamie, the rightful heir to the throne of Scotland and England, is plunged immediately into a brush with a Spanish galley, from which he emerges unscathed—and somewhat richer. This is but a mild foretaste of things to come.

In London, Jamie is attacked by an assailant whom he soon discovers to be an agent of Spinola, an Italian admiral in Spanish service. After this skirmish Jamie hurtles headlong into one exciting encounter after another as he uncovers a sinister plot threatening the safety of the realm.

As always with Jamie, the intensity of the danger is matched by the beauty of the damsels who cross his path. He meets a woman of exceptional beauty—and exceptional temper. As luck would have it (Jamie's brand of luck!) she has four sisters, each as stunning and as spirited as the next. High adventure swirls around Jamie and his lovely ladies as the action moves from the shady dockside taverns to the

(Continued on back flap)

(Continued from front flap)

throne room of the magnificent Elizabeth I, whose brilliant mind and sharp tongue add spice to this fast moving tale of blackmail and skulduggery.

Other books by Robert Kerr

The Stuart Legacy
The Black Pearls

The Dark Lady
ROBERT KERR

STEIN AND DAY/*Publishers*/New York

First published in the United States of America, 1976
Copyright © 1975 by Robert Kerr
All rights reserved
Printed in the United States of America
Stein and Day/*Publishers*/Scarborough House,
Briarcliff Manor, N. Y. 10510

Library of Congress Cataloging in Publication Data

Kerr, Robert, 1899–
The dark lady.

I. Title.
PZ4.K417Dar   [PS3561.E646]   813'.5'4   75-37904
ISBN 0-8128-1894-6

1893243

Contents

THE DARK LADY

The Dark Lady

'How much longer are you going to be, Mr Artist?'

The young man with the bright red hair was leaning over the ship's side as he asked the question. The young man with curls of fair hair of whom he asked it was standing in a dinghy moored under the ship's bowsprit. At his feet stood a large pot of black paint. In his hand was a well-charged paintbrush. He was engaged in repainting the figurehead of the ship. A few hours before it had been a pink and buxom maiden, naked, with bright blue eyes and golden hair. Now it was becoming a gleaming black African girl with lips of a startling crimson.

'Isn't she marvellous?' asked the painter.

The red-haired man looked as if he was about to say Yes, but instead he said, 'What I asked was, how long do you think you're going to be finishing her off?'

The young man with the paintbrush thought about this for a moment.

'I'd like to give her another coat – look at those breasts – marvellous! But I expect she'll pass.'

'Don't be too long about it, Jamie.'

For more than ten days the ship had lain quietly in this creek on the Friesian coast among sandbanks and islands. Before that, they had stolen out of the Elbe with the ship's papers showing that they were bound on the most innocent of voyages down into the Bay and, naturally, with the most innocent of freights in the hold – grain, which they meant to sell in La Rochelle so that the skipper could find the cash for a homeward cargo of salt.

7

The whole of Hamburg knew the story by the time they sailed – and most of Hamburg believed it. The trouble was that there were unbelievers, especially among those who were taking the Queen of England's money. As Alan Beaton said at the time, 'This port is fairly hotching with English spies,' his blue eyes blazing with the thought of it. 'They make a note of every ship that leaves and send a signal to their screen of scouts.'

What the English wanted above all was news of somebody shipping stores to the Spanish garrison at Kinsale in Ireland.

'Somebody like us,' he said. For beneath the grain in the hold were muskets, arquebuses, pikes and even a last or two of good German gunpowder. For all this they were going to find a market among the Spanish commissaries with the expeditionary force in Ireland. But to find the market they had first to reach the Irish coast. And that was not so simple.

There was the weather. No sooner had the ship emerged from the Elbe than she ran into contrary winds. For days they could make no headway at all and the skipper, a German, decided that it would be too risky to attempt the northabout voyage round the Orkneys. Better to take the route through the Straits of Dover and along the English Channel.

Two hundred leagues of salt water haunted by the pirates of half a dozen nations and patrolled by the English navy. With a bit of luck with the weather, they would slip past Queen Elizabeth's watchful frigates. A bit of luck which the skipper proposed to improve on.

So, one day, the ship crept into a Friesian inlet where no prying eye was likely to detect her. Sails were furled, anchors were dropped and the crew was set to work with pots of paint and brushes. A black ship became a green one.

'All very well,' Jamie Stuart had said, 'but our figurehead will give us away. Give me a pot of black paint.'

And he had set to work altering the carved, naked lady suitable to a ship named *The Sea Girl of Hamburg*.

'Now we ought to change the name.' Alan Beaton jerked a thumb towards the black figurehead. 'Except that – '

'Of course,' said Jamie from his place on the dinghy below. 'From now on, she is *The Dark Lady*.'

8

A cruel light shone in Alan's eyes. 'Don't you know,' he said, 'it's bad luck to change a ship's name?'

Jamie waved his brush contemptuously. A drip of black paint fell into the dun-coloured water. He watched it sink and leave an iridescent patch on the surface.

'Everything I do this month is lucky,' he said. 'I'm a Leo.'

Alan walked away, irritated as always by his companion's flippancy.

Before the new paint was dry on her new name, *The Dark Lady* was warped out of her hiding place behind the dunes and resumed her course southwards along the Dutch coast, picking her way cautiously among the yellow sandbanks until the skipper thought he could risk fetching a course into deeper water. For two days after that the wind blew from the nor'-nor'-west and the sea tugged restlessly at the ship.

'This will blow itself out,' said the skipper. 'It's what is going to follow that we won't like.'

And what might that be? Jamie did not ask. He soon found out.

Next morning he woke with a start, bewildered. Half of his mind was still involved in the terrible dream that had oppressed him – the vision of rows of gleaming, naked men straining forward and back, the rhythmic churning of forty oars, the regular spurts of powerful movement.

It had been real, so real that the remembered horror of it had followed him out of sleep, so real that . . . He strained his ears again. Yes, by God, there it was, far away, the merest whisper, the faintest pulse.

And now it had gone, vanished utterly. If it had ever been there. If it had not been a nightmare conjured up from the past.

Jamie looked round, not knowing what time of day it was, if day or night, and able to deduce nothing from the light. After a minute, he became aware that one ingredient he had become accustomed to was missing from his world.

The rigging was not clacking against the spars. The ship's timbers were not creaking as they worked against one another. The hammock which had been his bed no longer swung from side to side on an arc which he could measure against the

9

planks of the deck below him. Everything was still – as still as if the ship had reached some harbour.

'Perhaps we have . . .'

At the thought, Jamie twisted his way down from the hammock and went over, barefoot, to a port, listening. He could hear nothing. He could see nothing. Nothing but a vague grey light, something between daylight and dark, across which threads of darker cloud were drifting.

He went out on deck, shivering as the cold night air folded itself about him.

A dense fog shrouded the ship, a chilly and intimate presence. He could see only a few inches beyond his outstretched hand. The wetness hung in rows of droplets along the ropes and fell to the deck with small, smacking noises. The sails hung, soaked and motionless. He could see no higher than the lower edge of the canvas.

He made his way cautiously to the side. A shape he recognized was standing there. Alan Beaton with hair as red as a torch and eyes as blue as ice; Alan Beaton was leaning on the rail looking out into the opaqueness.

'Have we lain long in this state?' Stuart asked.

'Wheesht, man,' whispered Beaton.

Stuart repeated his question, more loudly.

'The haar closed in two hours ago,' said Beaton, with a frown.

'Speak English.'

'This,' said Alan, waving his hand round in the mist. 'We call it a haar in Scotland – a sea mist.'

'Speak up,' said Jamie. But now he too had lowered his voice.

'There is something out there.' Beaton pointed into the nothingness where, on some invisible line, sky met water. 'Listen!'

This time Jamie heard it, the sound he had heard in his sleep, very faint and slow, but unmistakable, a rhythmic swish gradually swelling up and then abruptly breaking off: a sound he knew too well, and for the worst of reasons. A vessel was being cautiously driven by many oars through the fog-shrouded sea.

10

'A longboat warping a ship in the calm,' said Beaton.

Jamie shook his head. 'No.' he said, 'Something bigger.'

The thin wail of a whistle had sounded in the distance and the noise of rowing had abruptly ceased. An eerie and total silence fell on the sea, broken when a faint puff of wind set one of the lighter cords of the rigging thrumming against a spar.

Jamie breathed deeply once and then sniffed the air quickly. He muttered an exclamation.

'What's the matter?' asked Alan.

'Don't you smell it?'

'Smell what, for God's sake?'

'Out there,' said Jamie, 'a good culverin shot away, is a Spanish galley. All ships smell. Spanish galleys stink. If you had ever lived in one you'd know why. Would you like me to explain?'

The stench was carried to their nostrils, as unmistakable as a whiff from a cesspool. Rank bodies and ordure, foul bilge water slopping a few inches below men's feet – a hundred and sixty poor devils living and toiling in their own filth. Jamie knew. He had rowed in one.

The skipper loomed up abruptly through the veils of mist – pink skin, blond hair, grey eyes, set in reddened rims. He spoke in his German English with his mouth close to Jamie's ear.

'You heard that?' He nodded seawards.

'A galley to starboard. Spanish, I should think.'

The German nodded. 'Frederico Spinola has eight of them based on Dunkirk. It will be one of his.'

'Spinola?' said Stuart. 'Spanish?'

'Italian. Genoese.'

'A pirate?'

The skipper laughed quietly.

'Carrying the King of Spain's commission as a privateer. Besides, he is rich in his own right. Banking money. Millions of ducats. Rich men are not usually called pirates.'

'Galleys? In the North Sea?' Alan was amazed.

But the skipper nodded emphatically.

'But when the sea is quiet as it is now,' he said, 'they are just the craft for a fast raid on the English harbours. Spinola

11

has sworn that one day he will burn all the shipping in the Thames.'

He pointed eastwards with his thumb.

The three men gave a start. The baleful shout of a trumpet came out of the mist, closer than they had expected. A minute later, another trumpet sounded, behind them and further off.

'That's two of them, calling one another,' said the skipper.

'We're lying between them,' said Jamie. 'The cannon ought to be loaded. Langrel shot to smash the oars would be best.'

He caught his breath. Out there on the starboard quarter, the fog had worn thin. And across a grey vacancy in the darker grey of the fog, moving between the invisible sky and the unreflecting sea, glided a long, low shape.

It would not have been possible to guess its length, in that light, but Jamie had no need to guess. It would be about a hundred and twenty feet from stem to stern.

Its oars were poised, motionless above the water, and lifted like wings. Its sail – a lateen, shaped like the thorn on a rose – hung without life. It had elegance, like a snake's. Given the right conditions of wind and water, this was the fastest thing afloat.

He could make out grey figures on the galley's coursier – the gangway that ran between forecastle and poop, a few feet above the rowers. Then, as suddenly and silently as it had appeared, the galley was swallowed by the half-night of the mist.

He heard creaking noises and felt a slight shudder go through the ship. Orders were given and carried out with almost no noise. This was a ship accustomed to clandestine work.

Fugitive noises beside him. Barefooted seamen were dropping expertly into the longboat. The skipper was going to tow the ship as far as possible from the spot where it had been detected by the galley.

Jamie felt his way, one step at a time, along to the captain's cabin.

There on the table, lit faintly by a tallow dip, a chart was spread out. Jamie peered down on it. The skipper pointed with one leg of the pair of compasses he was holding.

'We're here,' he growled in answer to Jamie's unuttered question. 'Drifting south-west at three knots in a strong current.

One galley is here. The other, there. They will try to find one another. And they will succeed, I think.'

The two trumpets sounded again, farther off than they had been before.

'But it is not so easy. In fact, it can be tricky. The current is shifting all the time and the shoals can shift, too.'

The chart showed that they were already dangerously near the outer shoals.

'Four fathoms at the last cast of the lead,' said the skipper.

The ship should not need as much as that to keep her afloat – but she was carrying more cargo than she ought to, with the military stores in the hold, beneath a full load of grain.

He could feel a tug and a tremor. The dead mass of the ship was beginning to respond to the urging of the rowers in the longboat.

Out in the fog the whistle sounded again. Then the slow beat of many oars, a rhythmic throb that seemed to come from all directions at once in the ghostly obsession of the fog, and seemed to grow louder at every moment. The skipper listened intently.

'With a bit of luck they will collide,' said Jamie.

They went out into the gloom of the deck. Jamie could tell from the skipper's face as he whispered with the leadsman that very soon they must anchor or run aground.

A man shouted in alarm.

Lurching out of the thick air, abrupt and sinister, came the spectacle of a beaked prow, pitch black, save where the carving on it was picked out in gold. It was higher by some feet than the deck of the ship. On it stood a row of men, helmeted and armed with arquebuses. On a tier immediately below were five cannon in a row.

The galley was moving unsteadily athwart the ship's course. Whistles blew shrilly. Orders were shouted in Spanish and German. Two rudders were put hard over. Jamie heard the crack of whips falling on naked backs. Cries of pain or rage. Too late to escape what was coming.

The crash seemed to lift the deck clean out of the water. Jamie was thrown breathless against the ship's rail. Green water poured on to the deck.

The galley had struck *The Dark Lady* a diagonal blow. Now it scraped along the ship's side. A loud splintering came from it, the sound of oars breaking like twigs. Screams coming from the rowers who had not been able to save their sweeps, fifty-foot spars of elm, from the impact.

Dark faces appeared for an instant, startlingly close, and were lost almost at once in the thickness of the air.

It was all over in a couple of minutes. The crew of each vessel made frantic haste to disengage their craft from the other. Boathooks and oars were plied.

Then, after a wild moment of rasping, swaying hesitation, the galley swung round. Her carved and gilded stern was visible for a second. Then it vanished behind the curtain of mist. But not before Jamie had read a name in gold letters.

A shout in Spanish came from the dripping opacity of the sea. 'What ship are you?'

Jamie made a funnel of his hand and opened his mouth. But he said nothing.

There was silence on the sea. Silence and emptiness.

Jamie turned to Alan Beaton.

'They say lightning never strikes twice in the same place,' he said. 'A common fallacy.'

'No doubt,' said Alan, soothingly.

'Listen. That galley is called *The Trinidad*. You saw her name. Well, on *The Trinidad* I served for six months as a galley slave. Then the Dutch captured her and I was freed. But it seems that somehow Spinola has won her back again.'

'If you aren't damned lucky, my boy, you'll be serving another six months on her before you're much older.'

Jamie shook his head.

'Don't believe it, Alan!'

'No?'

'No. The captain of *The Trinidad* was called Don Alfonso Saavedra. If he still has the job I'd like a word with him.'

As he was about to turn away, they were joined by a third figure, a dark young man with a badly scarred face and a soft voice.

'Who was that bastard who bumped into us?' said Alistair MacIan, white-faced because of a queasy stomach. He was a

14

Highland outlaw, a comrade of Jamie's. His costume, a shirt with a plaid belted about it, might have come straight out of the glens. He had climbed miserably up on deck from his malodorous bunk below.

'That was a Spanish bastard,' sneered Alan. 'But don't worry, Jamie is going to deal with him.'

Alistair's expression grew less wan.

'Does Jamie want to fight him?' he said.

Alan looked at him in disgust. Another mortal fool!

'Surely the weather is suddenly better,' said Alistair. 'Less of that – '

He made a seesaw movement with his hands.

'The weather is wonderful,' said Alan bitterly. 'With any luck it will stay this way for a week. We can't move. We will just ride here until we are gobbled up by those Spanish galleys. Are you ready to face the Inquisition, Alistair?'

'I'm a Catholic,' said the Highlander. 'At least. I think I am.'

'Brother, if you think that is going to save you from the *auto-da-fé*, you have a nasty surprise coming.'

The weather suddenly changed. Jamie felt that one cheek had become colder than the other. A sail whimpered. A cord clacked against a spar once or twice. For a moment, that was all. Then the skipper appeared. He leant over the ship's side. Orders in far-carrying German were growled out into the fog. He turned to Jamie.

'A wind from the east has sprung up. All this' – his arm was flung out towards the unfolding mist – 'will be blown away. Then we'll be able to see where we are going.' The skipper grinned and rubbed his bristling scalp with the knitted cap he was wearing.

Jamie decided it would be unmannerly – if not worse – to point out that the galley captain would be able to see *them*. And that a galley, with oars pushing and sails pulling, would be able to outsail a merchantman in any weather, short of a gale. He grinned back at the skipper.

'Good,' he said. 'Good.'

'A fight?' said Alistair eagerly.

'Very likely.'

'Good.'

15

Jamie smiled at the Highlander's twisted face which some women had the bad taste to find attractive.

'The wind,' said Jamie, 'is in the right quarter. It will blow us in the direction we want to go.'

There was a hint of derision in the skipper's shrug. He seemed to be saying that in these waters the wind was no reliable friend to honest seamen. But his attention was caught at that moment by something above them. He pointed upwards. Jamie looked. The weather was clearing fast; already he could see, between passing rags of mist, the peak of the mainmast.

The wind was freshening. Somewhere just below where he was standing, the sea was giving the hull a quick succession of little slaps. He thought that the ship had some way on her. The sounds he heard, a special mixture of squeal and clank, meant that the rudder was being used. The skipper, obviously a man who knew his business, was trying to enlarge his offing from the Flemish coast. He had no intention of being caught between the galleys and the shoals.

A seaman scrambled up to the crow's nest. Two others were fastening netting above the bulwarks. Defence against boarders. A heavy rumbling below told Jamie that the eight culverins on the gundeck were being made ready for action.

The skipper appeared at Jamie's side.

Straining his eyes, Jamie thought that a lighter area in the mist to the south was faintly suffused with yellow. No outline was visible. But somewhere over there would be the coastline of Europe, the low-lying muddy plain across which the Rhine and the Scheldt crawl their last few miles to the sea.

The sky was lightening fast. In twenty minutes' time, he would be able to tell whether they were going to have a free run to the Straits of Dover. After that . . . After that, it would be a question of keeping clear of the English navy.

He could feel the ship shudder a little as her sails took the wind.

'Yes, it was just about thirteen years ago . . .' The skipper had come back.

Jamie worked it out in his head. He must mean the battle the English had with King Philip's Armada.

16

Ten minutes later, he sighted Alistair MacIan and observed that he had now more colour in his cheeks, and that the glint of battle was in his eyes.

'You ignorant Highland robber, do you know what happened here thirteen years ago? No? The Spanish Armada was drifting on to those sandbanks you can see. The English fleet was waiting for the poor souls to drown. When what happened, do you think? God changed the wind and the Spanish galleons were saved?'

'Not all of them,' said Alistair softly. 'My uncle, Duncan, had the honour of looting one that God had mercifully put ashore on the coast of Ardnamurchan.'

'You will be able to tell that story to the admiral of the galleys.'

'What galleys?'

'Look there.'

On the eastern horizon, with the grey morning behind them, were two low black shapes. Something shimmered on either side of the vessels. Oars were moving in unison and catching the light as they rose and fell.

At that moment, he was aware that the ship's course was being abruptly altered. Very soon the galleys would be hidden by the poop.

The skipper was going to make a bid to outdistance the pursuit. A forlorn hope.

The Dark Lady, a sturdy Baltic cargo carrier, had a reasonable turn of speed. But with this sea, this faint breeze, any galley would overtake her in half an hour. Unless the fog . . . He scanned the sky overhead. But the treacherous clouds seemed to be thinning out.

Alan Beaton was beside him.

'The skipper says we should sight the English coast in an hour,' he said.

'And then what?'

Alan shrugged.

'There is a swivel gun up on the poop, James. Very useful against boarders, so they say. Can you handle one?'

'I can learn,' said Jamie.

17

From the poop he saw that the two pursuers were now in line ahead. The sea was rougher.

Half an hour later, the first cloud of smoke billowed out from the leading galley. The shot fell a cable's length astern and wide. The wind tore at the column of water it raised.

From below – the gundeck – a sound of men cheering.

The crew was a mixed lot – German, Dutch, Norwegian and one who looked like a Turk – but he thought they had been in a fight before.

The second shot whistled through the rigging above his head. By this time the first galley was near enough for him to see the brown blur of men's faces on her fo'c's'le. Beneath them were the black mouths of five cannon – twenty-four pounders, by his reckoning. Below them the galley's ram thrust its steel barb menacingly forward. Every few seconds the thrust of oars plunged that ugly grey lance into the restless green water.

The prow of the galley was suddenly hidden by smoke, pierced by darts of flame.

Over the water came a metallic, discordant noise like a hundred bells out of key.

'What the devil is that?' shouted Alan Beaton, crouched at the ship's rail beside Jamie.

'That is the slaves,' said Jamie grimly. 'Clashing their fetters. An old trick. It shows they are coming in to attack. It's meant to frighten you. If you listen carefully, you will hear the whips cracking to make sure that the noise is loud enough.'

The ship seemed to stagger once. A noise of wood splintering. A whistle blew. Shouts. Men scampering along the deck. Minutes passed. Another salvo from the galley.

So suddenly that Jamie was almost thrown off his feet, tackle screamed in the blocks, the big sails above him shuddered and snapped like musket-shots. The ship put about towards the galleys. In a few minutes she was running along the galley's side close in and her port cannon spoke one after the other.

The langrel shot, clumsy, articulated projectiles of no remarkable accuracy, were capable of doing cruel execution to a bank of oars at short range. Jamie thought the galley had slowed up. But he was too excited to be sure.

The ship lurched again. More frantic work with the tackle. The skipper – handling his old tub of a merchantman as if it were a pinnace – was driving the ship between the first galley and its follower. As they passed through the gap, Jamie could read the carved and gilded name on the stern of the leader. *Santissima Trinidad.*

This was a bold manoeuvre by the skipper because, apart from the stern-chaser which it may carry, a galley can only fire its cannon dead ahead. But the skipper was steering his ship directly across the galley's line of fire. If he counted on taking her unawares, he was taking a big risk. He had professionals to deal with. The second galley's forward guns fired a salvo.

The starboard cannon of *The Dark Lady* replied, raggedly. Then the oars struck the water again in a flurry of foam and the galley sprang forward. The ship, altering course once more, swept along the galley's side, raking her oars with cannon shot. A few minutes later she was working her way against a strengthening wind in the direction of the coast.

Jamie looked back. With the agility of their kind, the galleys had turned in their own length. Then, for a moment, they hesitated. Something had happened to make their admiral change his mind.

At that moment, the skipper's head showed at the poop steps. All his teeth were taking part in a grin.

'End of battle,' he announced. He waved a hand towards the sky. 'Gale coming up. They will need all their luck to reach Dunkirk harbour before it overtakes them. But before they go, we will give them another present to remember us by.'

The galleys were labouring against the wind as they went home. The sea was showing many white caps. It would be wet and cold on the rowing benches.

Alistair MacIan prodded the deck peevishly with his broadsword. 'When does the fighting start?' he asked.

'Just wait a little,' said Jamie.

'There might be good pillage on that ship,' said Alistair. 'These Spaniards are shamefully rich. Uncle Duncan was shocked at their luxury.'

The two galleys were sailing abreast when once more the ship passed between them. Jamie heard a rending crash above

19

him. A shot from a culverin had brought *The Dark Lady*'s mizzen mast down in a tangle of cord and sailcloth. The ship jolted under successive shocks as the port and starboard cannon blared into life.

The seaway between the vessels narrowed to a few yards. One after another, round black holes appeared on the dark, shining hulls of the galleys. One slowed down perceptibly; the other, amid a confusion during which its oars backed water and its rudder swung hesitantly, slewed inwards and struck the *Lady* a glancing blow which sent her lurching against the sternworks of *The Trinidad*. Between the three ships the sea churned madly. Groaning, the timbers strained against one another.

On the galley's stern gallery, men aimed arquebuses. Other men with swords and pikes got ready to jump down on to the ship's poop. Jamie and Alistair crouched to meet the attack. Three swarthy swordsmen in armour were the first to make the jump. Obviously, they had experience in this kind of fighting, for they timed their jump nicely to conform to the upward heave of the ship's deck. Jamie engaged at once, pressing his attack against a burly brute with a crimson headscarf and conspicuous ruby ear-rings. At his side Alistair was fighting in his usual vehement style.

After a few seconds a whistle sounded from the galley. A man's voice shouted in Spanish. The boarding party was being recalled.

Behind him Alan's voice spoke through a speaking trumpet from the maindeck below: 'The English fleet is in sight.'

The Spaniard who wore the ear-rings took a step backwards to avoid a lunge from Jamie. For a second he stood awkwardly, but just then one of his comrades on the galley aimed a caliver at close range. Jamie felt the wind of the shot pass his cheek.

When the smoke had cleared away, the boarding party had clambered back to the stern gallery of *The Trinidad*. The two ships were edging further apart. The ear-ringed Spaniard made an insulting gesture at Jamie.

I'll know that one next time, he thought. The hard black eyes, the cheekbones, and the ear-rings.

A second later, it was no longer possible to leap from one

ship to the other. Men with axes were hacking away at the tackle which held the broken mast.

From somewhere in the distance came the rumble of heavy guns.

'And now,' said Alan, 'we'll get on with our business. The English warships will look after the galleys. They will have no time for us and, with any luck, we'll be out of their reach by nightfall.'

'We'll need more than luck,' said the skipper, sourly. 'The carpenter will have to fit a new mizzen mast before we can chance a run through the Channel.'

Two weeks later, after hugging the French coast as far as Ushant, they headed into the Atlantic. There they sighted, through driving mist, the frail outline of a headland which the skipper recognized. He pointed. 'Ireland! Now it is for you, Herr Beaton, to find your Spanish friends.'

At nightfall, Alan and Alistair MacIan were rowed ashore in the longboat while the ship faded back into the sea mists and crept cautiously to the secret rendezvous they had agreed on. There, off that damp Atlantic coast, Jamie kicked his heels in boredom and caught an outrageous cold. Until one night Alan gave the expected signal from the shore. When he came aboard, the frosty sparkle in his blue eyes told the story.

'Boy, we're rich!' he cried as soon as he saw Jamie. 'Rich! Do you want your share of it in gold or in silver! Just say.'

'Tell me about the business,' said Jamie.

'What those poor devils of Spaniards need most of all is food,' said Alan. 'To get the grain we are going to bring them, they are willing to buy our muskets. In my opinion, the English will win this war,' he added.

'But what has become of Alistair?' asked Jamie.

Alan shrugged.

'He stayed.'

'Stayed, eh! What did he stay for, man?'

'For one thing, he can speak the language. And the truth is that Alistair has met an Irish girl.'

'Good God!'

'Haven't you noticed that women have a soft side for

Alistair?' said Alan. 'I remember my sister Mary thought him attractive.'

'Your sister Mary has damned peculiar taste,' snapped Jamie.

'Just so, man, just so.' Alan kept a malicious blue eye on the horizon.

'What kind of people are these Irish?' said Jamie, after a pause.

'Big, fine-looking fellows, brave as lions.'

'And the girls?'

'The girls,' said Alan Beaton. 'Magic. Sheer magic.'

'You said the men would make good soldiers.'

'It's my opinion that Alistair is minded to recruit a company of them for service in foreign parts. He can see the way matters are going in Ireland and, d'ye know, he has the idea he'd like to visit that place in Russia. What's its name?'

'The domes of the Kremlin! The palace of the Tsars! Moscow.'

Jamie was echoing a phrase he had heard often enough from a friend of his, a Scottish mercenary officer, Captain George Sinclair, who dreamed of marching with a Scots contingent when the Swedish king decided it was time to invade Russia.

'That's it. Strange how notions like that stick in people's minds. Well – one thing at a time! We aren't safely out of this business yet, James. We'll put the cargo ashore as fast as we can. We'll collect the money and – '

'How much?'

Alan smiled broadly.

'How many yellow-boys? More than you've ever seen before. But we've still to touch it. And there's no time to lose! The English already know that we are loitering in these waters. Their spies are at work all the time. The diabolical cunning of these people! Amazing!' His bright blue eyes were round with astonishment. Then a new thought occurred to him. 'When it's over, where do you mean to go, Jamie?' he asked. 'My sister will want to know that the next time I write to her.'

Alan's sister, Mary Beaton, was a beautiful girl James had met first in Edinburgh. He loved her as dearly as he was capable of loving any woman.

'I have a mind to see London,' he said.

Alan Beaton nodded with approval.

'It's a wonderful town to do business in,' he said. 'In fact, I am thinking I might go there myself. Provided the English spies don't know what we've been up to here . . . You will need to be careful how you travel there. The best plan would be for you to slip ashore in some port in Britanny – you have a French passport, haven't you? Then you can go up the coast to Calais and take the packet over to Dover.'

Jamie shrugged.

'There will be some way of doing it, I expect,' he said.

'See that I give you an address in London where I can reach you if I want to,' said Alan.

The Dark Lady heeled over suddenly as the wind filled her sails. Already the Irish coast was growing faint astern.

Jack Scream

The door of the Rose of York tavern down beside the river, a bowshot above the Bridge, was kicked open by somebody whose sense of authority was stronger than his manners. In the taproom, the noise of water slapping a stone quay outside was suddenly louder. It was loud enough for the elderly potboy to look up from what he was doing, which was rinsing out pewter mugs, and set eyes on the two men who had come into the house. Not that they were a sight either pleasurable or, in this part of the city of London, unusual.

The first of them, a muscular man beginning to run to paunch, had cold grey eyes which took the room in with a quick, left-right, up-down glance before fastening on the potboy. The second man, taller, thinner and just as unfriendly, stayed in the doorway leaning his shoulder against the hinge. It was the first man who did the talking.

'Name of Scream,' he said, without any preliminaries. 'Mr Jack Scream.' His voice was loud and pitched high, the kind of voice that ought not to be used for shouting. But apparently it had been.

'You asking me,' said the potboy after a few moments, 'or telling me?'

The grey-haired man put his little finger in his ear and shook it violently. He took a step forward. When he spoke again, his voice was even louder than before and higher-pitched. And his thumbs were hooked in his belt in an aggressive attitude.

'Asking,' he said. 'Or demanding information in the name of Her Majesty, Queen Elizabeth. Put it any way you like . . .

24

Jack Scream? Anybody of that name living in these parts?'

While the two men watched him, the potboy's gaze flitted slowly and incuriously across the ceiling where the reflected light from the river below executed a lively jig.

'Scream,' he said, thoughtfully.

'Jack Scream. Not a name likely to slip your mind if you heard it once.'

'Sounds to me like a Frog,' said the potboy.

'That's something which is not in the documents.'

After a short pause, the potboy seemed suddenly to awaken to interest.

'What does he look like?' he said.

The grey-eyed man thrust his chin forward.

'Like a man we want to meet, so we can put a few friendly questions to him, like! Big man. Fair-haired. Handy with the cutlass, they say! Not the sort of lodger for a respectable house. Could be nasty, for all concerned. See? Does all this call anybody to mind?'

The potboy was inspired suddenly.

'Has he got a limp? Chap in here the other night had a limp!'

Grey Eyes exchanged looks with his mate. Then he shook his head, and looked back at the potboy. There was no friendliness in his gaze.

'Know nothing about any limp.'

'Ah. Does he have a husky voice?'

The first intruder took his thumbs sharply out of his belt. 'At this time of year most people have a husky voice,' he said, and moved towards the door. 'Keep your eyes open and see you smarten up your memory. Remember! Jack Scream. Wanted for questioning by the law.'

'Tried the Mitre?' asked the potboy. 'They get all kinds there. Dutch, Portugals, now and then a blackie, even.'

The two men looked at him hard and went out, saying nothing. Grey Eyes went first, his companion flattening himself against the door to let him pass.

The potboy waited until the door had slammed and he had heard two men dropping into a boat which had been moored at the steps leading down to the river. He did not move until

25

his ears had picked up the splash of oars. Then he put down the mug he was holding and opened the door.

He looked down towards the river, a few yards away, and up to where the alley twisted and a jutting corner of masonry shut off the view farther along the street. There was nobody in sight either way. He shut the door thoughtfully and made his way wheezily upstairs.

He knocked at a door, opened it and looked inside.

A broad-shouldered, blond young man in his shirtsleeves was making elegant shadow passes with a sword. The potboy knew enough of the art to realize that this was a stylish performance, which might mean that the swordsman was a gentleman. Or might not. Who was to know! The young man paused in his exercise and looked at the potboy with a good-natured, satirical expression.

In one corner, a scabbard leant against the wall. Near it stood a signboard on which was painted in an ornamental Gothic lettering the words, 'Monsieur Jacques, Escrime'. The potboy looked at it gloomily and pointed his thumb towards it.

'Jack Scream,' he said, morosely. 'Been people here asking for him.'

The young man likewise looked at the signboard. A few months before it had hung outside the building in Copenhagen where, in an hour of dire need, he had set up in business as a French teacher of fencing. As a commercial venture it had paid him well. He was sentimentally attached to the signboard.

'People,' he said, in his low throaty voice. 'Meaning who?'

'Meaning rats,' said the potboy. 'Two rats.'

'Black rats or brown rats? There's a difference.'

'Black.'

'That's the bad kind. Did you know? The kind that brings the plague.'

'It's bad all right,' said the potboy. 'It brings trouble. It brings the lock-up, the rack, the rope. Horrible things. Poor innocent men can suffer just because – '

'In England? I don't believe it.'

'You'd be surprised.'

The young man, as if to brush away all despondent thoughts, executed a flashing series of passes with his sword.

26

'Very nice,' said the potboy without enthusiasm. 'Very pretty, I'm sure. But if I were you, sir –'

The young man stopped.

'If you were me,' he said, 'you would leave this town without losing another minute. Vanish. Take ship to the Indies and come back no more. That's it, isn't it? Well, thank you for your advice but, if you'll forgive me, I shall not be taking it.'

The young man slipped his sword back into its sheath. He smiled a little as he did so. He always liked that frail noise of the sliding steel.

'For one thing, I am not Mr Jack Scream. On the contrary, I am a Scottish gentleman named James Stuart –'

'You don't sound like a Jock to me.'

The young man made a showy gesture of regret that was as Scottish as could be imagined.

'My misfortune. Bad upbringing in foreign parts. But you've seen my passport. A mistake of identity somewhere. How it arose I can't for the life of me think. But rumour, gossip, slander! Keep clear of all that, friend!'

Stuart and the potboy had been looking thoughtfully at the signboard. Now their eyes met. Stuart was smiling amiably.

'Something else,' he said, clearing his throat. 'I have only just arrived here, after perils and hardships on the seas that would freeze your blood in the hearing. And now that I'm here, I mean to stay for a bit. Beautiful town. Nice people. Interesting things to see. The centre of the world's business they say. Maybe it is. Anyhow, I like it. As for this person Scream, forget him. He doesn't exist. He is a figment of the imagination, a phantom conjured up by wood, paint and human ignorance. Look! I turn him to the wall – gone!'

The signboard now showed a plain black surface to the room.

'You could burn it,' the potboy pointed out.

Stuart shook his head emphatically.

'Burn it! It's my luck. Where I go, it goes.'

He took a silver coin out of a purse and handed it to the potboy.

'To help you to forget things. By the way, did your friends happen to say what they wanted with Mr Scream?'

27

'They have questions to ask him. Questions . . . That's an ugly word, sir.'

Stuart shook his head disapprovingly.

'People shouldn't give way to curiosity,' he said. 'It can bring bad luck.'

He pulled his shirt over his head.

'And now,' he went on, 'if you please, hot water to shave with.'

The potboy paused at the door and looked back. On Stuart's shoulder was a curious red mark which seemed to form three letters on his flesh. But perhaps it was a trick of the light. The potboy could not be sure.

Stuart looked at his own image in a small mirror of polished metal which hung on the wall. 'How far can I trust him?' he asked it. He rubbed the shining bristles on his chin. 'No distance at all, Jamie,' they rasped in answer. It was sad but probably true. 'These are the risks of the trade,' he told himself. 'But at present they have got the wrong name. Somehow they've got it wrong. So the fact is that I've had worse luck before. And if the worst comes to the worst, I can always' – his eye, through the small window of his room, took in the urgent and ochre-coloured stream outside. It didn't smell the way it had done a few hours earlier, when the water was low, and a gleaming silver-grey stretch of mud was visible just underneath the window of the tavern. Then it had smelt like a drain, which, when he came to think of it, was one of the things it was.

Barges were working their way up from the lower reaches with the tide.

Rowed hard against the current, four oars on each side, and a man with a boathook erect in the bow, came an imposing craft. Under an awning which covered it amidships sat a grim-faced presence wearing a fur-trimmed cloak.

Some official going to inspect the queen's ships downriver or on his way to an audience with Her Majesty herself in that palace she had some miles down the estuary. In a flash of dripping sculls, the boat was out of sight.

Jamie's eyes ran along the huddle of houses on the opposite bank. That was the bad quarter of the town. He had been warned about it. Haunt of actors, whores, pimps, crimps and every kind of furtive creature. A row of painted signs faced him across the river: the Tabard, the Cardinal's Hat, and so on – whorehouses all of them, traps for foolish young men, hatching grounds of every kind of villainy.

'I can always find a hiding place there,' he said. 'No trouble at all. I have only to walk across that marvellous bridge –' From where he was standing, he could see the far end of it, shops crowding on top of it, and the grim row of skulls on poles above the roofs – 'and I am as safe as I would be in the Cour des Miracles in Paris' – which was a part of that city he had once known where even the bravest of criminal lieutenants did not dare enter.

A second later he put away the thought of flight – even the remotest possibility of it – as unworthy of him. After all, what was the chance that anybody would want to do him any harm? 'Jack Scream...'

He had brought the signboard with him in the boat from Hamburg. It was in that seaport, among the sailors, that he had first heard someone say with a laugh, looking at the signboard, 'Jack Scream.' Now somebody in London was asking for a man of that name. No doubt it was pure coincidence.

'Besides,' he said cheerfully, 'there is one thing that makes a lot of difference in your situation. You are rich, Jamie. By daring and prudence, to say nothing of the generosity of Alan Beaton, you have an impressive pile of big gold coins all tucked away in that strongbox at the jeweller's. For the first time in your life, you need only be careful. No foolish extravagances, no excess of vanity when you go to the tailors, and no girls! Above all, no girls! You have given up all that sort of thing! You are well-to-do, respectable – a sober citizen well on your way to making a fortune – so behave accordingly, James Stuart! Don't you agree, friend?'

The potboy, to whom the last question was addressed, had come in holding a jug of steaming water. He looked ill-at-ease.

'I was just saying to our friend here,' said Stuart, nodding to his image in the mirror, 'it's pleasant to have some money put aside. It gives a comfortable feeling. Don't you think so?'

The potboy put the jug down on a small table on which a basin was standing.

29

'It all depends,' he said, morosely.

'On what?'

'On how many people know you have the money. And on who they are. For instance, some of them might be women.'

'That's true. I was saying that very thing to myself as you came in.'

Stuart poured the hot water into the basin.

'Keep away from them,' said the potboy earnestly. 'That's my advice. Don't trust them. Not a man in your position.'

'Which is what, do you suppose?'

The potboy gave him a cold, penetrating stare.

'In my opinion, sir, you've done something outside the law,' he said. 'What it was, I don't know. Doesn't matter anyway. You are hiding something. The loot probably. And you are wanted by the police. All you need now is a woman of the wrong sort and you'll be swinging at the end of a rope before the week is out.'

Stuart, who had been soaping his face, stopped suddenly, with one cheek lathered.

'A man of the wrong sort might be just as dangerous,' he said. 'Perhaps I ought to grow a beard.'

The potboy shook his head. He spoke earnestly:

'No use! But sometimes you have a limp. Have it more often, even make it worse. They haven't heard about your limp. I mean, the law.'

He shrugged his shoulders and went out.

Stuart glanced out of the window. It was one of those days when London was painted in soft greys and tender pinks. Falling into the mood of the weather, he decided that it was, after all, and contrary to its reputation, a feminine city, like a sentimental middle-aged woman, recalling her loves and as beautiful as a girl because of it. But the river was something different, the enemy of sentiment, the tale-bearer of time. Sleek, hostile.

A cloud of screaming seagulls were diving, one after another, on something drifting past on the current.

He thought he saw a floating shape in the yellow stream. It could have been a body.

30

His nose crinkled.

'My nerves,' he said, 'are playing me tricks.'

It occurred to him that while, no doubt, he would be safe enough when he reached the distant bank, it would be rash to assume that, in an emergency, he could reach the Bridge, far less cross it. And probably there was a gate on the Bridge, shut at nightfall and manned by inquisitive officials.

He went closer to the window, pushed it open and peered downwards. Between the river wall of the Rose of York and the water below ran a narrow stone wharf which could be reached from the alley on which the front door of the tavern opened or, at a pinch, from his room. He tested the iron post on which the window was hinged. It seemed firm enough, fixed by mortar into slots in the stonework.

On the other hand, to reach the wharf would solve only half the problem. He had still to cross to the other bank where, in some house accustomed to welcome gentlemen in urgent need of shelter, he would be sure to find a good-natured, hospitable girl.

He resumed soaping his face, gravely at first, then more cheerfully as this familiar thought grew stronger. The idea of a woman, even a woman of the wrong sort – if anything of the kind could be imagined – invariably possessed this odd power to raise his spirits.

'I am young, rich and handsome,' he said, and looked searchingly into the mirror. 'No, not exactly handsome, but not repulsive. In short, I am the sort of man that any sensible girl would find attractive.'

He began to whistle a silly tune he had known since childhood, swallowed some soap, stopped suddenly and began to shave furiously.

Ten minutes later, washed, brushed and dressed, he stepped out into the alley and looked round. For the moment, no traffic was passing on the river.

He went down to the water's edge. The little wharf he had seen from above was empty. He examined it carefully. An iron ring was set into the river wall. Above, beside the tavern sign, was a hinged iron arm that could be swung out over the

31

water when a boat moored alongside with a cargo to be unloaded.

After his survey of the scene, Jamie made his way towards the busier streets of the city, where, sooner or later, he would catch sight of the red and white stripes of a barber's pole. He meant to have his hair trimmed, washed and – why not? – perfumed. Such indulgences were permissible to the man of means. It would be the preliminary to a journey of discovery in this strange city.

He restrained the natural exuberance of his gait. This was England, he remembered! These were English gentlemen, although they might not look like it. One did not swagger. One behaved with decorum. One observed the girls – if at all – with an air of indifference.

As he set out, he limped, remembering the potboy's advice. But after a few yards he had forgotten it. His sword was cocked, but at an angle three degrees short of provocation. He knew that the English were hot-tempered and quarrelsome. The last thing in the world he wanted was a fight.

In life one does not always get what one wants.

One Black Glove

Laid out temptingly on a merchant's booth was a lace collar of surpassing beauty – lawn which might have been woven by a team of subtle spiders, a delicacy of needlework which he could not recall having seen in Amsterdam; lest its virgin whiteness be thought too austere, the pattern was invaded by the most elaborate design in gold thread. It was just the sort of article which, in his days of irresponsible poverty, Jamie might have bought on credit.

But now he was rich and had no need of frivolous ostentation to raise his spirits . . . Still, he could admire fine craftsmanship when he saw it, he could wonder where the devil the English, who had no talent for the more refined arts, had come upon this masterpiece. At that moment, a voice sounded at his elbow.

'Pretty, isn't it? Not often you see goods of this quality.'

It was the shopkeeper, whose voice sank to a whisper like oil flowing over gravel as he went on. 'Expect you wonder where it came from, my lord. Indian stuff. Off a Portugal ship. Prize, you might say, condemned by the Admiralty Court – or ought to have been.' The merchant winked.

'Rather effeminate,' said Jamie.

'Effeminate, my lord! You amaze me. But even if it were, a gentleman of your sort could wear it without anybody thinking amiss. Now, if it were a question of ear-rings, I wouldn't advise you to indulge.'

Jamie strolled on, frowning. He remembered a pair of ruby

33

ear-rings against a swarthy skin. Two rubies. He came to a booth, outside which hung a board bearing the twelve signs of the zodiac. With a shrug, he entered. Great wealth, he thought, is making me superstitious.

'I am Leo,' he said to the bearded, black-robed wizard inside. 'What luck can I expect in the next few days?'

'I am a scientist, not a fortune-teller,' said the wizard, severely. 'But I warn you, be careful until the new moon. That will be ten pence, thank you.'

Jamie felt for his purse.

'And tell me, why are you thinking of some red, shining stones, rubies perhaps?' said the man smoothly. 'Or rather, do not tell me. But ask yourself. Good morning, sir.'

There is a simple explanation for a thing like that, Jamie told himself, once he was in the street outside. The man is an obvious fraud.

In ten minutes, he arrived at the jeweller's shop where, on Alan Beaton's recommendation, he had deposited his money. A few more coins in his purse would give him increased confidence in passing through the markets.

After all, he reflected, the man of substance has a duty to spread his abundance among the less fortunate. There was an apposite text in the New Testament which, in a moment, he would recall...

The jeweller weighed the coins and, as he handed them over, remembered that a letter was waiting for Monsieur Stuart. Jamie broke the seals. It was, as he might have guessed, from Alan Beaton – and another letter, sealed, was enclosed.

Jamie's heart missed a beat as he recognized the handwriting on the letter. It was from Alan's sister Mary. From the outer letter he learned that Alan Beaton would be in London any day now. If Jamie would be good enough to leave his address...

'Rose of York,' said Jamie to the jeweller, 'beside the river, if Mr Beaton should ask you.' Then he went to find a corner where, alone and quiet, he could read the letter from Mary Beaton, a girl he had met in Edinburgh and had seen last in Copenhagen. It was brief, as he had known it would be.

'Monster,' he read. 'This is to tell you that I have grown up

34

a great deal since I saw you last. It was just in time! So understand, please, that I will not be held to any of the stupid things I may have said when a child. They mean nothing at all. Nor do any wise ones either – if I said any.

'Now, we are going to Paris. Sir Robert, her ladyship and I. He has business there.'

(Sir Robert Anstruther was a Scottish diplomat, his wife was Mary Beaton's mistress.) The letter went on:

'I have always thought that I should marry a Frenchman. Imagine, then, how excited I am! M.'

Jamie folded the letter and put it away. What a silly child she was! . . . Stupid things. Wise ones . . . The last words she had spoken to him in Copenhagen were, 'I love you.' He had not taken them seriously. As for Paris, he would write her a letter of advice. It would begin, 'Nobody below the rank of marquis . . .' He knew the French nobility.

Having got this problem out of his way, Jamie caught sight of a barber's red and white pole outside a house which stood a bowshot from what seemed, to judge by the traffic that passed along it, to be one of the main arteries of the town. It was the place he was looking for, but before he reached it he saw through a window something else, a shop interior where strings of dried sausages were hanging from the ceiling. A cook shop. He opened the door and went in. As he sat down he was aware that someone had come into the shop on his heels. The man sat down opposite him.

Jamie was about to rise and move to another table when a glance at the newcomer told him that any gesture of that kind would be wasted. This was not a moment for niceties of behaviour. Nor was his neighbour a suitable target for a display of indignation.

He was a bright, furtive little man rather like a fox. His cheeks were pinched in beneath his cheekbones; he had a sharp nose and little brown eyes that darted this way and that without stopping. His manner was an uneasy mixture of the obsequious and the assertive.

He was talking even before he sat down and the talk rattled on, incessantly and with the greatest insouciance in the world. It was fast and was spoken – to nobody in particular – in an

35

accent that Jamie found hard to follow. What he heard was this:

'Gentleman! If ever! As soon as I set eyes on you, I recognized the signs. Never fail! Look at you, my dear sir. Clothes. Way you carry that sword. Breeding! Generations of it. Travelled. Educated. Want me to guess where you come from? Or would that be rude? Let me order you a drink. No, don't refuse. If I can't be hospitable to a stranger within the gates, so to speak, it would never do at all. Intolerable!'

The little man snapped his fingers at a plump woman who stood ready to take their orders. 'Sack, woman! The best you have in the cellar,' he said, 'and two platefuls of sausages. We're hungry, Mabel. Ain't that right, my lord! Easy to see. Yon Cassius has a lean and hungry look. Know where that line comes from? A great tragedy. See it sometime. Take my word.'

At his third attempt, Jamie broke into the flow.

'Look, Mr – ' he said, sharply. 'I don't know your name.'

'And why should you!' The little man made a wide magnanimous gesture with his arm. 'Jones,' he said, bowing over the table. 'Endymion Jones. As names go – of little consequence! And names don't go far, do they, my lord? A rose by any other name, etc. You will note that I haven't asked your name.'

'I am travelling incognito,' said Jamie.

'Very wise. But there is a special reason why I haven't asked it. Guess . . . Because you are going to tell me. You will insist on telling me. Just wait and see if you don't.'

The wine arrived. Jamie paid for his drink. Jones frowned but did not allow the incident to cast a shadow over their friendship.

'You may think it is an accident us meeting and so on,' said Jones. 'Not so. Fate! The moment my eyes fell on you, I said to myself, Endymion, here is the man we have been looking for. Youth. Birth. Riches. And a taste for adventure. Everything that brings a man good luck.' His voice fell almost to a whisper. 'My lord, how would you like to be very rich, *very rich* – just supposing. Maybe the richest man in the world, kings excepted?'

'At this moment, I'd settle for a plateful of sausages.'

36

'They'll come!' said Endymion Jones, leaning across the table, his little sharp eyes boring into Jamie. 'What won't come is fortune. It has to be seized. It has to be taken by the throat. Listen carefully to what Endymion says, my lord. Listen!' His voice fell to a dramatic chuckle. 'Would you like to see an island in the Indies? An island where no people live but where gold can be found by the ton! Like to see it on the chart. Then wait a little. Listen to the story.

'Ten years ago, a Spanish ship – a galleon – broke away from the Treasure Fleet in a storm, laden with Mexican gold and gems – '

'Rubies?' asked James.

'Why did you say rubies?'

'Just an idea that came into my head.'

'You must have second sight, my lord! Rubies, of course. And pearls. Sacks of them! That ship. Guess what happened to her. She struck a reef and went ashore on a sandy beach. And there she broke up – broke into fragments and only one of the crew was saved. What do you think of that? Only a story, of course, but what if I have the chart of that beach here, my lord?' – Jones tapped his chest. 'What if I'm willing to let it be seen by any man who'll charter a ship and hire a crew? The chance of a lifetime, my lord, wouldn't you say? What am I saying? The chance of ten lifetimes!' He paused to give this thought time to sink in.

'But there's a snag,' he said.

'There usually is,' said Jamie.

Endymion frowned and went on. 'The chance is not good for long! Not for long! Why? Tides, storms, sea beasts – what they can do to a ship! Horrible! And all that time the Mexican gold is sinking into the sands, sinking deeper all the time, for want of a ship, a crew, and a man of spirit. A man like you, my lord.'

The shop door had opened and shut again. Footsteps on the sanded floor. Then a new voice.

'Didn't I tell you not to come in here, Jones?' The voice was abrupt and Jamie looked up. A tall, lantern-jawed man, all in black, stood above the table, a heavy cane in his hand, looking down, bushy eyebrows drawn together.

37

'Didn't I tell you not to come here any more, pestering decent people with your lies? Now get out. Get out, I say.'

The voice was deep and unpleasant.

But before the tall man had repeated his command, Endymion Jones had scuttled halfway to the door.

'Good riddance,' said the tall man, contemptuously.

'Why didn't you leave me to deal with him myself,' asked Jamie, frowning at the newcomer. 'You interrupted an interesting talk.'

The eyebrows moved apart a fraction of an inch.

'Because your excellency should not have his time wasted by petty rogues. And because I don't choose to have him plying his trade in this part of the town.'

'It was a good story and seemed likely to get better as it went on. The Mexican gold on that beach in the Indies. Wonderful!'

The tall man flung out a contemptuous gesture. 'Twenty men in London spin that yarn. Often they are sailors. Sometimes they have a parrot on their shoulder. That's the kind to look out for above all.'

'Thank you,' said Jamie. 'I'll watch for the parrot.'

The tall man sat down with his cane between his knees. He clasped his hands, his fingers interlocked. One hand was covered by a black glove.

'Name is Porter,' he said. 'Alonzo Porter.'

Jamie nodded, and said nothing. Porter's hands interested him.

'Your excellency is a stranger in these parts,' said Porter. 'It will take you time to get used to our ways so – anything you want to know, just ask for me. Alonzo Porter. In this part of the town, what I say is what matters.'

'I understand, Mr Porter.'

Porter leant forward. He drew one hand out of the clasp of the other and struck the table once with the knuckles of the uncovered hand.

'Which reminds me,' he said, 'if ever you want some little job done, don't waste time on the likes of Jones. Come to me. I have men working for me who don't make mistakes, not of any kind. Naturally, it would cost you money, depending on what the job is. Nothing for nothing, Mr – ?'

Jamie nodded. He thought that he knew the sort of business Mr Porter's friends carried on.

'And don't trouble to give me your name and address,' said Porter. He paused for a second before continuing in a slightly harder voice. 'If I want 'em, I'll find 'em. It will take me less than five minutes.'

He passed over his face the hand covered by the black glove. He and Jamie looked at one another hard in the eyes.

At that moment the windows of the sausage shop shook. Outside there was a noise like rolling thunder. It was a noise which Jamie thought he had heard quite recently. He looked a question at Porter.

'You've guessed right,' said Porter. 'Gunfire. Below the Bridge is a ship exchanging salutes with the Tower. An ambassador is arriving in her.' He interlocked his fingers once again. They made a fascinating pattern.

'An ambassador?' said Jamie.

'All kinds come into London, sooner or later. Some good, some bad. Some rich, some poor. Good morning, Mr – ah – ' He rose to his feet and grasped his cane with his gloved hand.

Jamie smiled amiably. At that moment the sausages arrived. Porter went out of the shop.

'Interesting town,' said Jamie to the plump woman, who put the plate before him. 'In ten minutes I meet two rogues, one small, one big.'

'Some who talk big aren't all that big,' she said.

Jamie looked at her more attentively. She was a sturdy woman with some threads of silver showing in her dark blonde hair. She had fine shoulders and knew how to carry them.

'I expect you're right,' he said. He thought that she would probably know. 'You mean that a man like Porter isn't necessarily the biggest fish in this pond.'

There was some contempt in her laugh.

'Some of the water in this pond is so dirty, mister, that a fish has to be very big to be noticed at all . . . Porter!'

'One black glove. I wonder why.'

39

'You aren't the only one,' she said.

'Skin disease? Deformed? Lost a finger in some war?'

'Or lost the other glove,' she said. 'Why not that?'

'You make life too simple,' he told her.

The guns kept on shaking the window panes while Stuart ate the sausages. Soon after they stopped, he paid and rose to leave.

'What about Endymion Jones?' he asked.

She smiled.

'Endymion, poor devil! He's growing too slow for the purse-snatching. He is on the look-out for other work. He's giving the fraud game a run. Hasn't the brain for it. I told him, but he wouldn't listen. Wouldn't be surprised if he ends up snitching for the law.'

'Snitching?' The word was new to him. But Jamie thought he understood it.

She nodded emphatically. 'Snitching,' she repeated.

'Good day Mabel,' he said.

' 'Day, handsome. And not Mabel – Isabel.'

'Of course.'

Stuart strolled up the alley to the barber's.

When I come to a new town, he said to himself, climbing the three steps to the shop, it is important I should look my best. Besides, we rich people should give pleasure to the mob by giving them something handsome to look at. We must not be selfish.

It was the best excuse he could think of for something that was utterly frivolous, meaningless and time-wasting.

Hanging on a hook in the shop was a lute, for the use of customers while they were waiting. He sat down, plucking at the strings, fingering his way into a sentimental song he had known in Paris. He hummed it first, and then sang the words as well as he could remember them. He sang low, nursing his hoarseness which, in fact, suited the song rather well. It was half-sad, half-cynical, about disappointed love.

'You sing beautifully – makes me so happy.'

Before him, holding a towel, was the barber, simpering a little.

'It's a sad little song,' said Jamie.

'That's life,' said the barber, sniffing. 'What can I do for you, sir?'

'Haircut,' said Jamie. 'Not too much off. Maybe a couple of inches, enough to make it tidy.'

'Beautiful hair, sir. These curls your own?'

Jamie gave him an indignant look. 'What do you think I do? Roll it up in pins?'

'No offence, sir.'

'I should think not. Then I want you to wash it. It's full of salt.'

Some time later, lying back in the chair with a hot, dry towel round his head, like a Turk, Jamie heard someone come into the shop and growl some words to the barber. Then the new arrival picked up the lute and began to sing in a well-worn, but still resonant, baritone.

> 'Sweet violets, sweeter than the roses are
> Covered all over with marmalade...'

Jamie shot up in his chair and swivelled round. He had heard that voice before, singing that song. And there was the singer himself, gross, red-faced, black-browed.

He was the leader of a troupe of strolling actors. A year before, Jamie had seen him on the boards in Edinburgh in one of his famous roles – Romeo.

'Fletcher!' he called out. 'Lawrence Fletcher!'

Abruptly the song stopped. The singer looked round with suspicious eyes and bristling eyebrows.

'Fletcher, of course. But who the devil are you, sir?'

'Remember? Edinburgh. Captain George Sinclair. I was with him that night in the tavern when we sang.'

Jamie tore off the towel. Recognition dawned dramatically in the actor's eyes.

'Sinclair! And your name is – ?'

'Stuart.'

A hand as hard as an oak beam shot out and gripped Jamie's.

'Of course! Age, age! The faculties go one by one. Memory first. But by God, laddie, you are not so skinny as you used to be.'

41

'Money,' said Jamie. 'I eat better now.'

Fletcher looked dubiously at him for a moment.

'Money is a great help,' he said. 'But what has happened to your voice?'

'A cold.'

'Not infectious, I hope?'

'Not now.'

'You should take Dr Stephen's Water night and morning.'

'Thank you.'

'And Sinclair? Tell me, how goes it with my old comrade-in-arms.' (Fletcher had once been a sergeant in the Low Countries.) 'He was on his way – to where? I'll remember in a minute.'

'To Moscow.'

'To Moscow! Yes. He talked a lot about it. What is he doing now?'

'Still on his way to Moscow,' said Jamie.

Fletcher shook his head sadly.

'Poor Sinclair. Always a dreamer. No business sense.'

'But you can't say he was thin,' said Jamie. Sinclair was just about the biggest man he had ever seen.

'No, by God! Enormous. A Hercules!' said Fletcher. 'And, God, what a soldier! Did he ever tell you about the camisado at Sluys?'

'Yes,' said Jamie hurriedly. He had spent hours of his boyhood in the company of old soldiers, comrades of his father's, while they maundered among their reminiscences of forgotten battles. 'He told me. But I'd like to hear it again, from you. But at this moment, my hair's still wet. Could we meet?'

'Meet! Of course we'll meet. Come to the theatre – it's on the other bank. I'm on tonight in a new piece. I don't think you'll like it, but – '

'I'll be sure to,' said Jamie, and wrapped a new towel round his head.

When he emerged, dry and perfumed, Fletcher was being shaved in the adjacent chair.

He waved a lordly hand at Jamie and uttered grave, sonorous words:

'Stuart, you have come to the capital of all art and letters. What an experience for a young man! Do not misuse this precious time! ... Until we meet!'

'Ah, the theatre,' said Jamie. 'The theatre is called – what?'

Fletcher scowled.

'To the ignorant it is called the Swan,' he said. 'Sensible men just ask for Fletcher.'

First English Lesson

It was maybe two hours later. The precious time had not been misused. Jamie could say at the end of it that he had crossed London east to west and had seen a great deal of it, between the river bank where his stroll had started and the wall which closed it in from the country to the north. About two miles in one direction, and a mile in the other. He had fetched up in the end in a steep street above a grim old stronghold – a square keep with turret at each corner behind a moat and a curtain wall.

'What's that?' he had asked a man he met.

'That!' The man looked at him with suspicion, as if doubtful of his sanity. 'That's the Tower, mate. What's it for? To keep people in if the Queen doesn't fancy them. Such as foreigners, see.'

Jamie saw. The English didn't like foreigners. He bowed politely and passed on.

He liked the neighbourhood, crowded and – a thing that he always thought was a friendly feature of any neighbourhood – smelling strongly of fish. He found a tavern, a deep, cavernous dark establishment looking out on a small court. He made himself comfortable with a beaker of wine at one of the tables from which he could see through the archway leading out of the court. Looking downhill, he could catch a glint of light thrown back by the river.

Time passed. In a corner, a group of young men near him talked passionately. One of them had a sheet of paper on the table before him from which he read. The others laughed.

44

One of the listeners stabbed at the paper with his forefinger and uttered words which made the rest of them break into a gale of laughter. Another rose and recited some words with exaggerated gestures. They shouted him down. They talked quickly and all together, so that Jamie could not understand a word that was said.

'What is it?' he asked the girl who carried round the wine. 'I've learnt my English at the wrong school.'

She looked him up and down. By St George, he thought, you are a bold beauty. You are telling me with that glance that English cannot be learnt at school at all. That you must be born speaking it. That it is the private language of the English people.

'Oh,' she said, contemptuously. 'Them! They are only making up a play. They are paid for doing it. God knows why.'

Silence had fallen on the table in the corner. The man who had been reading was now writing busily. His companions were drifting away. But the writer remained at the table and his pen went on moving, fast and nervously across the paper.

Jamie's eyes went back to the serving girl – the ripe lips, the lustrous black eyes, the gleaming brown hair, the dazzling skin.

'I must come back here,' he said. 'I think I could learn English in this place.'

'Why not?' she said, with a lazy movement of the shoulders. 'Everybody ought to try to better himself.'

'It depends on the teacher,' said Jamie, slipping a coin across the table. Her hand went out as swiftly as a snake's tongue. The coin disappeared into a pocket hidden under her apron.

'That's for the first lesson,' he said.

Her eye ran over him. 'Wrong amount.'

'Too much or too little?' he asked. She shook her head almost imperceptibly; a slight smile was leaving her lips as she moved away.

He called after her to bring him a pen, ink and paper. He was going to write a letter to the girl named Mary Beaton, advising her how to deal with the amorous advances she was sure to encounter in Paris. He would like to give the girl honest advice. And for some reason he did not wish her to have a social triumph among the French. There was a tradition in his family that he was the rightful King of Scotland. He did not take it too seriously, but now he wrote as if he did.

'Madam,' he began, 'we learn with alarm that you contemplate marrying in France. You may say that this is no business of ours. You could not be more wrong. We require to be consulted when one of our subjects proposes to marry outside the Kingdom. It is true that Scotsmen in France have all the rights and privileges of Frenchmen, as recently confirmed by our cousin, Henri. So it might be argued that, likewise, Frenchmen are Scots. This is a piece of casuistry which, madam, we cannot accept. At least, we have the right to be heard before any irrevocable step is taken.

'You are young and inexperienced. The world (which includes France) is full of scoundrels. Worse still, some of them are not men of property. Unlike ourself! Through prudence and industry, etc., etc. We are quite changed. Age and wealth, etc., etc.

'As to France, counts are two a penny. Marquises are more deceptive. They may have coats of arms, dating back to *The Song of Roland*' – he scored out that. She would not know what he was talking about (there he was wrong. She did) – 'to the First Crusade, and still have not a penny in the bank. Most dangerous of all are the moody, lounging sort, squires from Gascony, often Huguenots, with a name so long that you fall asleep listening to it, a rolling eye and funny way of talking French. Look out for them. Sometimes they serve in the cavalry. That is even worse.'

He went on to warn her against certain streets in Paris. No girl over the age of ten could safely go into the Latin Quarter. Churches (which, as a Protestant, she was unlikely to enter) were sometimes haunts of those with vicious inclinations. Milliners were bawds. The impudence of footmen knew no bounds, and so on.

From another room came a delicious smell of cooking. Suddenly, Jamie felt hungry.

He ended the letter abruptly, signing with a flourish, 'Given

46

under our hand, James R.' Then he added a postscript: 'Mary. There is a stall in the Rue St Antoine, near the church of St Paul, which sells flowers. Pick the most beautiful rose you see in it and wear it for me. Tell the florist that le Sieur Stuart will pay. The florist will make disrespectful advances to you – but that I must leave to your sense of propriety. J.'

When he had finished eating, the light was beginning to fade outside. In the outer room of the tavern, he looked around for the serving girl. She was not to be seen. That was a pity! The time was ripe for his first English lesson. He noticed that the corner table was empty. The writer of plays had vanished. His companions, too, were no longer there.

Jamie hesitated for a minute or two in the doorway under the tavern sign. The scene entranced him. Already lights were glimmering in some of the windows which looked out into the little court. Farther off and lower down, lights flickered on the surface of the river.

At that moment he was conscious of something nearer and of a different kind. Noises were growing more definite on the floor above him. Voices were raised in anger. A man's. A woman's. The floorboards of the tavern were thin.

A door opened above so that the noise was suddenly louder. The voices were unmistakably angrier. The door slammed, shaking the whole building. There were light, rapid footsteps on the stair leading down to the entrance passage of the tavern. Coming towards the place where Jamie had been writing. Immediately afterwards, he was aware of a noise behind him and a cloud of perfume.

Someone, moving in a great hurry, had tried to brush past him and had not quite succeeded. He turned abruptly and his elbow met something that was soft and hard at the same time. It proved to be an arm within a cloak.

Something fluttered on to the floor. A black mask of fine lace. Jamie stooped at once to retrieve it and, when he rose, found that he was looking into the face of a young woman. The face was brimming with anger.

In an instant, the rhythm of life quickened for Jamie, as he had known it do before, for the same kind of reason.

Brown eyes flecked with gold, hair tumbling like copper

47

shavings; a small nose, exquisitely moulded; lips which passed on the malice of the eyes; cheeks flushed by nature, or emotion. But he had just time to decide that there was more than youth, beauty and fury in this face – although he was the last man in the world to despise those gifts of heaven. There was also ... While he sought for what it might be, the unknown girl snatched the mask from him and put it back on her nose. He noticed that she was carrying a riding whip.

'Too late,' said Jamie.

Through the slits of the mask her glance sparkled in his. It took her a second to grasp what he had said.

'Too late?' she threw the words at him. 'What do you mean?'

'Too late to put the mask on again, madam. The harm has been done.'

For a second her gaze rested on Jamie, then suddenly her look, which had been furious, turned into perplexity; her lips, which had been twisted with anger, melted into a brief smile.

'But it is not beyond repair,' she said, with a cool little gesture, something between a nod and a bow, between recognition and insolence.

'Your hair,' said Jamie, his fingers executing a small dance in the air.

'Curls are coming in,' she said, contemptuously. 'Didn't you know?'

'Since you seem to be going, madam, let me call your carriage.'

'Carriage! What do you think I am? An old woman? A cripple? I have a horse. If that lazy lout of a groom will only bring it round!'

'If only he won't!'

She looked him up and down. He noticed her knuckles whiten on the whip. He had gone too far.

He remembered a saying of his father's when he – Jamie – was old enough (say fifteen) to receive worldly advice. 'A gentleman, Jamie, is one who knows how far he can go too far.'

Standing at the tavern door, Jamie did not think that he

had passed beyond the shadowy border which divides the adventurous from the merely impertinent. But how was he to be sure?

This was England, where the code of conduct was notoriously different from anywhere else. The Channel raged between one set of proprieties and another. He was in a world of unknown values, although fairly sure that his instinct for effrontery would somehow carry him through.

It was true that this girl had been, for some reason, trembling with anger and agitation. The situation was one in which the normal standards of conduct might not apply.

With a last sidelong glance, not angry but startled – and with that something else in it which he could not define – she gathered her black velvet cloak about her and swept past him into the pool of evening light in the court outside.

While Jamie's eyes followed her, another voice spoke in his ear – light, ironical – a voice Jamie had heard before. A man had entered the tavern from the courtyard.

'Well, well! So Daniel walks into the lion's den! I thought we should meet again, sooner or later. But I hardly expected it to be in London.'

Jamie was looking into the quizzical eyes of a man he had met in Copenhagen, an English diplomat, agent, spy – whatever might be the proper description – named Edward Carey.

'I have taken your advice, Carey,' he said. 'You said once that I should come over to the other side of the street. And now, see – I have done so!'

'I wonder,' said Carey.

The girl in the black mask had taken a few steps into the court outside. Now she turned back, impatiently.

'Miranda,' said Carey. 'I am sorry I am late. But you are early. This is Monsieur Jacques, sometimes called James Stuart. He is either Scots or French as the mood takes him and he is on one side of the street or the other. I am not sure which. Stuart, Mistress Miranda Vane. She is a cousin – of a kind – of mine.'

Bowing, James had time to admire her curtsey, which for a furious girl was remarkably graceful.

49

'Which side of the street are you on today, monsieur?' she asked, insolently.

'The sunny side,' he told her.

'I expect Edward will bring you to call on us one day. That is to say, if you have time to spare.'

'Stuart has always time to spare for girls, beautiful girls.'

'Perhaps we will be able to show him several.'

'One will be enough,' said Jamie.

As they turned away, he began, 'You will want my address –'

Carey waved his hand easily. 'Don't trouble,' he said. 'We are sure to know it. You will find London is quite a small place, Jamie.'

'For some reason your beautiful cousin does not like me.'

Carey shrugged. 'But, as I seem to remember, you are an expert in overcoming those first impressions. As it happens, you are the one man in England I would trust with her name at this moment.'

'Don't trust me too far, Carey.'

'Today, I would trust you with all the family secrets, Stuart. You are safe,' said Carey, with an odd smile. '*Au revoir.*'

Still thinking over that last remark of Carey's, Jamie walked out into the courtyard where the masked lady waited. Impatience was quivering to the tip of her riding whip.

Horses were being led out of a stable somewhere. The two – Miranda Vane and Carey – walked over towards the sound of the hoofs on the cobbles. Jamie followed them with his eyes for a few seconds.

Anger, malice, recklessness, and something else – Jamie puzzled over the girl's appearance. What was the final ingredient which had given that unusual quality to the face from which the mask had fallen. Something, at any rate, in addition to beauty itself.

The clatter of horses' hoofs on the cobbles faded into silence.

'We have company today,' he remarked to the serving girl.

'The quality,' she said.

50

'Just my class.' Jamie nodded amiably.

She shrugged.

'I have not forgotten that you are going to give me an English lesson,' he said, and strolled out of the tavern yard, pulling his cloak more closely about his shoulders. It was getting colder.

It was lucky he had brought to England a fur-lined cloak.

Jamie thought of the pair of brown eyes and the tumble of copper curls, the latest fashion. A lady of the court. Birth. Breeding. A profile cut with a diamond in the crystalline air. And something else, the quality he had not been able to name. The quality which, for a reason he could not fathom, was somehow suitable to a child of the aristocracy visiting a tavern in the City of London, set in a huddle of shops and offices and warehouses. Visiting it for some reason of her own. And in the company of Carey, a kind of cousin, whatever that might mean.

Whatever it meant, it did not mean that Carey had been in the room upstairs. No, Carey had not been there with his cousin. But someone else had.

'Don't trust women. A man in your position,' the potboy had said.

On the other hand, if women were to be trusted, would not life be infinitely more tedious? . . . Moreover, English women were notoriously more unpredictable than the rest of their sex. At the academy in Paris where his education (such as it was) had been completed, travelling companions had assured him of this, without explaining it. *'Les Anglaises!'* Their accounts had usually ended in soft whistles, raised eyebrows and suchlike symptoms by which male bewilderment is used to conceal male defeat.

Jamie thought that he was beginning to understand something of what those gestures had tried to convey. And for some reason – it might have been the wet air blowing in from the distant sea – Jamie was aware of a vibration of danger, stimulating, as it always was. He took his way, downhill, towards the Bridge.

The tide had turned and water was rushing greedily between the arches – he counted twenty of them – as if it were

51

pouring through the rapids of some stream in an untamed country.

In certain states of the river, shooting the Bridge would be a chancy business. One would need to be handy with a boat.

He set out across the Bridge towards the south bank, the disreputable quarter where the theatres were, where other places of entertainment beckoned to the wanderers, the sailors who had stumbled ashore after voyages like wasting diseases, the soldiers who had survived terrible wars on the Continent, the refugees of fortune, worried about duns or the value of their passports.

Halfway across, the houses parted and he could see the stretch of water, eastwards, downriver, beyond the Tower. Above the livid stream, there was a low fume out of which rose a multitude of delicate vertical lines. Masts. Shipping. Vessels lying in the river, loading or discharging.

Jamie went on, impressed by the signs of mercantile power, and, on the far side, asked the way to the theatre. When he reached it, the flag, a white swan on a red ground, was being pulled to the top of the staff. Somebody was ringing a hand-bell. The play was about to begin.

He took out a penny and handed it to the man.

'A seat will cost you another penny,' said the man.

'Tonight,' said Lawrence Fletcher in a voice that might have been announcing the fall of Imperial Rome, 'I was awful.' He stopped wiping the greasepaint off his face with something that resembled a dishcloth. 'Awful!'

He looked at Jamie for the reassuring denials that were the expected response to his self-accusation. Jamie said nothing. He had thought the performance lacked the bravura of Fletcher's Romeo seen in Edinburgh all those months ago. Further than that it would be presumptuous to go.

'Sooner or later,' Fletcher said, 'the machine runs down. The clock stops!' He rolled awful eyes. His voice echoed through some dismal cavern.

Since this ignorant youth would not feed him with the expected lines of comfort, he, Fletcher, would give a specially brilliant display of self-pity. Unaided. Solo.

52

'It was not a very good play,' Jamie conceded.

So far as he had been able to follow the plot, it had been concerned with a Persian king who had fallen passionately in love with a Greek princess – or, perhaps, with a Greek prince. It had been hard to be certain which, especially as Jamie had a problem of his own to solve which distracted his attention from the action on the stage. Was the woman who sat next to him in the theatre making amorous advances, or was she trying to steal his purse? She seemed too old for the first, and too well dressed for the second. But how was he to know?

This was a strange city. The English – it was universally conceded – were a strange people. His father had always insisted that they could not be put in the same category as any other nation in the world. 'After all,' the old gentleman had pointed out, 'they cut off your aunt's head – and she a queen! I admit that they may have had some excuse. Still!' His father had always insisted that Mary Queen of Scots was his sister and therefore Jamie's aunt. But Jamie had never quite believed it.

'The play!' Fletcher's brow had cleared. His voice rang out like a trumpet of doom. 'Terrible! Unspeakable! Written by a miserable hack to please a nobleman who was looking for a part to suit his catamite, whom, God forgive me, I employ. The boy can't act, which is just as well in the circumstances. And these, Stuart, these are the conditions in which an artist has to work today! The English drama – dead, boy, dead! How can the modern theatre compete with the bearpits? Or the poor player with the sword-swallower or the tightrope walker? But enough! Come again soon and hear me in one of my finest roles. Look on greatness before it vanishes for ever. In Edinburgh, you have seen me as the tragic lover. You will see me now as the great, the gross, the irresistible Sir John – Falstaff! In the meantime!' – his voice suddenly ceased to be declamatory. 'A drink. Two drinks. Oceans of drink! How are you off for money?'

Leaving the theatre, Fletcher plunged into a warren of dark little streets. Walking in front Jamie caught sight of a tall man who impulsively took the arm of a fair-haired youth with –

was it possible? – a painted face. Fletcher sneered, 'A patron of the theatre! ' At that moment, he put his shoulder to the door of a tavern. Light spilled out and a confused noise of talk. They went in.

Over the second drink, Jamie spoke of the girl he had seen at the tavern on the other side of the river. Fletcher listened to the description closely. 'Lady Miranda Vane. Red hair, brown eyes. A cloak of black velvet.' Pause. 'A lady of the court, Stuart,' he said, with a thunderous frown. 'Let me warn you. She is very likely to be a maid of honour. In that case, to seduce her would be treason.'

'Seduce her! I have only just seen the girl.'

'Quite so, Stuart. But I have heard something about you. So remember. Treason!'

The actor, with a smirk of relish, drew a finger across his throat.

After the fourth drink, singing broke out in the tavern and Jamie lost count of time...

When he was crossing the Bridge going northwards, a church bell in the City began ringing out the hour. What hour? While he was puzzling over this, another bell, softer and sweeter, began to strike. Then another and another. Different bells, of different sizes, at different distances over the roofs of London.

After that silence fell on the empty streets.

Empty? Silent? In less than a minute, neither the one nor the other.

Instead, sounds that were positive and emphatic, sinister and unmistakable. If they have once been heard, there is no doubt at all about their meaning.

Men fighting!

In the darkness ahead, there was a scuffle. Men – two, no, three – struggling. No sound but the thud of blows and feet scraping on the cobbles. Then, at the end, a scream of pain, followed by what sounded like a bellow of rage. And the thump of a cudgel on a body. Jamie quickened his pace.

He could think of a dozen reasons why he should avoid this obscure brawl. Ordinary prudence, plus the special arguments that could be advanced against his taking any part whatever,

54

at that moment, in a breach of the peace in a London street. He went over the problem in his mind, but, alas, at the same time he ran forward, his hand on the hilt of his sword, uttering shouts which any dispassionate observer, if there had been one, might easily have mistaken for a summons to battle.

Just then, the writhing knot of men sprang apart and became three distinct, violently active figures, one of which came towards Jamie with a cudgel uplifted.

Jamie, peaceful of intention but forced to defend himself, drew his sword swiftly and made a brisk slash at the other man's wrist. The cudgel came down sharply; its bearer, with an appalled glance at Jamie, turned and fled.

He was yelping with pain, or, more likely, with fright.

Another figure picked himself up from the cobbles and scuttled towards Jamie. He was a puny little man. Before he had time to think what he was doing, Jamie had barred the fugitive's way. He seized the little man by his doublet and held him up, panting, to the weak, yellow light of a street-corner lamp. By that time none of his assailants were in sight.

Blood ran down the side of the little man's nose. His tongue licked out to catch it.

'By God,' said Jamie in amazement. 'Jones! Ulysses Jones!'

'Endymion,' the little man snarled. 'You let me go, whoever you are.'

Jamie freed him.

Ahead, the street was empty once more.

'Don't you remember me, Endymion? I'm an acquaintance of yours. What the devil have you been up to? Brawling like that in the public thoroughfare. I'm surprised at you.'

Endymion Jones looked at him distrustfully out of haggard, twitching eyes.

'No business of yours. I was doing nothing. Nothing at all. Those two set on me. With cudgels. I'm lucky to be alive.'

'You are. They might have had knives, stilettos, pistols even.'

Jones nodded. 'You're right there. Foreigners.'

'Ah! Foreigners. I thought one of them was English.'

'You did? How would you know? I go by what I hear. I

55

have ears, haven't I? One ear more than one of those bastards has.'

Endymion grinned wolfishly, and held something up.

Jamie noted that his fingers were covered with blood. He bent forward and looked more closely at the small, sparkling object in the little man's hands. An ear-ring torn from an ear.

'You've been up to your old tricks, Endymion,' he said. 'Snatch and run! You are too old for it, Endymion. Mr Porter won't like it at all.'

'Screw Mr Porter,' said Endymion, spitting blood out of his mouth.

'Language! Disgraceful. Tell me what happened.'

'There was I walking along as quiet as you like, when those two set on me, like I said. But you saw! You were a witness. In the fight I got one of them by the ear – in self-defence – and that came away in my hand.' The ear-ring.

'Emeralds,' said Jamie.

'You colour-blind or something? Rubies!'

'Rubies and diamonds.'

'I'll let you have it for five pence, sir. Just to be rid of it.'

Jamie shook his head.

'Rubies bring bad luck. Any gypsy will tell you.'

'Don't say that, sir. Don't say that! I was brought up religious.'

Jamie nodded gravely. He had an idea.

'Do you know what you ought to do, Endymion. Find a church and put this in the collection box. I'll walk along with you and see you do it. Now you say that these men were foreigners?'

'One of them was. Can't say about the other.'

'French, German, Spanish, Italian – what do you think?'

Endymion Jones peered up at him with a knowing glint in one screwed-up eye.

'And why would you want to know that, mister?' he said.

'I'll tell you if you tell me why those two villains attacked you . . . Because you know something, wasn't that it? Something they don't want you to know . . . What is it you know, Endymion?'

It was a shot in the dark but he did not think it was too far from the mark.

'D'ye want to have me killed, mate!' said Jones.

'No, but somebody else does. Somebody has just that idea.'

Somewhere in the confusion of roofs around them, a clock struck the quarter. A thin little shimmer of sound, as if a cracked pewter mug had been hit lightly by a spoon. It came from some steeple close at hand.

'That's it, Endymion. That's the church we're looking for.'

Jamie slipped out his sword as he led the way forward. The two who had attacked Endymion might not be content with the failure of their work. On the other hand, he did not think they would risk a fight on more even terms – if Endymion had the pluck to face them.

He stayed with the little thief until he had heard the light chink of the ear-ring as it fell into the heavily padlocked box in the dark porch of the church.

'What is it called, this church?' he asked.

But when Endymion told him, the name did not seem to belong to any saint in the calendar.

'You wanted five pence for the ear-ring,' he said. 'Here it is. You have enemies, Endymion.'

The little man cocked an eye at him. 'Maybe I have,' he said. 'But nothing like the enemies you have, mister.'

Jamie would have liked to ask him more. But suddenly he found himself alone in the street. He was about to walk back to the Rose of York when a thought occurred to him and he turned on his heel. It was time for his first lesson in English.

A Ship for Virginia

'The hours you keep!' said Alan Beaton, indignantly. He was sitting on the bed in Jamie's room in the Rose of York. 'Eleven o' clock of a fine morning and you aren't dressed yet!'

'I had a late night,' said Jamie.

Alan sneered. 'What's her name?'

Jamie had not heard. 'And maybe it's safer for me to go out after dark,' he said. 'All these people going around asking for Jack Scream . . .'

'Who the devil is he?'

Jamie tapped his chest.

'It's a long story,' he said. 'But somebody in this town has heard about a ship from Hamburg. How he heard, what he thinks, I don't know and I'm not going to ask him. I don't want to meet him, that's all.'

Alan shook his head. 'You've changed, Stuart. You're not the man you were. All this worry; this caution – you're fairly trembling with nerves!'

Jamie nodded, smiling pleasantly.

'It's the money that's done it, Alan. You see in me a man who is corrupted by wealth.'

'And why the devil do you speak in this husky voice?'

'Because girls like it. You try it. But I'm told I should take Dr Stephen's Water.'

Alan shook his head emphatically.

'No. That's for scurvy. Do your teeth rattle in your mouth like marbles?'

'Certainly not.'

'Then it isn't scurvy. Now all this money you have . . . Probably you won't be interested in getting any more?' said Alan.

Jamie looked at him thoughtfully. 'It all depends,' he said. 'We might talk about that.'

'Do they know the name of the ship?' asked Alan.

'*The Dark Lady*? I don't know. Likely enough they do. Where is she lying now?'

'In a little harbour not so far away. She's changed her name.'

'I liked the name,' said Jamie.

'A rose by any other name.'

'That's the second time somebody has said that in the last few days. Alan, I'm hungry. Aren't you? There's a cook shop around the corner. Come on.'

After a plate of sausages, Jamie felt strong enough to tell about the fight Endymion Jones was involved in, and the ear-ring he tore from an assailant's ear.

Alan shrugged.

'This town's hotching with little thieves like that.'

'Maybe,' said Jamie. 'But I had seen that ear-ring before. On a sailor in Spinola's galley – you remember – *The Trinidad*?'

'You're sure?'

'I'm always sure, Mr Beaton.'

Alan Beaton's thoughts went back to another subject.

'You made him put it in the church box,' he said severely. 'That was cruel. After all, it *is* the little man's living.'

'He wanted five pence for it. I gave him five pence. If he had taken it to a fence, it would have been traced back to him, quickly. And something horrible would have happened.'

'Meaning the rope?'

'More likely the rack. They are rather free with the rack here. In Scotland, they use the Boot. The effect is the same. Tell me, what do you think this is all about, Alan? Why is this man with the ear-rings in London?'

Alan thought for a little. 'Why are you in London yourself?' he said. 'But this man who has lost a piece of his ear . . . Let

59

me think. Now, what if he were a deserter from Spinola's galleys? What if he had brought news about his admiral's plans?'

Jamie shook his head.

'You'll have to do better than that, boy. For one thing, he wouldn't pass the news on to a little rat like Jones. He'd find a better market. Besides, you haven't explained why he would want to beat the life out of Jones.'

'Your turn, genius,' said Alan Beaton, sourly.

Jamie collected his thoughts for a moment: 'He has come here for recruiting. Spinola is hard up for crew. He can get all the oarsmen he wants from Spain. Slaves. But he wants able seamen. That's harder. And this is the best place in the world to find them. So he sends One-ear over to London with a pocketful of ducats and orders to pick up any seamen who happen to be on the beach. One-ear takes on Endymion Jones as a likely lad to lead him to the taverns and bordellos where the game is most likely to be flushed. And Jones, being what he is, pinches some of the ducats and makes a bolt for it. One-ear is angry, naturally. But he has to go warily. He can't go to the justices like you and me. The authorities will not much like what he is doing. Recruiting crew for ships to be used against the queen! Instead, he hunts Jones down all on his own. And gives him the hiding of his life. How's that?'

'Not bad. Not bad at all,' said Alan.

'Not bad! It's marvellous!' And for a moment, he really thought it was.

'Why didn't he kill Jones?'

'Because I arrived on the scene, Alan. As simple as that.'

Alan grunted. 'What does it matter, anyway?' he said. 'What do we care about this Spinola, one way or the other?'

'The answer is Nothing. Nothing at all. Just remember, though, I have a prejudice against Spanish galleys.'

'No prejudice should stand in the way of business,' said Alan, primly.

'Go on,' said Jamie. 'You have something on your mind.'

Alan thrust his head forward and lowered his voice.

'Not far from here there is a kind of castle –'

Jamie nodded.

60

'The Tower,' he said. 'Where the Queen of England puts people if she doesn't like them.'

'It's somebody like that I am talking about. He did something that was careless . . . Treason. He is called Lord Southampton.'

'You mean that he seduced one of the queen's maids of honour?'

Alan shook his head irritably.

'Nothing of the kind! Why do you say that, man?'

'Because, believe it or not, that is treason in this country. Go on, though, go on.'

'If you'll let me talk for a minute! This man I'm telling you about was mixed up with Lord Essex in that plot against the queen and was sentenced to you know what – '

Jamie drew in his breath noisily through his teeth.

'No,' said Alan. 'The other one.'

'The chop?'

'That's the way they execute a nobleman here, more respectful.'

'Go on, man.'

'He's been kept a prisoner in that place the Tower, expecting every day to be his last. Watched all the time. Only a cat for company. And a thousand rats. So what happens? His mind has turned to serious things!'

'Religion?'

Alan frowned.

'Business,' he said. 'He is rich – oh, very rich – these English lords are up to their necks in money – and he plans to charter a ship and send it to Virginia. He plans to make a settlement there. Think of it! Jamie, it's the most wonderful country in the world, enormous and empty.'

'Maybe it is. But where would we come in?'

Alan's eyes were like the sun flashing on blue ice.

'You must be crazy, Jamie,' he said. 'We have the ship. You need a ship to go to Virginia.'

'Yes,' said Jamie. 'Yes. Very interesting.' But his mind seemed suddenly to be remote from the topic. 'One thing occurs to me. What if Spinola is planning to rescue Lord Southampton from the Tower?'

'What makes you think he knows Southampton?' Alan asked, irritably.

'Nothing at all. But could you think of a better way to annoy the English government than breaking into the most famous prison in the land and carrying off the friend of Lord Essex, the arch-traitor?'

Alan shook his head.

'Very nice,' he said. 'But have you thought of all those English ships of war between here and the sea? Even if your friend Spinola reaches as far as this, he would only be at the beginning of the business. He would still have to swim a ditch, climb a wall, find the keys to the cell. Then, perhaps, his lordship would be rescued! No. Don't be a damned fool, James! It can't be done.'

'No? Let us take a stroll along the streets.'

'It may cool your head, Mr Stuart.'

The Smell of Danger

A few days passed before something else happened. Jamie
found a sealed note waiting for him at his tavern. He read it
carefully and with some excitement. Then he did exactly as he
was told in it. Whom did it come from? Carey, perhaps? Or,
possibly, from someone else. The initials at the foot of the
sheet were illegible:

At the river steps nearest your alley, call a waterman and ask
him to drop you at the landing stage for Vane House. See that
he does not overcharge too wildly. They are all robbers.

He bought the beautiful lawn collar which had somehow
been intercepted on the way from India to Lisbon. With that,
and a new pair of perfumed gloves, he felt he could meet the
challenge of an evening with the English aristocracy.

In the late afternoon, he was rowed upstream until he had
passed the point at which the City wall ran down to the water.

After that, gardens bordered the river in which, one after
another, fine mansions were set. This was the suburb of the
grandees, stretching out towards the west, to the cluster of
buildings where the heart of English power beat! The palace
of Whitehall. Where the queen reigned, where Cecil spun his
web, where Parliament sat, grumbling at the times when its
members could be cajoled to Westminster from their estates.

The buildings beside the river had not the elegance of the
palaces he had seen in Paris, but, in their dusky, redbrick way.
they had warmth and the assurance that wealth conferred.

Ahead, when the sun was sinking into a pink fume of cloud, he caught a glimpse of a mass of roofs and turrets which he thought must be a royal dwelling. Beyond it, the spires of a church rose clear of the river mist into the evening sky.

Jamie was put ashore at the end of a gently sloping garden. He gave the boatman twice what he had asked. A woollen cap came off. A scowling, weatherbeaten face broke into a ferocious smile.

'God bless your excellency.'

Jamie looked at him sharply. 'We shall see one another again, I think,' he said.

'At your service, sir. Jabez Walker. Everybody on the river knows me.'

'Walker. I'll remember that. I'm Stuart. James Stuart. At the Rose of York.'

He nodded and turned away. Jabez Walker looked after him for a minute before settling down to row.

It had occurred to Stuart that in London watermen might play much the same role as the strange tribe of caddies did in Edinburgh. Go-betweens, messengers, informants, counsellors – and probably pimps, too. And some day he might want a messenger for one purpose or another.

Ahead of him, a broad paved walk led to a flight of shallow steps. Vane House, now that he could see it, was a red-brick building crowned by a tiled roof partly hidden by mock battlements. Dignified, absurd, endearing, he thought. And the house of a person of quality and wealth.

At the front door, he was met by an elderly servant who, wheezing slightly, took his hat and cloak and hobbled ahead of him through a rush-strewn hall and, by way of an ornate oak staircase, to a small, panelled room with thick Turkish carpets on the floor. In one corner there was an immense fireplace in which logs were smouldering. A great, shot-torn, yellow flag, which he recognized from its crown, castles, lions and other devices as an ensign from a Spanish royal vessel, hung against the wall. The air was heavy with perfume from a basin filled with lavender.

The old servant bowed and, murmuring something, left Jamie alone in the room. So far it had all been exactly as he

64

could have foretold. But what happened next came as a surprise.

In a few minutes, the door by which the servant had disappeared opened, and, one after another, four beautiful young girls trooped into the room. He had just time to note the fact that they were blonde in that gentle, exciting English way, with no head exactly the same tint as another, no pair of eyes the same blue, grey or green as the next one. Only the cheeks blushed to the same soft pink.

Each charming young breast was displayed. But Jamie, a man of the world, knew that what on the Continent would be regarded as a token of shamelessness was, in England, the badge of virginity. He had just decided that they were close relatives, probably sisters, aged between fourteen and nineteen, when they came up to him, one after another, curtseyed and kissed him on the cheek. They had to reach up to do it. The youngest went on tiptoe.

'In England,' he said, 'you have invented the most charming way of opening a conversation. But how does one go on?'

'We are Kate, Molly, Jane, Liz,' said the girl who he thought was the eldest and was certainly the darkest of the quartet. She pointed in turn to each of the girls. 'We are Miranda's sisters. She will be here as soon as the queen gives her leave for the night. Until then, you will have to be content with us.'

Looking from one to the other, Jamie did not think that the interval of waiting would hang heavily on his hands.

'Are you going to marry Miranda, Mr Stuart?' asked the youngest girl. She was very fair. If pink can be pale, she was pale. He thought she was called Liz.

Jamie looked round at the shining eyes, the smiling lips, the flushed cheeks of this quartet. Angels? . . . He did not think so.

'It is high time she was married,' said Jane. 'Already she is twenty-one. Soon she will be an old maid.'

'And Mother,' said Molly, 'will certainly not allow any of us to marry before Miranda, so – '

'The outlook is black!' said Liz, with an enchanting smile.

'Even for vain Jane,' said Molly, putting out her tongue at

65

one of her sisters, who lifted her chin with a touch of *hauteur*.

Jamie thought that Jane – if she was Jane – had some reason to be vain, although no more than her sisters.

'But you are not the marrying kind, are you, Mr Stuart?' said Kate. 'Edward has told us all about you. Faithless, heartless, a fatal seducer of women. That is the protrait he has painted of you.'

'A ghastly slander! Although,' said Jamie, 'I am sometimes willing to be seduced.'

'You mustn't seduce Miranda,' said Jane. 'She is a maid of honour. You would go to the Tower for it.'

'Like poor Lord Southampton.'

'You mustn't call Henry by his title now that he has been attainted. After what he did, he is lucky to have his head on his shoulders,' said Liz, shuddering.

'Oh!' cried Kate, 'And whatever you do, don't speak of Lord Southampton to Miranda.'

'Why not? Everybody knows. Besides – Miranda – !'

They were all talking at once.

Jamie held up his hand. It seemed the only way he could break into the heavenly chorus, if that was the proper term for it.

'It is a question of marriage,' he said. They looked at him in astonishment.

'Not your marriage!'

'Mine! I can see that I am in a dilemma,' he said.

'Tell. Do tell. Perhaps we can help.'

'As I see it, there is only one solution,' he said.

'What is that?' one of them asked him, or, perhaps, all of them asked; he could not be sure.

'I shall become a Moslem. Then I can marry all of you. But, first of all, I must be sure that I know your names.'

They rattled the list off: standing in a semi-circle before him. 'Kate, Molly, Jane, Liz.'

At that instant the door opened, and Miranda Vane came into the room, her cheeks rosy from the sharp air on the river, her hair like a beech leaf in winter dusted with small sparks of light raindrops.

'And Miranda,' she said, completing the list. Coming over,

66

she kissed Jamie on the cheeks. He thought her kiss was more perfunctory than her sisters' had been. But, of course, she was older, more worldly – and perhaps he was becoming spoilt.

'Even a Moslem is not allowed five wives,' said Kate, sternly.

Looking at Miranda, he was inclined to believe that Lawrence Fletcher was right: 'She is very clever, my boy. It is said that she writes poems and speaks five languages, not bad for a girl whose father – a gentleman by birth by the way – has the reputation of being a highly successful pirate. Also, she is believed to have a secret lover – a dangerous game for one in her position, although most of them play it. It's a wicked world, Stuart! Incidentally, the game would be even more dangerous for the lover. See you remember that.'

The little face, exquisite but alive with intelligence, was no longer angry, but he thought that some feeling was quivering beneath the surface, some strong emotion, repressed with difficulty. A russet beauty amid this bevy of gold, she had a quality which made her sisters seem to be so many pretty girls and no more. But what the quality was, he could not define.

James found himself believing in the lover, and wondering what kind of a man he would be. A wild young noble squandering his estates, a grim soldier home from the war, or a serpentine foreign diplomat who would whisper secrets of state to one who could, then, whisper them to Cecil in the chambers of Whitehall? After all, the renowned English intelligence service had probably women agents and, if it had, they would be like this girl.

In the corridors of the palace he had seen from the river, there would be no lack of opportunities for dalliance and, in the wrath of the queen, an additional incentive to court danger. It was likely, too, that this lovely little bird of prey would seek her quarry in unusual places – and even that she had not yet found what she was seeking. But she might have found him in a tavern in the City . . . and lost him again.

With this last cheering thought in his mind, Jamie Stuart looked with greater interest at Mistress Miranda Vane.

'Edward Carey will be here quite soon,' she told him. 'He has some business with Mr Secretary. Do you know who I

mean by Mr Secretary? He is a little hump-backed man with
eyes that can see into stones.'

'Can they see into hearts?' he inquired.

'Cecil does not waste time on hearts. Minds – that is what
fascinates him.'

'With hearts one can play more complex games,' he said.
Miranda looked him sharply in the eyes.

'I can see that one might. As if in chess, a dice box could
interfere in the game! You must teach me.'

'I shall be content to learn,' he said.

The others laughed. 'Edward was right about you,' said
Kate.

'He said you are probably the rightful King of Scotland,'
said Molly.

'Either I am that or my grandmother was a – ! I don't
think she was.'

'Or your grandfather was a fatal seducer,' said Liz, the
youngest, blondest, sauciest of the five.

'But – ' Miranda raised one finger in the air. 'If you are
really the King of Scotland, then you may soon – God
forbid! – you may some day be King of England!'

'So that's why you have come to London!' cried Liz.

James raised his hands in horror.

'My father warned me I mustn't on any account be a king.'

But, before him, five girls swept down in a full court
obeisance, while five pairs of eyes sparkled in his.

Jamie decided that some special acknowledgement was
required of him. A simple bow would not be enough. He
unbuckled his sword and put it on a chair. Then he performed
the old acrobat's trick he had learned as a boy – the double
somersault which left him standing where he had begun,
breathing hard and red in the face.

The Vane girls clapped their hands with the right mixture
of admiration and mockery.

'Did Edward tell you I could do that?' he asked, when he
had recovered his breath. They shook their heads. 'When I
become King of Scotland I shall make it compulsory at court.'

'You must be – '

He held up his hand.

'Let nobody know! I am a Transylvanian gypsy,' he said.

'Can you tell fortunes?' asked Kate.

'It is high time,' said Miranda, firmly, 'that you met Father.'

Father – Sir Ferdinand Vane – interrupted in his study, at a table strewn with charts and account books, was much as Jamie had expected. Suspicious blue eyes peered out of a florid face – a typical Englishman. He seemed to have a crippled leg which, when he rose, gave him the excuse to make a great noise on the floor with a stick. He looked hard at Jamie, as if he had sighted a doubtful craft on the horizon.

'You're lame,' he said, searchingly. 'Too young for gout. How did you get it? Fighting?'

'Pulling an oar on a Spanish galley,' said James.

'Ah-ha! You must tell me about that. Got mine' – thumping the floor with his stick – 'in a little affair off Ferrol. Spanish coasters. They were imprudent enough to attack us. At least! – War! Terrible! Ten minutes of excitement and a lifetime of discomfort. Keep out of it. What did you say your name is? Stuart . . . Stuart, eh! You're not one of – ah, well. You're staying to dinner? Good. Keep an eye on these girls of mine! Don't trust them!'

He winked and hobbled back to his chair.

'For some time Father,' murmured Kate – it was Kate? He was not sure – 'has been carrying on a private war with the King of Spain.'

'So have I,' said Jamie.

'Father has made a great deal of money in his war.'

'In my case, the king has had the best of it. But the game goes on.'

'Mr James Stuart.'

The light, ironical voice, the quizzical eye, the neatly trimmed beard – Edward Carey.

'I see that you are making yourself at home among my little cousins.'

'Yes. I have decided to marry them. All of them.'

'Very wise. But this is the first time I have heard you talk about marriage.'

'Things have changed with me, Carey. I have become prudent. Respectable. Money has done it.'

'Oh dear! I *am* sorry.'

Jamie put the past resolutely behind him and turned his attention to the scene in that fragrant room in Vane House. There were new arrivals, most of them red-faced young men who had spent the day shooting in the fields outside the City. They still had traces of mud on their boots. They were treated by the Vane sisters with the cool disdain which, Jamie knew, was, in any country, the first step in the dance of flirtation.

There was, too, one tall, elderly man who was apparently a person of some consequence. He had a dark complexion and a narrow rim of beard, flecked with grey. His manner was insinuating and, for some indefinable reason, unattractive. Jamie thought that he was probably a member of the queen's council. But what was strange was that somewhere, at some time – and quite recently – Jamie had seen the man before.

When dinner was served, Jamie found himself seated at table next to Miranda Vane. He asked her in a whisper who the stranger was.

'That?' she said. She spoke coolly but Jamie thought he detected some nervousness in her voice. 'That is Lord Henry Howard. He is not the sort of man you will like. At least, I don't think you will.'

'You don't like him yourself, do you?'

'Maybe I don't.' Miranda frowned. 'Not that it matters much, does it? See how Father looks at him, as if he was a toad whom it would be nastier to tread on than to let live.'

'I wonder . . . Somewhere I have seen the man before . . .'

'Slinking out of some back door, I expect.' He was surprised by the venom in her voice.

But by that time, he had remembered something he had seen in the darkness of the streets when he had left the Swan Theatre with Lawrence Fletcher . . . A tall man who had taken a boy by the arm. He had not seen the face, but the shape of the man was unmistakable.

'Lord Henry is interested in the play,' he said.

There was a pause before she spoke again. 'You know more than you tell, James.'

'And you, Miranda? Do you tell all you know?'

For a long second their eyes met. There was something in

70

hers that surprised him. If it had been anyone else he would have called it fear.

Farther up the table, Sir Ferdinand was telling a story he had heard from one of his captains about a ship which had hovered off the Irish coast recently with no good intentions and then, suddenly, had disappeared . . . What had it been up to? . . . That was obvious, wasn't it?

'No question of it! Selling arms to those Spanish villains. Excuse me, Lord Henry. They are friends of yours, I think.'

'God forbid, Sir Ferdinand. I know what my enemies say of me, but – '

'It was a joke, my lord. Only a joke.' Sir Ferdinand made appeasing movements with his hand and turned away. 'What is the latest news from Ireland, Edward?'

'Any day now, we should hear who has won the battle,' said Carey. 'But, so far, silence from the Lord Deputy in Dublin. He is not, of course, in Dublin. He has taken the field against the rebels . . . As for that ship you spoke of . . . They think she ducked into a French harbour, but nobody knows for sure.'

'How could anybody be sure?' cried Sir Ferdinand. 'There were thirty pirate ships in the Western Channel last month.'

'And some of them were thought to be English,' said Lord Henry. Sir Ferdinand raised an eyebrow, cleared his throat and said nothing.

'His lordship has won a point off Father,' breathed Miranda Vane to Jamie.

In the parlour – the warm room with the panelled walls – after the meal, Jamie listened to the teasing chorus of talk around him and wondered why the English girls were so much better at the game than the boys were.

He beckoned to Liz.

'You should fence with people in your own class,' he said. 'These boys – '

'We are sharpening their wits,' she said.

'Liz,' he said. 'Tell me why I must not speak of Lord Southampton in Miranda's hearing.'

71

For a moment, she became serious.

'Because . . . James, has everything in life gone well for you? Everything? Always?'

After a minute, he answered. 'I see. So that was it?' he said. She nodded.

He looked into a small circular room which opened out of one corner. Its walls were hung with Spanish leather. At that moment a voice – too sleek, too careful, too loaded with too many overtones – sounded at his shoulder. It spoke in French and was accompanied by a heavy cloud of some peppery perfume.

'Don't you miss Copenhagen, Monsieur Jacques?' asked Lord Henry Howard.

It was an odd experience to look into those pale grey eyes. As if there was nobody inside. As if someone had been there recently but had gone out.

Jamie held up one finger. 'H'sh,' he said. 'That's a secret.'

'Would you call it a secret?'

'It is a special kind of secret,' Jamie insisted. 'The kind everybody knows.'

'Not much of a secret, then.'

'You may be right. But it's the best I can do. But to answer your question, my lord. No. Tonight I miss nothing. Everything I want is here,' he said.

'Including the hint of danger?'

'Especially the hint of danger.'

Lord Henry sighed. 'That is excellent. Provided you see the danger in time.'

'I can smell it, Lord Henry.'

The untenanted grey eyes passed over him and looked away. The voice was quiet, rather sad.

'The smell is easy to recognize, so they tell me. Salt, like the sea, with a trace of gunpowder.'

'Not at all. Sweet and heavy . . . Sold in a shop in Venice. But it comes from farther East, as so many things do. Religions. Habits.'

'When you are tired of danger,' said Lord Henry, 'you can arrange to have it abolished.'

'I shan't forget.'

'But don't leave it too late. There isn't much time.'

'Thank you.' Jamie nodded politely and moved away.

'Lord Henry and I have been talking about danger,' he said to Carey. 'He tells me it smells of salt with a whiff of gunpowder.'

'His lordship's special brand of danger has no smell and almost no taste. It comes in tiny phials.' Carey's smile died. 'Do not take him too lightly, James. He writes every day to a kinsman of yours who is at present James the Sixth of Scotland. Lord Henry hopes that one day King James will be King of England. When that day comes, Lord Henry believes he might be Secretary of State. God knows, he has worked hard enough for it! In that friendly little enterprise you, James, are thought to be a possible obstacle . . .

'Oh, don't tell me you would refuse to wear a crown. The other James Stuart, your royal cousin, doesn't believe you, and the fact is, if the time came, you would behave like any other man in these circumstances. You would protest your unwillingness and snatch your rights. Don't deny it. So – don't be surprised if Lord Henry talks to you about danger. He is telling you what King James is planning for you.'

'How much does Lord Henry know?'

'A little. The rest is his instinct. They have a good deal in common, these two – the king and his crony.'

Jamie grinned. 'So this is what happens when I cross on to the other side of the street,' he said.

Carey nodded pleasantly. 'After all,' he said, 'it is the same street.'

'There is one advantage in being on this side of it,' said Jamie. 'I have a better view.'

At that moment he could see Miranda Vane talking earnestly to Lord Henry Howard. Their heads were close together. There was a frown between her brows. Once or twice she shook her head. Once she stamped her foot. Then she turned sharply away from him. She was very pale and her lips were twisted with anger. Anger?

The little episode made an odd impression on Jamie.

'It does not mean that I understand what I see,' he said. But Carey had moved away.

73

Now, Jamie thought, it was time to make his departure.

In the hall, he took his farewell of four of the five sisters in four separate bows, each more extravagant than the one before. They looked at him critically.

'You can tell he has been brought up in France,' said Kate, dispassionately.

'You can tell he is an acrobat,' said Liz.

'And a fatal seducer,' said Molly.

'A king would not bow so gracefully,' said Jane. 'So that settles *that*!'

At this moment Miranda joined them. The colour had come back to her cheeks. Her eyes glittered.

'What a wonderful fur,' she said, running her fingers over the sealskin of his cloak. 'A gift from a woman?'

'It was a cold night,' he said.

'There are cold nights in England, too,' she said, 'at this time of the year.' She walked at his side towards the door that led out of the house.

'Do you ever think of visiting the City again?' he asked.

He felt her stiffen beside him. 'No,' she said in a dry voice. 'Never. Never again.'

For some reason, Jamie felt relieved. Walking towards the door, he was aware that her hand was seeking his arm under the cloak.

'The moment I saw you, I said she is like me,' he told her. 'She is one of the same tribe.'

'This is a new kind of flattery.'

'Yes. Quite new. I have never tried it before. Usually in flattery one confers on a girl the qualities she doesn't possess or deprives her of those she does. In either case, the result is the same.'

She looked at him doubtfully.

'You are out of your depth, Jamie.'

'That is true,' he said. 'I am trying to get into yours.'

She changed the subject.

'One of my sisters was speaking about you after supper,' she told him. 'She said she was sure you were stupid because you seem to have no sense of danger. I told her that, on the contrary, you are afraid of everything in life except its dangers.'

Both statements seemed untrue to Stuart.

'And you, Miranda, is there nothing that frightens you?'

She laughed and gripped his arm tightly.

'Dishonesty and corsets,' she said. Her glance caught his for a flash and, then, swift as a swallow in the air, darted away.

His arm slipped round her waist and he pulled her towards him. Of one danger, at least, she was free.

At the last moment, between the glimmering candles and the night, he thought he heard her add, 'Come again, Jamie', but her voice was low and he could not be certain.

'Soon?' He caught her wrist and held it for a moment.

'In a few days,' she said, 'we are going to a house that Father has in the country, not far to the east of London, between here and the sea. It has good hunting. Have you a horse, Jamie?'

'I suppose I can hire one.'

'See that it's a good one,' she said.

He nodded.

'I think Father will ask you. He seems to have taken a liking to you. He is an eccentric man.'

He thought that, for a moment, she hesitated, as if, for some reason, she would be glad to have withdrawn the invitation.

He found that moment of doubt irresistible. He took her and kissed her hard. She said nothing but a spark of excitement flamed in her eyes. She was not the daughter of a pirate for nothing. He began to tell her so.

But by that time he was speaking to no one.

A servant, carrying a lantern, led him down to the river steps. In a few minutes, out of the tremulous darkness of the water a boat came into sight.

Slipping downstream, Jamie thought about Miranda and thought that he would be wiser not to think of her. Clever. Too clever. A girl with a streak in her that was wild and might be wicked. That way she had of raising her eyebrow should be warning enough for any man. Even if there was not the special

75

danger due to her place at court. The crime of seducing a vestal virgin. All of which the little she-devil was exploiting to the full! In short, James, as tempting a morsel as you are likely to come upon in all this crowded, dangerous city!

As if there were not troubles enough for an innocent wayfarer like himself! The man of good sense would have no doubt what to do. He would smile – sniff this English rose – and avoid its thorns.

When he reached the steps beside his tavern, Jamie had thought of something else. Turning to the boatman, 'Do you know Jabez Walker?' he asked. 'If you meet him, tell him to call and see Mr Stuart.'

The boatman listened and raised his hand in acknowledgement.

'Tell him to come and find me at the Rose of York. If I am not on the jetty here, I shall be in the tavern.'

The boatman vanished into the blackness of the river. Quarter of an hour later, when Jamie, still pacing to and fro in the alley beside the tavern, was about to go indoors, a large form hoisted itself ashore and held up a lantern. By its light Jamie saw a ruddy, rather brutal visage.

'Sir?' inquired Jabez Walker.

'Have you a length of rope?' asked Jamie.

'No, sir,' said Jabez Walker, hoarse with horror. 'Not that! Not a gentleman like you! Nothing is as bad as it seems to be. Believe me!'

'Don't be a fool, Jabez. I want the rope for quite a different purpose. Listen. Do you see that window in the tavern? It's my window. Do you see that hoist beside it?'

'I do that, sir.'

'If I had a rope . . . do you follow me?'

Ten minutes later, Jabez Walker rowed away once more. Jamie carried a length of rope into the Rose of York.

Traitors' Gate

Too late Jamie decided that sack, the favourite drink of the fashionable Englishman, disagreed with him. In the evening after his visit to Vane House, he drank too much and diced too recklessly. The day would have ended gloomily if he had not restored his self-esteem by defeating the attempt of a pickpocket and his wench to snatch his purse. Jamie had not been brought up in Paris for nothing. He woke, penitent, next morning. So much for all your promises of wise behaviour, Stuart, he said. You must do better than this, or people will not take you seriously as a man of property.

On his way to breakfast at the cook shop, he met Alonzo Porter who stopped in front of him. Porter spoke with unpleasant emphasis. 'Mr James Stuart,' he said. 'Late of a certain ship. Now living round the corner at the Rose of York? What an honour for our parish! Can I be of service to your highness?'

Jamie nodded amiably. 'You can tell your friends, the pickpockets, to leave me alone,' he said.

'It will certainly be done.'

'Their methods are clumsy. I am used to something more refined.'

'But if I am not mistaken, pickpockets are not the worst danger your highness has to fear,' said Porter. 'So if you are in need of any protection . . .'

'I'll keep you in mind,' said Jamie. 'I see that you haven't found your other glove yet. Good morning, Mr Porter.'

He touched his hat politely and passed on.

77

At the cook shop Alan Beaton greeted him with blue, accusing eyes.

'You look awful,' he said. His Scots speech was very noticeable.

'Talk business or shut up.'

'Can your highness read small print at this hour? Or do I wait until you're feeling stronger?'

'You can stop calling me your highness. Too many people are doing that this morning. And you can keep your small print until I have eaten.'

Jamie beckoned to the serving woman. 'Isabel!'

Later, Alan rolled out a chart on the table showing a coastline deeply indented by waterways and fringed by ropes of islands. Mountains and forests were shown and there was a sprinkling of legends like: 'Here is gold. The seeming road to Cathay' and so forth.

'Virginia,' said Alan.

Jamie shook his head. But it would have been useless trying to explain to Alan that every man carries his own Virginia in his heart, and that it cannot be captured in a cartographer's net.

His own private Virginia was very bare, very beautiful, above the trees and under the clouds – only there were no clouds. Waterfalls like bridal veils hung over the still waters of its lakes . . .

Jamie put one finger firmly on the chart: 'Give me something to write with.'

'What are you going to write?' Alan frowned suspiciously.

'This is the place where we feast,' said Jamie, jabbing at the chart. 'The girls wear a great deal of gold. The music is wonderful.'

'Don't be a damned fool, James. Listen! I have something to tell you.' His voice suddenly became solemn. Jamie waited. 'Lord Southampton would like to see you!'

'In the Tower?'

'In the Tower. He has heard about you. I do not know where he heard it or what it is. But now he wants to meet you.'

'Let's go, then,' said Jamie.

'It isn't as easy as that,' said Alan. 'In fact, it can't be done. People aren't allowed to go into the Tower. Once they are in, they can't go out again. I have a special pass because I have done business once with the Master Gunner. He had some old cannon to sell and I found a market for them in Algiers. Ever since then we've been friends. But you, Jamie – that's different. I don't see how it can be done.'

'I could swim the ditch, climb the walls and so on. Remember you are talking to a man who once escaped from Edinburgh Castle.'

'I'll bet a woman had something to do with that one.'

'Maybe. It wouldn't surprise me if a woman had something to do with this one, too. No. Nobody has told me anything. It's just a funny feeling I have. Don't you sometimes have a tingling at the tips of your fingers?'

'Every time I touch one of the yellow boys.' Alan rubbed two fingers against his thumb. 'It's like the music the fairies make.'

'The trouble with you, Beaton,' said Jamie severely, 'is that you keep your soul in your purse. Tell me, what kind of a man is this Southampton.'

Alan knitted his brow. 'Older than either of us by some years. Tall. Handsome, I suppose. One of the spoilt darlings of the world until misfortune struck him. Now as sad as you would expect. A bit of a poet. And a bit like you.'

'Me?' Jamie was really surprised.

'Yes,' Alan nodded vigorously. 'I don't know what it is, but there's something. I thought, that's what Stuart will be like when he grows up.'

Jamie rose with a clatter and a snort.

'Come on, Mr Beaton.'

Alan rolled up his chart.

'Yes, but where are we going?'

Jamie, on his way to the door, grinned back at Alan.

'To the Tower of course.'

'That's not the way to the Tower, idiot.'

Jamie was striding towards the alley which led to the river.

'Come on and don't talk so much!'

With Alan Beaton still grumbling and expostulating by his

side, Jamie was standing at the head of the steps beside the Rose of York. He was shouting for Jabez Walker.

Ten minutes later, the waterman appeared, his face breaking into the appalling convulsion which was his notion of a smile.

'Your excellency! What is your will?'

'Jump in, Alan. This is a Scottish gentleman – excuse his accent. Now, Jabez, you know a way into the Tower, don't you?'

'Tower, sir? Only the way I deliver fish of a morning from Billingsgate Market. I give a call and the porter opens up.'

'Couldn't be better.' Jamie settled lower in the stern of the wherry. 'Bend to the oars, Jabez.'

'Where are we going?' said Alan, nervously.

'Where do you think? To the only gate on the river – the only way for a gentleman to go into the Tower of London. To Traitors' Gate, of course.'

'Jesus!' said Alan.

'And if you think we aren't traitors, Jabez, just ask the King of Scotland. He can tell you.'

'Hold your hat, Alan,' said Jamie as they swept towards the Bridge. 'It's going to be rough here.' With a sudden swoop and a roar, darkness and a jarring, they shot between two piers of the Bridge and emerged into smooth water.

In a few minutes, 'Keep your heads down, gents!' said Jabez.

He uttered a shout in two notes. Jamie thought he heard 'Fresh fish', then they passed from daylight into gloom under a low arch in the waterfront of the fortress. Below it was a heavy iron grating which ended in a row of spikes a few feet above the water.

They came into a small dock surrounded by a stone quay, green with slime.

'It isn't myself I'm frightened for,' said Alan. 'It's you, James.'

From somewhere in the blank wall in front of them came a thud and a clang. A heavy door opened slowly, pushed from the other side. A tall man in the queen's livery appeared, carrying a lantern.

80

'Fish,' said Jabez Walker. 'Two prime Scotch salmon. Look at 'em.' He winked.

Jamie smoothed down hs collar, adjusted the angle of his hat and stepped on to the quay.

'Lord Southampton,' he said. 'He is expecting us.' Turning to the waterman. 'Come back in half an hour, Jabez,' he said. 'We shan't be very long.'

'I don't know you, sir,' said the man in livery, either a warder or sentry or, probably, a turnkey.

'Of course not,' said Jamie indulgently. He passed a coin into the man's hand.

'Thank you, my lord.'

'That's all right. And don't trouble to come with us. Mr Beaton knows the way.'

Jamie passed through the doorway, forcing the man in livery to step to one side.

Alan breathed at Jamie's neck.

'Of all the cheek!'

'Gentlemen don't have cheek, Alan. They simply know how to behave as the occasion demands. Lead on!'

Jamie laid one gloved hand elegantly on the hilt of his sword and let Alan pass in front.

'Above all,' he said. 'Don't ask the way. Instinct will lead you to my Lord Southampton. Should anyone have the impudence to ask questions, we have come on behalf of the King of France to value the crown jewels. Alan, you are walking too quickly.'

Nobody asked questions. Instinct, helped by Alan's memory, led them to a cobbled walk where rooks sat on the branches of ancient trees. Jamie saw two tall men in black walking towards them.

'The second one will be the keeper,' he said.

'Yes,' said Alan. 'He is called Captain Hart.'

Captain Hart was a grim-faced old soldier who cast a wary eye on them as they approached.

'My Lord Southampton,' said Jamie, bowing with that exact degree of respect that was due to a peer imprisoned for high treason. 'My name is James Stuart.'

81

Southampton turned out to be a lanky, sombre young man, heavily bearded, who looked at him doubtfully.

'So they have caught you,' he said.

'How did you know they were after me?'

'In a prison there are no secrets, Mr Stuart.'

'True,' said Jamie, adding, 'Virginia.'

Southampton's face lit up.

Ah, yes,' he said. 'Come to my quarters. We can talk there in comfort – at least, we can sit down.' He gave a sidelong, tentative smile. At once, he was striding ahead, eagerly. Jamie thought he was probably anxious to be out of earshot of Captain Hart.

'In fact, I am here of my own free will, my lord,' said Jamie. 'They have not caught me yet. In any case, who are "they"?'

'That is like asking a mouse who is the cat.'

He sketched a rueful gesture which, somehow took in the battlements around them, Captain Hart, and the entire police system of England.

'And what if there are more cats than one?' asked Jamie.

'That isn't my problem,' said Southampton, smiling sadly. 'I have one cat. That one is enough.'

They climbed a stair into a long, narrow room which might have been pleasant enough if its windows, set high in the wall, had not been so heavily barred. Jamie saw that Southampton had gathered a great many books to while away the days of captivity. There was a faint odour, none too agreeable, which Jamie could not identify. On top of a pile of books a large, black cat was sitting. It rose to greet Southampton with arched back and erect tail.

'I told you I had a cat. She keeps the mice down.'

Mice. That was what he had smelt. It was better than the usual prison smell.

'Virginia,' said Jamie, waving a hand towards a table on which a pair of compasses lay over a chart.

Southampton's face lit up: 'Ah! Do you ever dream of founding a kingdom, Stuart; where everything is at the beginning, where everything is new. All the mistakes have still

82

to be made. And the men and women stand amazed in an empty world?'

'There was a moment in life when I did,' Jamie admitted. 'It was a beautiful day in the mountains of Scotland. A solitary eagle was motionless in the sky above the glen. Sometimes I think of it still. Yes, it would have made a good kingdom.' He smiled, at the thought of it.

'And you are a free man!' Southampton's glance swept round the room and the barred windows. 'You have no need of dreams.'

'I am free, as the fox is free when he hears the hounds give tongue over the hill. But we were talking about Virginia.'

Southampton leant forward and spoke with a sudden intensity.

'Virginia will keep. My gaoler will be here in a minute. You know Miranda Vane, Stuart.'

It might have been a question. But Jamie did not think it was. He nodded. Southampton was about to say something which was going to cost him an emotional effort – it was visible in his face. At that moment, Alan and Captain Hart came into the room.

Southampton mumbled words so rapidly that Jamie was not sure if he heard what was said.

'If she only knew what Howard has done – and is doing!'

'What has he done?'

But Southampton turned to the two newcomers.

'I have been talking about Virginia to Mr Stuart,' he said. 'We think alike.'

'The question is, where are the settlers to come from?' said Jamie, speaking as if the problem had been much on his mind. 'From convicts, beggars, discharged soldiers? – I speak as an ex-convict myself. We do not necessarily make the worst of settlers.'

'Or men who can be paid well to live abroad,' said Alan. 'The Spaniards have no lack of colonists.'

'Or money,' said Southampton with a smile. 'It all comes back to money.'

'It should not be hard to find money in a town like London,' said Alan.

He began to speak with enthusiasm of the opportunities that lay before a well-found fleet making the Virginian voyage – the fertile soil, the timber, the docile savages, the hope of gold. The prospects of the way to Cathay of which the best authorities were persuaded. Jamie was impressed. He had never heard Alan be so eloquent. Charts were spread out, the globe was spun round, passages from the reports of returned mariners were read, the price at which *The Dark Lady* could be chartered was discussed – a matter which Alan Beaton would take up with the skipper and his partners in Hamburg.

After a time, Captain Hart interrupted the talk: 'The governor will be making his rounds very soon. It is near the time for the gentlemen to go, especially' – he frowned at this point – 'since they have not given up their swords. Contrary to the ordinances of the Tower!'

'If I have a bottle left in my bin, Hart,' said Southampton, 'let us broach it before they go.'

While the captain was out of the room on this business, locking the door as he left, Southampton turned to Jamie. He spoke in a quick vehement murmur.

'Miranda,' he said. 'Once I would have asked her to marry me. She was hardly more than a child then. And I was under the spell of Robert – of Lord Essex. He had a magic. Among other things, it brought him to the Tower! He did not want me to marry Miranda. No! Everything must be as *he* wanted. So he found a wife for me and arranged it so that I must marry her or be disgraced. And Miranda found another lover – a man I admired. Whether she still loves him I know not. Perhaps you do, Stuart. Howard knows her secret. You may wonder how.' He shrugged. 'Through some friend. He has strange friends for a nobleman. He will tell the queen if Miranda does not do what he wants. Which will be to take part in some black treachery – I know my Lord Howard!' He paused for a moment and shot a long, hard look at Jamie. 'Stuart, I have heard about you. Now I have seen you. You are as I expected you to be. A man like you can beat Howard. You can save Miranda from his blackmail. You are the man to do it.'

'If he does not destroy me,' said Jamie.

Southampton made an impatient gesture. Then he went on, speaking rapidly.

'There is a little rat of the London sewers named Endymion Jones,' he said. 'Find him. He owes me a debt. That is where the work begins . . . When you talk to him you will understand.'

Somebody was making a noise with a key. The door opened. Captain Hart came in with a gleam in his eye, a bottle in his hand.

'Plenty more where this came from, my lord,' he said.

Ten minutes later, Jamie and Alan took their leave.

'Give her my love,' whispered Southampton at the door.

'Love?'

'Love,' he repeated, frowning briefly.

Endymion Jones . . .

'It would be interesting,' said Jamie, 'to inspect the crown jewels. It seems a pity not to. But, perhaps, in the circumstances . . .'

They found their way back to the door that led into the little dock where they had arrived. The same warder was on duty. With the greatest possible ostentation, Jamie handed him a coin.

'I shall tell Her Majesty how well things are done here,' he said.

'For God's sake, my lord,' said the man, hoarse with anxiety, 'say nothing of it!'

'I see! Modesty – modesty!' said Jamie with a kindly laugh.

He led the way on to the stone quay of Traitors' Gate. The warder shone a lantern once or twice. There was a splash of water and a crash of oars. Jabez Walker brought his wherry neatly under the spiked grating.

On their way upriver to the point above the Bridge where the sign of the Rose of York came into sight, Jamie talked to the waterman.

'Do you chance to know a little runt name of Endymion Jones?' he said.

'Know him, sir! 'Course I knows him. Weaselly chap, not

85

much higher than that – ' Walker's hand marked a level somewhere between his waist and his shoulder. 'Married a stale whore, Bessie Jennings, and lived on her until she found a thief she fancied better. What we call a high lawyer. He was more of a man. Understand? Then she tipped Jones off Fleet Bridge into the mud one dark night and took her traffic elsewhere. Follow me?' Jabez opened his eyes in alarm. 'If you have anything to do with him, sir, look out for your purse. But, excuse me, you were saying?'

'I'd like a word with him, that's all. So if you see him, tell him.'

'Funny thing is I haven't seen him these last few days. But if I do, I'll – '

'He'll turn up. Sooner or later. If he isn't on the mortuary slab.'

'Endymion Jones!' said Jabez, in something like wonder. 'Well, it take all kinds to make a world, as they say.'

'And while you're about it, Jabez. If you hear of anyone who has lost an ear lately . . . Might be walking about with a bandage on his head. One of the seafaring sort. And might be foreign.'

'That should be an easy one, sir. I'll pass the word around. It's surprising what you hear on the river. The point is you would like to meet this one-eared sailor?'

'Not meet him. I'd like to know where he lives and what he is doing.'

'Foreign sailors – one ear or two – they usually does the one thing, sir,' said Jabez Walker with a shrug.

'Everywhere it's the same!' said Jamie, sadly.

With a practised twist of the oars, Jabez brought the wherry alongside the steps below the tavern.

'At ten o' the clock, sir, in a boozer called The Cock, on the waterside, everybody knows it. Not a place for the likes of you but – I can't leave the boat.'

'Of course not.'

'I'll be there. Maybe I'll know nothing. Maybe not.'

'That's life, Jabez.'

Jamie paid once, twice, three times, and stepped ashore after Alan.

'Now I must go and work,' said Alan. 'Yes,' he answered the question in Jamie's face, 'I'll write to the skipper of *The Dark Lady*, telling him what Lord Southampton said.'

The evening shadows were beginning to steal out of the corners. Soon they would take over London. The time had come when men, even a young man who has been gilded by the pagan sun of the Renaissance, who has bought a charming new lace collar, and cuffs to match (more or less) and still has money in his pocket, when even such as he feel the first twinges of melancholy, of theology, of doubt, and ask – as Jamie asked – 'Is it not time for my second English lesson?'

But the tavern, when at last he reached it, was empty. It was apparently an off night.

No poets and their supporters making jokes with one another. No beautiful girl coming down the stair in a flaming temper. No long period of literary exercise when he would write a letter to warn a delicious little lamb against the ravening wolves of Paris – for in this mood of sadness and doubt he could not entertain as the faintest possibility the notion that Mary Beaton was able to eat up all the ravening wolves in Paris and ask for more.

Incidentally, he wondered had he sent off that letter, so wryly loaded with wit and wisdom; one of his best efforts?

'His best efforts!' How arrogant, how contemptible!

He remembered a remark his father had made on one occasion. 'There is no gift more dangerous than that of writing charming letters.' A gift (he could see it now!) compounded of light-mindedness and insincerity, unlikely to deceive any but the stupidest of girls.

The letter was not in his pocket. He could not remember seeing it anywhere in his room. But, really, would that prove anything? The incomparable English Secret Service could have opened it and read it. But, with the matchless subtlety of its kind, it would have re-sealed the letter and sent it on to Paris. Which proved, what? ...

As for his second English lesson, a different serving girl was on duty. Jamie did not trust her accent.

Darkness had fallen by the time he sauntered down to the river to look for The Cock. Darkness and a comfortable feeling that he was, after all, surrounded by a great deal of wealth – warehouses crammed with spices; carpets; exotic drugs; dyes; ivory from walrus or elephant; rare metals; counting houses where merchants were totting up the take for the day; the piercing odours of tar and salt fish, with all that they conjured up of voyages through frightful suffering to fabulous treasure.

All of which was pleasing to a man of substance like himself – almost a merchant! In Venice, he would certainly be a member of the dread Council of Ten. Meanwhile, it was undeniably soothing to feel that he was at his ease, a rich man amid riches, gnawed neither by hunger nor envy.

The girls? They could wait. There would be time later for all that kind of thing.

Jamie turned into the narrow alley which shuffled down from one of the main streets towards the river. Down there, as he found out after questioning passers-by, was the tavern Jabez had mentioned.

When he found it, his expectations were realized. It was ill-lighted, the serving women were surly and suspicious, the drink was cheap.

Jamie waited quietly for Jabez Walker to arrive.

When he did, Jamie listened carefully.

'Chap with his ear bound up. Of course, could happen to anyone, sir. Might have been done by order of the justices, see what I mean. Anyhow, this chap, foreigner – pardon me for saying so, seeing you're a bit of a foreigner yourself – he's been taking men on for a job. A job! A voyage, he says. Now, wouldn't you think he'd want seamen for that sort of work, instead of the sort he's taking?'

'What sort are they?' said Jamie.

Jabez spread his vast hands over the table. They were red, chapped and as hard as the wood of the oars he pulled. He lowered his voice as he went on.

'Wrong 'uns, sir. In trouble with the justices; knock you down as soon as look at you; old, beat-up watermen; hookers – '

88

'Hookers?' Jamie asked.

Jabez looked at him in surprise.

'You know what hookers are, sir? Walk about with a long stick. See an open window, they slip a hook on the end of the stick and pull out a hat or a coat that somebody has left inside. Then off they go – work another street. Hookers. That's the sort he's after. For what kind of work? Sailoring? A week at sea would kill most of them.'

'For what, then?'

Jabez looked around sadly and shook his head.

'Ah, that's the point, ain't it. Ask me, it's some job not too far from here, not too long from now. All this while he keeps them in the attic of Old Mother Brown's house across the river. Women and booze. What it must cost him! No, it's going to be some day soon. Maybe I'm wrong.'

Jamie thought that very likely he was right.

'Old Mother Brown's,' he said. 'I could slip in there one evening and have a drink with the girls.'

Jabez Walker looked worried.

'For the love of God, sir, no! Not your class at all. Now, if it's girls you want – '

'Where is Old Mother Brown's, Jabez?' said Jamie.

A smile spread, slowly and with infinite precaution, over Jabez's face.

But it was to the Rose of York that Jamie was now making his way through the crooked streets of London. When he came to the alley in which it stood, all was quiet. Perhaps too quiet.

Nobody in the street. Nobody skulking in the doorways . . . Neither sight nor sound of human life. Nothing at all but the crawling on his scalp.

For which there was no accounting. Unless –

Before he noticed it, there had been the faintest scratching noise – but it was hardly a noise – as if somebody had rubbed his coat against a wall, as if . . . But a thousand explanations were available. In a vast, crowded city like London, silence does not happen, any more than it does in an empty meadow on a sunny afternoon.

Jamie entered the Rose of York.

'Anybody been asking for Jack Scream?'

'No, sir,' said the old potboy. 'Not a soul here. Business quiet, sir.'

In the candlelight Jamie's face had the grave serenity of a Florentine angel. He went upstairs. Intuition had become suspicion. He went into his room and looked thoughtfully around. Then he pulled his sword out of the scabbard as gently as he could. But when he slid it under the door, it was obvious that it would not do what he had wanted, which was to be a wedge to keep the door shut when somebody wanted to push it open from the outside. He sheathed the sword and tried the dirk which he had taken to wearing more for ornament than for use.

The dirk was better. When he cautiously opened the door, it acted as a wedge would have done and stopped the door. He did not think that it would resist a second, determined shove from the other side, but it might give him a few seconds of time to do what he had to do.

Next, he threw the window wide open. Using his sword at full arm's length, he pushed out the hinged iron hoist on the wall outside until it stood at right angles to the building. It creaked damnably when he moved it but that could not be helped. The loose end of the rope – Jabez Walker's rope – which he had tied to the hoist, dangled over the window ledge and hung down to the floor.

Surveying the room again, Jamie saw that his defences could be strengthened by a measure so obvious he was astounded it had not occurred to him before. With infinite caution, he pushed his bed against the door: nobody could break into the room without waking him. He was just about to blow out the candle when he remembered something. He looked down from the window to the black river below. The boat was there. All was well. He went to bed clothed, cloaked and booted. In three minutes he was asleep . . .

Jamie was still hardly conscious – how many hours later? – when he found that he was rowing across the river in the dinghy which Jabez Walker had left moored to the wall below his window. A great deal had happened in the last few seconds before he was completely awake, actions that he had performed by instinct, events that he had understood before he had seen them.

Asleep, he had become aware of furtive noises and sharp concussions as the door of his room was pushed against the bed. Still asleep, or almost asleep, he had leapt to the window ledge, seized the rope and launched himself into the air. Barely awake, he had landed with a crash on the dinghy moored at the quay below and set about unmooring it, hastily, not knowing how Jabez had left it.

Now the boat was in midstream. The night was bitterly cold. The current was strong. He was rowing towards the distant bank with all of his strength. It needed that and a bit of cunning besides, because he was less than a hundred yards above the Bridge and he did not care for the look of the water that was plunging seawards between the piers.

At length, he found an iron ring on the further bank, near some slimy wooden steps, and made the boat fast. By that time he was fully awake.

The question was, what was he to do now? It was too late for the theatre and he did not want to visit Old Mother Brown's before he had taken the advice of Lawrence Fletcher about that establishment.

At this hour, there was still a chance that the actor might be entertaining friends in that alehouse he had taken Jamie to once before. It was somewhere not far from the Swan.

At length, he found it and pushed his way into a huddle of customers and a reek of beer.

The actor stopped in the middle of a harangue.

'God,' said Fletcher, 'look who's here! Don't you know it is out of bounds? And what may you be looking for, Mr Stuart?'

A bed and a job,' said Jamie, suppressing a yawn.

'Any more for any more?' shouted Jamie to the grey sky above Southwark. Then he struck the drum before him a resounding series of whacks. 'Good people,' he said, 'good people! The show is about to begin. The greatest show on

91

earth. The most famous actor in England – what am I saying? – in all Christendom. Lawrence –' and he gave the drum a resounding thump – 'Fletcher' – thump – 'in his latest triumph. The man who can conjure the hearts out of your breasts' – he looked around before going on in a slightly lower voice – 'if you have any, you miserable little toads, you sweepings of the Cockney gutters, you – ' For the public had ceased to press into the Swan Theatre.

The enthusiasts for the drama were either already inside waiting for the play to begin or they had decided that this new offering of the great Fletcher's had no appeal for them. At this moment, he caught sight of a citizen hurrying past with no evident intention to come into the theatre. 'You,' he called out. 'You, mister. This means you!' The man paid no attention.

'How much have we taken?' Lawrence Fletcher asked, rubbing thumb and forefinger together. Jamie glanced at him, grimaced and went on counting the money at the turnstile of the Swan Theatre until he had finished. Now that he had a job and – almost – a bed, he had discovered in himself an unsuspected talent for business. Much more exciting, he could use his fencing skill when there was duelling on the stage.

'Two hundred and twenty-three pence,' he said, finally.

Fletcher scowled, although as the theatre's income for a day it was average good.

'And some of it mighty strange coin,' he said. 'The rewards of art! Makes you wonder!' He rolled his eyes in despair.

A bell rang.

'Time you were on,' said Jamie.

'What about yourself? That fencing show you gave. Be careful! The drama is a question of split-second timing. Last night, what happened? The poor devil playing Laertes was left looking about the stage wondering how to fill in the pause.'

'I was only a couple of seconds behind time.'

Fletcher nodded vigorously.

'Right,' he said. 'But, on the stage, time isn't what it *is*!

92

It's what it *seems* to be. Laertes. He didn't know what to do. You must admit, people were beginning to laugh.'

'It's time you were on,' said James.

'And another thing,' said Fletcher. 'There's no need to be so clever about that fencing anyway. Remember. *He* has to kill *you*. You've got to make it seem natural. Otherwise what's the point of lowering the lights and substituting you for me? Do you understand? Just say if you don't.'

The bell rang again.

'That's the second bell,' said Jamie.

'So no more of this show-off stuff, if you please.'

He was going, when Jamie called out, 'Hey!'

'Yes?'

'Do we accept French money?' He held up a coin.

'Less twenty per – ' said Fletcher. He hurried off.

On this side of the river, thought Jamie, you're in another world.

He was growing used to his new career as keeper of the turnstile at the Swan and custodian of the funds, if any, of Fletcher's troupe.

'It's a key position, boy. Historic! You are in the direct succession from Judas Iscariot. As it happens, you have all the qualities which the job requires. You are honest. You can count. And, most important of all, when somebody makes a snatch for the till, as sometimes happens, you can fight him off.'

As well as these duties, Jamie was brought on the stage when there was a fight, to 'give a bit of zest', as Lawrence had put it. 'No harm if you play it a few minutes longer than it needs. The customers will love it.'

In fact, as Jamie found out, it was during those moments of high drama, when the house was cheering both sides on, that the pickpockets and the cutpurses – the nips and the foists – did their best business in the theatre.

'They are the curse of the drama,' said Fletcher, with indignation. But he didn't say no to the case of sack which turned up mysteriously at Christmas and was generally supposed to come from the organization of the thieves.

Another world, thought Jamie, and turned with a smile to

the unwashed, ragged, impudent but undeniably attractive doll who had appeared before him. He knew her kind. He knew where she came from. He had learnt a great deal about the South Bank in a couple of days. He was even beginning to pick up the local language, pedlar's French, as it was called. And he had a special interest in this little flower of the South Bank.

'Yes, angel?' he said amiably to the grand-daughter of Old Mother Brown.

'You asked about him,' she said, 'the fellow who lost his ear. Still want to know?'

Jamie nodded.

'Two came in from the high pad,' she said. 'He wanted them to go along with him. They wouldn't – not on any account.'

Jamie understood from this that a couple of highwaymen who had deserted the open road for a more comfortable billet in the town had refused an offer that the one-eared stranger had made to them.

'Wouldn't, eh!' he said. 'Ever seen a French penny, dear? Take it in your hand. Don't be frightened. Now, why do you think they wouldn't?'

'Didn't like the way of his talk. Said they were good Englishmen.'

'Is he not English?'

'He's English all right. But he's not the good kind of English, if you get me.'

Jamie reflected. 'Where do they booze, Jenny, those two fellows?'

She shook her head, 'They've gone. Left the vill.'

It was easy enough for him to understand what she meant. The thieves' slang was not called French for nothing.

'Skipped?' he said.

She nodded.

'It can't be helped,' he said. 'Do you think he might ask me to join him? I'd like a job as much as any man. Maybe somebody could slip him the notion.' He winked at her. 'Anyhow, you have a friend in me, Jenny. Give us a kiss, girl. And tell your gran that Scotch Jimmy will be along to see her when the show's over at the Swan. Remember, darling?'

'Oh, your hair,' she said, dreamily. 'You ought to have been a girl.'

He had put away his sword, hidden his fur cloak and borrowed some shabby clothes from the Swan's wardrobe. He did not shave, nor, for that matter, wash. He looked as he meant to look, every inch a rogue at odds with the watch!

When he dropped into Old Mother Brown's for a talk with the well-painted harlots of the establishment it was compassionately assumed that his abstinence from pleasure was due to a passing touch of the old Spanish pip, not surprising in a young man of spirit. In spite of this failing Jamie was on good terms with the ladies, from the little Jenny who was still being trained for her profession, to the blowsiest old hag, sodden in gin and bald under her wig. His manners were thought to do honour to the house, while as for his accent – 'Say what you like, girls, that French talk makes something in me turn over.'

'Takes dam' little to make you turn over, dear!'

'Not so much of that, girls!' came the warning from Old Mother Brown.

That evening, after he had seen Jenny at the turnstile, he was chatting to some of the inmates when Jenny whispered to him.

'He's here, Jamie. One-ear.'

'Remember what I told you, darling.'

A little later somebody stumped into the room and gave Jamie a long, hard stare. He was beyond all doubt the man who all those weeks ago had leapt on to the deck of *The Dark Lady* from *The Trinidad*. No mistaking him.

After his survey, he went on into another room in the house. Jamie waited to hear Jenny's report.

'He don't fancy you,' she said. 'Something about you scares him. You're bad money, he says. He's had some trouble already with the lot he's got. Knives out. Bottles flying. In the end, two of 'em went off with two of the girls.

'You don't know where they went to?'

95

Jenny shook her head. 'They'll keep clear of my gran,' she said, sombrely.

Jamie nodded. 'If they have any sense!' he said. 'Well, if you hear anything – ' He slipped a penny into her hand. 'Oh, and tell him to try warm olive oil. Tell him I said so. But wait till I've gone.'

'Oil?' Jenny's eyes were big.

'Yes,' he said, 'for his earache.'

As it turned out, it was from Lawrence Fletcher he picked up the next scrap of news.

'Remember you telling me about a fellow who lost his ear-ring?' said the actor. 'Funny thing but I saw an ear-ring that might have been the twin of that last night, made me think of you. Yes, it was on a man who had a plaster on his cheek. In the boozer, he was.'

'Did he try to recruit you, Lawrence?'

'No. But I'll tell you something. He was asking about the shipping between the Pool and Greenwich Reach, asking most particularly. Number of ships, when they unloaded, and all that. He seems to be in business, your friend.'

'He's in business all right,' said Jamie. 'The question is, what kind of business?'

'Ah, m'm . . .' Fletcher scraped his chin with his thumb. 'Talking about that, reminds me. You haven't a shilling you could lend me, I suppose? Until tonight. We're running short of greasepaint. Some of those boys of mine use it for extramural occasions, if you know what I mean. That's my opinion. Strange thing, the stage, Jamie. On one hand, the immortal spirit of man, on the other – vice! Sodom and the stars. Thank you, my boy. You couldn't make it two, I suppose?'

It was the time of day when Jamie was accustomed to stroll down to a jetty on the river bank below a tavern called The Cardinal's Hat. This house was not really a tavern. And it was not any more called The Cardinal's Hat, not officially anyhow, for England was a Protestant country and cardinals were out of favour even for the names of whorehouses. Except, of course, in popular speech.

On the jetty, by arrangement, Jabez Walker would bring

Jamie any news there might be from the Rose of York across the river. This time, Jabez brought a verbal message and a letter. Mr Beaton had called asking for him. It seemed that it was very important.

Jamie broke the seals of the letter. It was an invitation from Sir Ferdinand Vane asking him to come down and stay a few days at Sir Ferdinand's house in Essex. He was promised some duck shooting in the marshes and some hunting of no particular class. But reasonably good sport for those who were healthy enough to endure the English country scene with winter coming on. Mr Stuart would not be there alone. Among others, Lord Henry Howard had been invited. And Sir Ferdinand's girls were particularly anxious to see Mr Stuart. He was asked to send word to the secretary at Vane House if he proposed to do Sir Ferdinand the honour, etc.

A stream of directions followed on how the house was to be reached; where he could hire a decent horse; sections of the road where he ought especially to be on his guard, etc.

Lawrence Fletcher shook his head when Jamie showed it to him. 'There is something not right about this. No, I don't like it. Look. What is certain? They are after you – '

'But who are they?' asked Jamie.

'That's the problem. *Your* problem. Then you have this invitation. Out of the blue, so to speak. And this girl who's in trouble.'

'She's not in trouble.'

'How do you know, Stuart? And Lord Henry. I could tell you something about him.'

'You needn't.'

'A snake. A viper. Poisonous! And he has this girl in his power. Oh, I should be very careful if I were you. Of course, it's flattering – '

Jamie exploded with annoyance.

'Flattering! A prince of the blood royal is invited by a well-to-do pirate! Who is flattering whom, I'd like to know?'

'Prince . . .' said Fletcher, turning down the corners of his mouth. 'I don't mean to be rude,' he said.

Alan's advice was different. He had crossed the river in Jabez Walker's boat and arrived, full of his latest visit to

Lord Southampton in the Tower. His eyes were rounder and bluer even than usual.

'For this Virginian voyage, he wants to form a company. But the trouble is that he is not allowed to do it so long as he is in a State prison. So some other way must be found.'

'In London,' said Jamie, 'there are a hundred men who have the means to found a company. Every day they do that kind of thing in the City. Listen now, Alan, I want your advice.'

'Go ahead.'

At the end of Jamie's story of the invitation from Sir Ferdinand, Alan said, 'I would accept it, if I were you. If you stay here, you are sure to be discovered sooner or later. Theatres and whorehouses – just the places for them to search. And I like what you tell me about Sir What's-his-name Vane. How many ships do you think he owns?'

'Five,' said Jamie. 'One for each daughter.'

'Five!'

'Beautiful, all of them.'

'He might just be the man,' said Alan, 'for the Virginian adventure.'

An Angel of Mockery

Jamie rode eastwards out of the City on the useful horse he had hired – dappled grey with the hint of a rusty sheen on its crupper, a sturdy little beast with no pretensions to style. With him rode Tom, the young groom, whom Jabez Walker had supplied to his specifications – 'a young man who will keep his mouth shut and his eyes open, and if he can use his fists, no harm at all.' The waterman had nodded, winked and understood.

Next day he had come back: 'You want Tom, sir. Go into the Three Kings in Cheapside, know where I mean? Go through the back bar into the stableyard and call out Tom, see. He'll answer. Sure to. Don't worry about his looks. And don't ask him too many questions, sir. Would only make him nervous.'

Looks? A broken nose and not many teeth in front. Also a long scar down one cheek, barely healed. A way of walking that suggested that two feet were more than a man could reasonably be expected to manage. Age? About the same as Jamie's.

Jamie had asked, after one quick survey of this human disaster: 'Can you look after yourself if things get rough? Not that they will.' Tom had said nothing. It was quickly apparent that he was not the talking kind. But from somewhere, a belt or a pocket hidden in his doublet, there had flashed a long pointed knife – one, two! and it had vanished again. Jamie put no more questions.

They rode in silence through a landscape which was grey,

cropped and sombre. It suggested that in England the winter was about to begin. About the time when, in other countries, it was already far advanced. To the south, there was flat country broken by grey stretches of water which reminded Jamie of Holland where he had spent years of his boyhood. To the north, the land rose into low hills. In spare, black forests the hunters were out. He heard horns and the barking of dogs. Once or twice, a shot.

Night was closing in when they came in sight of Sir Ferdinand's house at the far end of a long avenue of freshly planted trees.

It was built round a courtyard which they entered through an archway. Jamie looked round with interest. This, he thought, was a house that had been in the family for a long time and, then, somebody had decided it was not grand enough for him and had rebuilt one side of the yard with a certain amount of fancy brickwork, especially about the chimneys. Somebody with money to spend.

Somebody not too long ago. Somebody who had done well. Out of what? With the enlivening thought that he might be looking at the proceeds of a career in crime, Jamie dismounted.

Something seemed to have put an edge on the wind. It had come a long way and now it was ill-tempered. Sniffing it, Jamie imagined that he smelt the sea; but maybe it was only one of the tricks that fancy plays! A lantern was coming towards him across the darkness of the yard: a stable hand was coming for the horses. Jamie handed the reins to Tom.

Seeing light showing below a door, he entered a hall where, behind a pierced wooden screen, a log fire was crackling in a huge chimney. Just at that moment, two burly, weather-beaten men came towards him. They were wearing heavy knitted jerseys and sea-boots. Between them, they were carrying a heavy chest. They gave him a quick glance and passed on out of the house. Jamie thought that one of them had winked as he passed. The door slammed behind them.

After all, he had smelt the sea.

Somewhere, not far away, a boat would be lying moored

alongside a jetty. A fishing boat? He did not think they were fishermen. And what had they been carrying? It was not a herring box.

A servant held out a hand for his cloak and led the way up a broad, oak stair. Jamie found that he had been given a darkly panelled room in what was apparently the older wing of the house. Its main piece of furniture was a large bed, sumptuously hung with crimson velvet. Its canopy was adorned with a trophy of ostrich feathers at each corner.

'Magnificent,' said Jamie to the servant.

'Slept in by Her Majesty when she visited us.'

Jamie was being allotted the best bedroom.

When he came downstairs, later, he was greeted in the hall by one of Miranda's four sisters – Liz? He could not remember. The youngest. Yes, she was Liz. He found to his delight that the English ceremony of welcome did not vary from town to country.

'At last I have you alone!' he said.

'If you begin that way, God knows how you'll finish!' Her eyes danced with mischief. 'You *will* do your tricks, won't you? That is one of the reasons you have been asked.'

'Do you mean my tricks with cards? Or would you rather I did the one with the rope? I throw it into the air and climb to the top.'

'That will keep until after supper,' said Liz.

'Ah, supper. A pity you mentioned that. I am dying of hunger. I shall disgrace you. Tell me, who else is coming?'

She uttered names that meant nothing to him. '. . . and Lord Henry Howard,' she finished with a little frown. 'He is here with one of his friends. Miranda insisted he should come. I don't know why. I don't like him and I like his friends even less.'

Somewhere, someone was brewing punch. Nutmeg hung in the air like clouds blowing off a tropical island. A chest, heavily carved in black gleaming wood, stood against the panelled wall. Once it had been bringing silks from Asia. And then, he thought, somewhere between the Cape and Tagus Bar, it had been rudely transhipped. There were more ways than one of doing business.

101

One after another, the Vane sisters appeared, Miranda last. 'She is clever,' said Kate, 'to be always the climax of our story.'

'It is her right,' said Liz, 'as the eldest.'

She greeted Jamie with a downcast, almost sulky, air, which he found indescribably alluring.

A troop of young men followed, cheeks scrubbed by the air, blue eyes inflamed. And, after a time, Lord Henry Howard, with his plump white face and his plump cleft chin, his little eyes roving this way and that. His companion was a tall, lanky young man with pale hair and a small, disdainful mouth. His ear-rings were too long and elaborate for Jamie's taste.

'Who is he?' he asked.

'Let me introduce you,' said Kate, with a shrug. 'But haven't you met him?'

'Not exactly.' He thought that it was some time since he had met the kind. And he thought he knew what the kind was.

'Captain Chandler – James Stuart.'

Chandler ran a weary, hostile eye over him. Then, he drew down his eyelids as if he wished to see no more.

'You are here for the hunting?' said Jamie, bowing politely.

'Like yourself,' said Chandler, in a voice as sleek as it was cold.

'Some people prefer to hunt in couples,' remarked Jamie to Miranda when the two were out of earshot. She gave him an anxious glance.

'If I were you, Jamie', she said, 'I should – ' For a moment she hesitated. 'They are not your kind.'

'No,' he said. 'I hunt alone.' He gave her a smile of real pleasure. Then he found his way back to the stables where Tom was giving the horses their feed.

'Listen carefully,' he said. 'Two men are here. Howard and Chandler. They'll have a servant. Perhaps two. Keep an eye on them. Understand?'

Tom nodded and went on with the task of fitting a horse's nosebag in place.

102

'It may be just that I don't like men with dimpled chins, and drooping eyelids,' said Jamie to nobody in particular. When he walked into the house again, the aroma of punch was stronger.

'May I talk to you, Liz?' he asked the blondest of the Vane sisters. Her eyes were bright with excitement. He reminded himself that she was very young.

'Certainly you may talk to me. But you must not make love to me, Jamie.'

So she was not so young after all.

'Those two gentlemen at the further end of the room. One is Lord Henry Howard, the other walks as if his legs were one size too large for him. Tell me more.'

'Lord Henry was anxious that Father should have him down to talk about some shipping thing. What it is, I don't know. Why do you ask, Jamie?'

He looked thoughtfully at the pair.

'Shipping,' he said. 'You surprise me.' Chandler did not look like a man who would be interested in the sea.

'I think it's shipping. There are different kinds of shipping, you know. Some of them are quite respectable, I believe. Maybe it's that kind which interests him.'

'I don't think so,' said Jamie.

'I don't think so, either. But you ought to ask Miranda. She is the cleverest of the famous Vane sisters, and I am probably the stupidest. What do you think, Jamie?'

'I think we should inquire into the whole business without a moment's delay,' he said, solemnly.

Taking the girl's hand in his, he turned it over and kissed it on the wrist.

'Ah,' sighed Liz. 'Wonderful.'

She was an angel of mockery.

As the evening wore on, they played cards. Kate Vane told fortunes and Jamie taught Liz a song from Paris. She had a singularly pure little voice and accompanied herself on the lute. Jamie found that he drank a great deal of punch.

'Your father's friends interest me,' he said to Miranda.

'You mean Lord Henry's friend,' she said quickly. 'But why do you say that?'

103

'Mr Chandler cheated me at hazard twice, so clumsily that I had the idea he meant me to notice.'

'Why should he?'

'Ask yourself. Perhaps he had the notion I might accuse him. Then he would be insulted and feel obliged to challenge me. He did not like the way I turned the pack over and ran my fingers over the backs of the cards. It was touch and go whether he would slap my face. Later, he told one of these young men that most Frenchmen are liars and cowards, too. He looked me rather hard in the eyes as he said it. Luckily, I am quite deaf and did not hear him.'

'I'll tell Father.'

'Please do nothing like that, Miranda. Let the comedy go on.'

'So long as the comedy remains a comedy,' she said, with a frown. It was as if she was nervous.

Once Upon a Time

Miranda and Jamie had lost the hunt. It ought to have been hard to do with the horns blowing, the hounds giving tongue, and the men calling, but they did it.

The higher ground above the fields was broken into shreds of coppice and heath with stretches of rough grassland in between. After ten minutes, when it was clear that the chase had taken a different direction from theirs, Miranda, who was in the lead, reined in. She was riding a fiery little devil of a dark bay with a white star on his forehead and one white sock. Jamie had to push his grey to the limit to keep up.

'Shall we go back?' she said, 'or shall we ride on a little further and look at the sea,'

'It is too early to go back.' Before he had finished the sentence, she had touched her bay into a gallop through neglected woodlands dotted with ancient trees of ruined grandeur.

After a while, she called something back over her shoulder. It might have been to tell him that they had passed beyond the bounds of the family lands. Trotting sedately for a mile or two along the verges of ploughed fields, they came at last to a low sandy hill, crowned by a group of splendid pines. Miranda held out her whip. 'There!' she said.

It was the sea, insinuating tentacles into a land almost as low and level as the water. Scanning the scene, Jamie thought that he recognized one feature in it. The idea crossed his mind that she might have brought him there in order to see it. He looked at her.

105

The colour in the little face was quickened to a new brilliance by the exercise and the wet, cold air. Hair, eyes, lips – all seemed to quiver. Nothing about her was still. Everything seemed to be on the brink of a delicious explosion of laughter, temper, mischief. Jamie rode nearer to her, but not too near. He did not trust that glistening little demon she was riding.

'Do you see that island in the distance?' she said. He could see a thin stroke of pale light in the grey distance which might have been an island. He was prepared to believe it. 'Millions of birds come there every year from the north, to winter.'

'I see a ship in that long winding creek down there,' he said. 'Very like a ship I've seen before somewhere.'

'Yes,' she looked him in the eyes, serious. 'Yes. It's been here for the last few days. I have heard some of Father's men talking about it. It's German or something. An Easterling.'

'If it's the one I am thinking of, it has a black girl as a figurehead.'

She said nothing.

'A man I know,' said Jamie absently, 'wants to sail a ship – one just like that – over to Virginia. He has the idea that he could make a kingdom for himself there. He has been reading books. That's too exciting for a young man.'

'He should take more exercise.'

'That's difficult. You see, he's in prison.'

She looked away quickly.

'What will he call his kingdom when, at last, he escapes from prison? I suggest New England,' she said.

'I shall tell him you said so, next time I see him,' said Jamie.

'People have strange notions sometimes,' she said, looking over the flat country to the distant ribbon of the sea that had been stretched across the vista, faintly, like an afterthought.

'Yes. Like the strange notion somebody had to ask Captain Chandler down here for the hunting.'

'Lord Henry Howard has a peculiar taste in friends. What do you think Captain Chandler is, Jamie?' It seemed to need

106

a great effort to draw her gaze away from the sea, so that for one instant, she could dart a look into his eyes.

'If it were not your father's house,' he said, 'I might be wondering. If I were in Paris, I would be fairly sure. Yes, I think I should know where I was. But this is England. All the rules of the game are different.'

'In Paris,' she said, 'what would you think he was?'

For a moment it looked as if he was going to tell her. Instead, he said, 'You are frightened of Lord Henry, aren't you? Don't tell me, I know, You needn't be frightened, Miranda.'

She looked round, startled; the beautiful colour flushed her cheeks; her eyes were alight.

'Blackmail,' said Jamie, 'is a game that two can play.'

For a moment he thought she was going to force the little bay headlong down the steep slope. And then ride like the wind towards the sea. And when she reached it? – what?

Her knuckles whitened as she gripped the reins harder. The whip was lifted. Her face was the scene on which some sudden, obscure moment in a drama was staged – panic, rejection, hatred? Then it was all over and her voice was cool and level as she said:

'What *is* Captain Chandler, do you think?'

He shrugged.

'Why did you change the subject, Jamie? We were talking about Lord Henry and his friend.'

'A jack of all trades,' he said. 'All trades from extortion to killing. A killer, Miranda. Or I am much mistaken.'

Miranda pulled her horse's head sharply away from the sea.

'Marriage!' cried Miranda Vane as they rode back together.

Had they been talking about marriage? Jamie could not remember. It was not his favourite subject.

'I don't think I shall ever marry,' she said.

'That will be a great blow to your sisters. They told me that, until you marry, they can't. Your mother won't have it . . . Love,' he said, inconsequently.

107

'Love is the trouble. Without love, I shall not marry. And I can't love.'

'No?'

'No. Never. Never again.'

'Ah! Tell,' he said.

'Of course not.' She spoke angrily. He thought that she frowned. He was riding at her side and he could not see her face. But she made the quick movement of the head that usually goes with a frown.

'No? Invent a story then. Something that might have happened and did not. Tell it in verse if that will make it easier. You are a poet, I'm told.'

'One of my sisters has betrayed me. Which one?'

He shook his head.

'No,' he said. 'I heard it somewhere else. You must remember I am in touch with literature. In the world of drama I am very important. I take the money at the door. Didn't I tell you? Please. Make up a little fairy story. Shall I begin it for you? *Once upon a time –* '

'Not so long ago. You are a devil, Jamie!' she cried.

'Go on, Miranda. Continue the fairy-tale.'

'Once upon a time, there was a man.'

'A *man*?' he said, surprised.

'Yes. This is a story about a man, James. He wrote things – I don't know what.'

'Could we make it that he wrote plays? As he is imaginary. anyway.'

'Why did you say plays?' she said.

'The first thing that came into my mind. I'm a man of the theatre, after all. But make it something else if you like. Books on navigation, say.'

'No. Plays will do . . . One day he met a girl. She was younger than he, quite young, reckless, inexperienced, simple. Simple enough to think that he could love her as she loved him. But he was married – a wife and children! Besides, he had his writing, the things he wrote.'

'The plays.'

'The plays,' she made only the faintest grimace as she spoke. 'How could he love her with all his being as she loved him – or thought she did – when he was in the power of this god – or devil – of creation? She hated it, with a jealousy she did not feel for his wife or his women – if he had any woman; she was not sure. But she was not willing to have anything less than all his love – *all of him*! And she was young, greedy, stupid, strong – '

'And beautiful,' he insisted.

But Miranda swept on.

'Then, one day, she knew that she had won. It is not a thing a man tells a woman. If he does, she need not believe him. But she saw it like a sickness in his eyes. He wrote, more than ever, but it was in the hope that he might tear her out of his heart – if he could. But he couldn't. He swore that she had enslaved him, heart, passions, mind. Every particle of him was hers. There was no good or evil in the world for him apart from her smile or her frown.'

She paused.

'And she?' said Jamie. 'The girl in the story. What did she feel? The joy of victory?'

'What do you think?' she asked. 'What would be the feelings of a girl who had gone through that double twist of fortune? . . . Triumph? Alarm? . . . No. That would be much too simple! The girl in the story was growing up. She was learning fast. She was being wooed in language more beautiful than she had ever heard. It made her drunk. But – *but*! – she was seeing a god humiliated. And she had been in love with the god.'

'Ah! This business of love is very tricky.'

'Yes. Think how lucky you are, Jamie!'

'Please go on.'

'People said that he wrote better than ever before. Do people write better under torture? He swore he would kill himself, and her, too. They had terrible scenes. He accused her of having made him betray the God-sent power which was the best part of him, which he had been sent into the world to realize. And he said the worst of it was that he no longer cared for his work. Then he told her that if she loved him at all, she would go to the queen and tell her everything, that one of her Virgin Majesty's maids of honour was no longer a maid. Once the girl would have done that joyfully. She all but did it unprompted. Now – she would still do it. She was willing enough. But no more than that. Love was mixed with compassion, and compassion is a neighbour of contempt.'

They had arrived at the verges of an open heath, a stretch of untamed land broken by clumps of gorse and sandpits. Miranda kicked her horse into a canter, calling out something as she went ahead. He could not hear it. But it was probably a warning about rabbit holes. When they pulled up five minutes later, Jamie's horse was breathing noisily.

'Compassion,' he reminded her. 'You were speaking of compassion.'

'Don't ask me to explain,' she said. 'Or excuse. *He* understood. Nobody better! It was as if he possessed a secret chart of the labyrinth of the human heart. There were times when the girl thought he must have lived once before and been a woman. And then, what do you think happened? If you were inventing this tale instead of me, what would be the next turn in the plot?'

She turned to look at him, almost fiercely.

'She would tell the queen,' said Jamie, 'and the queen would say, "How dare you disturb a poet who is one of England's glories! Go, my girl, and find a new lover!"'

Miranda smiled and shook her head.

'No, Jamie. Something quite different. She wrote a letter to the queen, telling everything, but, first, she took it to him so that he could read it. Of course, she would not have done that if she had been the simple, loving girl with whom the story began.'

'He would see that, of course?'

'Who better! He crumpled the letter into a ball and threw it into a corner of the room. He spoke with a quiet politeness – oh, poisonous! And he told her to go away. He said that now he was writing as he had never written before. And he had found a girl whom he loved.'

'He had invented her.'

Miranda shrugged her shoulders impatiently.

'Maybe. What mattered was that he did not love *her* any

110

more. The spell was broken. She left him there – and the letter, too. She was distraught.'

There was a moment of silence.

'Ah! Enter the villain!' said Jamie softly.

She looked startled.

'I suppose we must have a villain.'

'It helps the story,' said Jamie. 'The villain had been watching these two. Now he finds the letter.'

Miranda hesitated for a moment.

'What if he did *not* find the letter! What if he, the lover, read it to him – the villain – and then crumpled it up in disgust and threw it on the floor, or in the waste basket? Then, next day, the girl comes back for the letter and it is not there. It can't be found.'

Jamie's eyes lit up with excitement.

'Because it *had* been found,' he said. 'So the villain could blackmail her for a sin – excuse the word – of which she is no longer guilty! My God, when I think what Lawrence Fletcher could make of this story! But what about the man who had been her lover? He is write, write, writing better than ever, he thinks – Ah! But he has a new girl!'

Miranda frowned.

'Who is Lawrence Fletcher?' she said, coolly.

He brushed the question aside impatiently.

'Who found the new girl for him? Or was it a boy?'

'How do I know!'

'Don't tell me, Miranda. Don't say it was Lord Henry! – *Good God*!'

'It's time we went home, Jamie. Mother hates it when we are late for dinner.'

She touched the little bay with her spur. Within seconds they were at full gallop.

This is something, thought Jamie, looking round at the scene in Sir Ferdinand Vane's hall that night. This is something of which Carbon de Castel Jaloux would have approved. Carbon was an old acquaintance who had been the greatest gourmand in the school they went to in Paris, looking on food with the same solemn passion that other men look on women.

111

On the long table, hewn from a single elm trunk, as Sir Ferdinand explained, were set out sixteen main dishes, having as their centrepiece a pasty, the crust of which had been moulded by the master cook into the semblance of a baronial stronghold crowned by brilliantly coloured heraldic banners. How many score of birds, wild and domestic, were immured within those walls of flour?

It was plain that the English, famed throughout Christendom for their coldness towards the arts, for their deep and dangerous melancholy, had a more genial and aesthetic side to their character.

With glistening eyes and hands which they brought together with loud smacking noises, the guests approached the table, round which stood a ring of waiting footmen. Beyond them was Lady Vane, her caving knife hovering above a vast chine of beef.

Sir Ferdinand called on a chaplain to say grace and kept interrupting him with groans of pain, snappings of the fingers and other symptoms of spiritual discomfort. The feast began with the impetus of a charge of horse.

'Your father's gout seems to be troubling him,' said Jamie to his neighbour, who happened to be Kate Vane. She shook her head.

'He always does that,' she said. 'Father thinks parsons are apt to go too far.'

'Or too long?'

'It's the same thing,' she said.

Some time later, heaven knows how long, Sir Ferdinand made a speech. A speech of welcome? Jamie thought that it might be, but the truth was that he could not hear a coherent sentence for the talk around him. And, in any case, he was engrossed in the problem of how to describe the colour of Kate's hair.

'Mouse,' she said.

'I have seen mice a hundred times but never one that was that colour.'

'Mouse,' she said. 'We are all mouse except Miranda.'

'And what is she?' he said.

Kate smiled, a slow, incendiary smile.

'What do you think, Jamie?'

His hand found hers, or hers found his, under the table. What colour was Miranda's hair? He was still wondering as one of the main walls of the pastry castle fell with a crash and a white cockerel flew out.

'I love your English cooking,' he said. 'Tell me, though what happens – afterwards?'

'Can you wonder! You know what night it is?'

'Ah! Yes, of course. No, I am afraid I've forgotten!'

'Twelfth Night,' she said. 'We do a play. After we have had something to eat, of course.'

'Of course.'

How did I ever think the English were lacking a sense of the poetic, the dramatic – in short, a feeling for the wonder and absurdity of life? He tried to explain his bewilderment to the girl sitting next to him at the table but she, for some reason, was no longer Kate. Now she was Molly. Who? Liz? Who then? What on earth had happened? In his confusion, Jamie could only smile weakly at the enormous complexity of life.

Some time later he understood that, while the chief parts in the play were to be taken by girls, he was to be one of the Seven Champions of Christendom. Which one? He was not sure. His part was to face, in the last act of the play, an adversary who had blackened his face and was wearing a turban. Jamie recognized him. He was the tall friend of Lord Henry's, the disdainful, equivocal Captain Chandler.

They were seven a side, dressed in all kinds of obsolete pieces of armour. Jamie's coat of chain mail had probably last been worn at Agincourt, said Sir Ferdinand. They were each given a wooden sword and told that, at the blast of a hunting horn, they were fighting in a mêlée, Christians against Saracens.

Jamie saw that Captain Chandler was among the Saracens. He caught the captain's eye resting on him thoughtfully and turned to Miranda.

'This combat will be worth watching closely,' he said, waving his sword.

'Don't hit him too hard,' she said. 'It will break.'

113

'That's the point, is it?' He made a stabbing motion. 'I should never have left the stage.'

Sir Ferdinand blew a blast on a hunting horn.

'You're on,' said Miranda.

It was a sham fight of a kind Jamie had been brought up to look on with a mixture of alarm and contempt; confused, clumsy and dangerous.

In Paris, his fencing master had warned him, 'If you find yourself mixed in a brawl, where you do not even have time to check the credentials of your adversaries – the number of their quarterings, that sort of thing – my advice is leave at once and call the constables.'

The gist of this memory from the past had just come into Jamie's mind; he was seriously involved with one adversary when he felt a heavy blow above the right temple and staggered forward, off balance for a moment. He had no doubt at all what had happened. Chandler, next along on his right front, had struck him with the flat of a wooden sword as heavy as a cudgel. He could hear Chandler breathing murderously, could see or imagine, which is almost the same thing, his contemptuous smile, his drooping eyelid.

Taking the hint, Jamie overplayed the part of helplessness. He stepped back smartly just in time to escape a swing to the head from Chandler's weapon. Simultaneously, he thrust with his own shortened sword at the vulnerable inch below the captain's ribs. He heard his adversary grunt like an angry pig. From that moment to the end there was some dodging but little attempt at guarding.

In the end, Jamie, his head singing, thought he had struck two blows for each one he was given. The captain had a slight scalp wound. Then the horn blew again and it was over.

Jamie turned to Chandler with an amiable smile. 'Did I hurt you?' he asked. Chandler gave him a poisoned look and said nothing.

'That man made a set at you?' said Sir Ferdinand. 'I saw it all. He did not hurt you as much as he imagined? No. I thought not. And you paid him in his own coin. By God, boy, it was worth watching.'

'I love your simple English sports,' said Jamie.

114

'Come and have a glass of wine with the women,' said Sir Ferdinand.

He led Jamie to a room in which there was a dazzling display of cakes of all kinds, lavishly decorated with swags and wreaths of icing sugar, and an array of bottles of Malmsey. Once more, Jamie was impressed by the stubborn energy with which the English fought against hunger.

After a time he exchanged good-night kisses with a great many young women. The Vane sisters wore, each in her own way, a mocking expression which seemed to have just alighted on their faces and would, in a flash, be replaced by – by what?

He thought them five reasons for love and five reasons why love could not, in the nature of things be a lasting passion. Kate, the kind one; Molly, the romp; vain Jane – but one day she would forget the looking glass, and then! – Liz, youngest, blondest, most mischievous. And Miranda, who walked with him to the foot of the stairs and lit his candle.

'Miranda,' he said. 'I have a confession to make. I have five sins on my conscience.'

'Jamie, don't you know? You must never tell a girl you have anything on your conscience – except her.'

Clever girl. She was using a perfume very faintly, so that – like her reputation – it would be suspected only by intimate friends. He admired the rich hues of her copper curls.

'My friend Chandler seems to have disappeared,' he said.

She frowned quickly. 'Whatever he intended before,' she said, 'now he will certainly try to kill you. Be careful, Jamie.'

They kissed a little longer than the rules allowed, and on the lips, which the rules forbade.

He went upstairs and in his room found Tom, the groom, with some news ready to pour out of his toothless mouth.

'That captain,' a jerk of the head, 'he's a cruel brute.'

'How d'you know, Tom?'

'Way he treats his poor horse, sir. You should see its sides. Horrible. And another thing – '

'Yes?'

'He's going to leave early in the morning. He knows the way you mean to take, sir. Sir, you'll change it, o' course.'

Jamie shook his head.

'And, sir, the captain talked to somebody tonight in the stableyard. Man with one glove.'

'You're sure it was only one?'

Tom nodded. 'Cross my heart.'

Here was news! Alonzo Porter straying far out of his parish.

'Tom, do you think we can handle all of them?'

Tom grinned.

'I shall certainly not change the route, then.'

'Just what you say, sir.'

Tom left.

Jamie in a few minutes blew out the candle and drew the heavy curtains together so that he was in total darkness.

Sometime during that night, in the total blackness of his bedroom, when he was asleep behind the heavy satin curtains which he had drawn round the vast bed on which the Queen of England had slept, Jamie was aware of a disturbing, yet not unpleasant sensation.

The curtains had been parted, admitting the darkness of the room to the darkness of the bed. Someone was climbing into bed beside him; a warm body between the chilly sheets. A smooth naked arm was encircling his body.

He turned round on his back, babbling some words of question or protest. At once a finger was pressed against his lips. He tried to speak again. Someone, in the darkness of the room, laughed almost inaudibly.

'So you wish to preserve your incognito, do you?' he told the darkness of the bed. 'Very well. I respect your wish. I understand – completely. But you won't mind if I carry on the conversation for the two of us? You see, I usually have company when anything like this happens to me. Not that it has ever happened before. You can interrupt at any time you wish...'

There was a slight trembling of the bed.

'That is precisely what I had in mind. After that, I assume you would like me to continue in French? *Non? Tu ne parles pas français? Ah, quel malheur! Eh, bien. Tu parleras en*

115

anglais. Et moi, je repondrai en français. C'est à toi de commencer, mademoiselle.'

He spoke both parts in the dialogue that followed.

'At least you know that I am a girl.'

'Tu, me permettras à dire, chérie, que c'est la chose la plus incontestable de la vie ...'

'But which of us am I? Remember. We are five.'

'Ah, quel question!'

'Which of us would you prefer me to be?'

'Tu dois parler français!' Was it a man's voice or a girl's?

'Unknown,' said Jamie. 'We are in a state of hopeless confusion ... Besides ...'

Lips came out of the darkness and settled on his.

Silence fell on English and on French alike ...

After a time, the rings of the curtains made a faint trilling sound and someone slid from the bed, again with that laughter, that barely audible recognition of the sly comedy of life. Just before Jamie fell asleep, he was aware that the bedroom door had been softly closed.

During the rest of the night, Jamie dreamed that his first experience was repeated.

Dreams can be a commentary on life, an improvement on life, a realization on another plane of something that has failed to occur in this one.

In the morning, he found a hair on the pillow; it was russet brown. How vivid had been his dreams!

At the Holm Oak

In the stableyard next morning Jamie found Tom waiting with the horses. It seemed that Chandler with his servant had left at first dawn. Liz, the youngest and blondest of the Vanes, was waiting to bid Jamie goodbye.

'I want to kidnap you,' he said.

'There is a law against it,' she said.

'In England,' he said, 'there is a law against everything. I shall hope to see you all in London soon.'

'But Miranda will be on duty with the queen.'

'Ah, pity! Tell her I commit treason in my heart every day.'

When he turned to wave he saw that the girl was already talking earnestly to one of the grooms who had emerged from the stables.

After half an hour's riding, Jamie came to a black, shaggy wood filled with majestic, half-ruined oaks. There the road he was taking to London dwindled to a bridle path which twisted through sunken tracks that were hardly more than ruts, a little wider than the other ruts.

Tom rode up alongside him. 'Here!' he said. 'Be just the place for him to try it.' Tom showed his knife and hid it again in an uncannily swift plucking movement, which made Jamie think that his groom must once have been a success-ful pickpocket. As for what Tom apparently meant, Jamie agreed. If he had been going to commit a murder on the highway, it was here, certainly, that he would have planned to carry it out. The loneliness of the spot, the cover which the

118

ground afforded – everything favoured it as the scene of a crime.

They rode on, slightly increasing the pace, holding the reins taut, listening for the snap of a twig, the drumming of some startled bird, the sequence of small sounds which occurs when a man, standing in soft ground, shifts his weight from one foot to the other. Nothing. Then a horse stamped somewhere But it was too far off to interest them.

At the moment it happened, Jamie was studying a magnificent holm oak, which grew a few yards off the path. There was a clear space round the lower branches. He had seen trees of the same kind when he was travelling abroad. They had been just as straight and graceful. But their leaves could not have given shelter to so many men as this giant.

Jamie's mind was, just for a second, transported far away from the English wood.

It happened with such speed and violence that all he remembered afterwards was blurred, confused and strangely unreal compared with the image he retained of that remarkable tree. When he pieced together the impressions that followed in the way explosions follow one after another when a trail is laid from one powder barrel to another, what emerged was something like this.

A shot was fired, from quite near and a little behind him. He was almost sure of that, although the three shots that followed came so fast on the heels of the first that he might have been mistaken in the order his mind gave to events. He heard a yelp. Somebody had been hurt! That was odd because he had not felt anything. It must have been just then that he became aware of the masked men swarming about on the ground under his horse's shoulders. To his joy, they had swords in their hands.

Swords! This was a game he could play.

Sometime in the distant past, maybe when he was on one of those tactical rides dear to his old teacher, Antoine de Pluvinel, he had lived in imagination through a situation just like this: cavalry vedette surprised in a wood by guerrilla fighters. This preparation – or perhaps mere animal instinct – would account for Jamie's action.

119

Slash! with the sword which seemed to have come into his hand. Slash! at a masked face on his right. At the same moment a hard tug at the reins and a cruel stab with both spurs. The horse reared and snorted with fury as if it were straight out of a crack cavalry barracks and were not a mere hack from a London livery stable.

A masked figure thrust up a hand to try to shield himself from the brandished hoofs, and stumbled aside. Then Jamie let the reins fall loose, and crouched with his head on his horse's neck. The poor brute's ears were flat on its head with panic and anger.

When Jamie pulled it up again, after a minute, and looked round, he saw no sign of Tom. What he did see was one of the masks, levelling a horse pistol. Jamie kicked a gallop out of his horse and made for the man, leaning well forward in the saddle and holding his blade low.

Someone was pouring out a stream of ferocious curses in French. His drill master had said more than once, 'The human voice is an instrument of terror, messieurs. Use it!'

Below the black mask of the man aiming the pistol, he saw a sneering mouth. Jamie snarled and raised his hand as the smoke of the shot billowed out. He knew that his point had struck Chandler, but more than that he did not know. He was aware only of his horse falling away from under him while he was thrown through the air. One hand broke the fall. He turned head over heels on the ground and, for a moment, lay quite still.

When he opened his eyes, his horse was quietly cropping the grass of a small patch between the trees. Tom had vanished. Two masked men stooped over a third who lay on the ground, groaning.

Above Jamie stood Captain Chandler, his mask torn off, his left eyelid drooping, the expression on his face one of passionless malignity. He held a pistol pointing at Jamie. When he spoke, his voice was soft, too soft.

'Move,' he said, 'and this will blow your head off, King James.'

Behind him appeared a man as tall as he, but older and

120

dressed more sombrely. He had kept his mask on but Jamie recognized him without difficulty.

'Good morning, Mr Porter,' he said. 'I see you have not found your glove yet.'

When Miranda arrived at the foot of the stairs, by the door leading out to the stableyard, Liz was already there.

'Gone! Of course he has gone', said Liz. 'In fact, he was a quarter of an hour late in leaving – but still there was no sign of you!'

'It was your morning on duty, Liz.'

'And he has gone. However, if you are so anxious to see him, all you need do is ride fast to the holm oak in the Old Forest. The holm oak in the Old Forest,' she repeated. 'He will be passing it on his way to London. And – you'll see Captain Chandler there, too.'

'How do you know, Liz?'

'Because that is where Chandler has arranged to meet a friend. He made Hutton – '

'Hutton?'

'The groom – tell him how to get there. And there he means to wait. That's what he said. Why? God knows! So it's a case of two birds with one stone.'

'Hutton!' Miranda called out.

'What do you mean, Miranda?' said Liz.

'Horse!' Miranda called again and when a stable hand appeared: 'Saddle me the little bay. As quickly as you can.'

'Miranda?' asked Liz.

'Do you think that a meeting of Jamie Stuart and Chandler would be a friendly one?' said Miranda, scornfully. 'Chandler is a killer by trade – that among other things – and the holm oak is where he means to practise his trade.'

'Miranda! You can't think that!'

'No?' said Miranda, smiling. 'No, perhaps not. But I mean to go and make sure.'

She ran upstairs to get her riding clothes. Liz paused, irresolute for a moment. Then Kate appeared.

'Miranda is in a great hurry this morning!'

'She is going to prevent the loathsome Captain Chandler

121

from murdering her beautiful Jamie. In the Old Forest.'
'And you, Liz? What are you doing?'
'I am going to see that Miranda is not murdered, too.'
Kate's eyes followed her little sister up the stair.
'On that fat little pony of yours? Don't be so silly. And he
isn't all that beautiful! He's Scotch!'
'French,' said Liz. 'It's as fast as yours.'
'We'll see about that!' said Kate. 'Molly! Jane!' she
called out, running up the stairs.

'The quick way or the slow way?' said Alonzo Porter. 'The
quick way is surer. Knife under the ribs, a stone tied to the
ankles and heave him out of a boat into deep water. Then
it's over.'
'Orders are orders,' said Chandler. 'We are to find out
where he has hidden some piece of parchment the Scotch
king wants. So it had better be the slow way: a match between
the fingers.'
'Wastes time,' said Porter.
'He meant to kill me,' said Chandler, venomously.
'Another inch and Stuart would have killed me. Sword
thrust at the left lung. The slow way,' Chandler persisted.
'Make him feel it.'
'I'm all for a bit of fun like the next man,' said Porter. 'If
it doesn't take too long.'
'With the match it will be no time at all,' said Chandler.
'That tree will do nicely,' he went on, pointing to a
straight young chestnut. 'We'll tie him up to that. It will be
easier that way. 'You –' he called to the groom. 'Take off his
doublet and shirt. And keep a good eye on him. He's
dangerous.'
'Have you ever played with match, Mr Stuart?' he said.
The pallor of his face was faintly flushed with excitement.

'Where do you think you're going to?' Lady Vane called
across the stableyard where the last of the six riders was
disappearing under the arch into the road beyond.
The five Vane sisters and a stable hand. Miranda, Kate,
Molly – one after the other – the stable hand, red-faced with

122

excitement. And then an interval, and then Jane Vane, Vain Jane, as her sisters called her, who had kept them waiting while she put something on her face. Liz was stamping with impatience when, at last, Jane appeared, cool, beautifully tinted, beyond all question the perfect picture of an aristocratic English girl whom the world should pause to admire and obey.

'Where is my horse?' she said. 'Where is Betty?'

'Damn Betty!' said Liz. 'And damn you too, Jane. The others have gone.'

'Vulgar!' said Jane.

Within a minute, they were galloping one after the other through the archway, while their mother was crying, 'These girls of mine! Mad, all of them.'

There were three ways through the forest to the holm oak. Miranda, who had her father's hunting horn slung over one shoulder, took the middle way. Hutton, the stable hand, rode after her. Kate and Molly took the path to the right. Jane and Liz, who had punished their horses to overtake the others, bore off to the left where the going was most difficult, slithering down a steep slope where the horses' cruppers slid over mud, splashing through a wet greenness and, then, clambering awkwardly up a muddy bank.

'Meet at the holm oak,' Miranda had said, 'unless I blow the horn. Then make for the sound.'

Two hundred yards short of the tree, she blew. At that moment, Jane and Liz were riding delicately through a noble grove of beeches, the horses' hoofs rustling in the red carpet of leaves.

'Miranda likes to blow that horn!' said Jane.

'She *is* the eldest,' said Liz. 'Where do we make for now?'

They chose a point somewhere ahead of the sound as they judged it.

Miranda and the stable hand had met Jamie's groom, Tom, leading his own mount and a pack horse. They could not understand all he said, but it seemed there had been a fight. Tom had a graze wound from a shot in the thigh but – quick glimpses of a bloody knife and a toothless grin – had been able to do some damage to the enemy.

123

'Where have they gone?' Miranda said.

'Leave it to me, my lady,' said the stable hand. 'No trouble at all to find 'em with the ground being soft like it is.'

'Take the lead, Hutton,' said Miranda crisply as her four sisters came into sight through the trees. 'And press on as fast as you can.'

As they cantered forward through the trees, Miranda pulled out a small pistol which she had brought in a saddle bag. Kate and Molly held swords which they had pulled down from the armoury wall; Jane had a bow slung over one shoulder and carried a quiverful of arrows gracefully at her hip. Liz had hidden a dagger in her bosom. Now she brought it out and felt the point with her thumb.

The Vane sisters were armed for battle. Their eyes, brown, grey, dark and brilliant blue, sparkled with excitement.

Hutton rode with his eyes fixed on the ground. Once or twice he paused in doubt; then pressed on again. At last he stopped and held a hand up, listening.

'They are near, my lady,' he said, when Miranda rode up to him. 'Best now on foot.'

'We'll play with him a little while longer,' said Chandler, lighting a second match. 'Pull down his breeches. We'll try a new trick.'

At that moment a young woman appeared unnoticed through the branches. Quickly she raised her arm. A stab of flame, a cloud of smoke. A shout from Chandler's servant, 'Look out!'

While Hutton laid hands on as many bridles as he could, Tom limped forward, knife in hand, and slashed at the rope that bound Jamie to the chestnut tree. Vain Jane fitted a shaft to her elegant little bow. Kate and Molly advanced, swords at the ready, beautiful and determined. Liz looked at her dagger doubtfully.

'They're girls. Only girls!' shouted Porter. 'What are you frightened of?'

There was a moment of hesitation, Jamie tying up his points, while Tom with his knife held Chandler at bay. Then Jamie, picking up his sword, made for Porter who had his back to an oak tree and could not manoeuvre. In any case he was no match for a blade of Jamie's class. After a noisy exchange of passes, Porter's sword sailed shimmering through the air. His hand – the one in the black glove – was lifted helplessly against the tree behind him. Jamie drove his dagger furiously forward and pinned the black hand to the tree.

He was turning to face Chandler when a sound of tearing made him turn again. Porter had wrenched his sleeve away from the black hand which was only an object of carved wood inside a glove. He was free and running to his horse.

Jamie, doubtful between the two, was about to run after him. Then he saw Chandler with a flying leap reach the saddle as his horse scampered off through the trees. Hurrying off, Chandler passed within a foot of Liz who, on an impulse she never regretted – or understood – drove her dagger through his thigh into the leather of his saddle. He screamed with pain as he galloped into the woods. The victory of the Vanes was complete.

Laughing with relief, Jamie took the sisters in his arms, two at a time. 'The fighting Vanes!' he cried, covering them with kisses. 'Look out for my fingers. They are burnt.'

The girls covered them with kisses.

'If you don't get some clothes on, you'll catch cold,' said Miranda, running her fingers over his shoulders.

'Where's Liz?' cried Kate. 'Good God, look!'

Liz was lying unconscious on the ground with no colour in her face.

'Liz is useless in a crisis,' said Miranda, with a frown.

But Hutton spoke up.

'Begging your pardon,' he said, 'but Mistress Liz pinned that Chandler to his own saddle. And all with that knife you would hardly pare an apple with! Took a bit of doing, I reckon, her being only a slip of a girl.'

'How beautiful she looks,' said Jamie, 'an angel!'

'Mother will be furious,' said Kate.

'I'll ride back with you and bring the news of victory to your father,' said Jamie. 'What a day for the Vanes!'

'What a beautiful shirt, Jamie!' said Jane. 'But why does it have a crown embroidered on it?'

'Why do you think, silly?' said Liz, opening her eyes and lifting her head from the ground.

The colour was flowing back into her cheeks.

'Remind me to send that black glove to Mr Porter,' said Jamie, pointing to the object hanging from the oak tree. 'Without it, he won't be the same man at all.'

The ride back to the house was leisurely and cheerful. Lady Vane raised her hands in horror at their story and went off to find bandages for Jamie's fingers. Sir Ferdinand swore that, so help him God, he would have Chandler up before the magistrate who would condemn him to be branded as a common highwayman. It was no empty threat, either, for, in these parts, as Jamie found, Sir Ferdinand himself was the sole fountain of justice.

With difficulty Jamie persuaded his host that Chandler had probably been punished enough by Liz's dagger. There was also the difficulty that Chandler had spent the night before the crime under Sir Ferdinand's roof. Jamie insinuated that the reputation of the house might, unjustly, suffer in consequence.

'There is more to this business than I know about, young man,' said Sir Ferdinand, tugging his white beard irritably.

'There is,' said Jamie. 'And more than I know either.'

'Lord Henry Howard. Would he have a hand in it, do you think?'

Jamie shrugged.

'He looks like an old pussy and acts like a fox,' said Sir Ferdinand. He gave Jamie a long, searching look out of his suspicious blue eyes. It seemed he was going to ask some more questions. Then he decided not to.

'Lucky you can look after yourself, Stuart,' he said.

'Yes,' said Jamie. 'Very lucky.'

Next day, he rode back to London.

'Two been looking for you, Mr Stuart,' the potboy at the Rose of York said dolefully, as he looked into the distance over Jamie's shoulder.

126

'Two what?'

'Rats.'

From the way the potboy's eyes moved, Jamie knew that whoever they were they could not be far away. He turned sharply round and found that he was looking into the muzzle of a large-calibre pistol. It was held, about a foot from his head, by a burly, cold-eyed man with an authoritative manner.

'Ah!' said Jamie. 'Did you not have a friend?'

The man with the pistol said, 'Just look to your right.'

There, sure enough, was a taller, thinner man who was also holding a pistol.

'Somebody would like to have a word with you, Mr Stuart.'

'And what if I excuse myself?'

'Now you're not going to be a trouble, sir, are you?'

'That depends on who Somebody is, and what Somebody wants with me.'

'I expect it's only to ask you a few questions, sir. Now we'll go along, if you please. The boat is at the foot of the steps. We can always snap on a pair of handcuffs if you'd prefer it that way. We have 'em handy. Just in case. But take my advice, sir. Be more comfortable for everybody if you were to come quiet.'

Jamie nodded

'I'll be back in an hour's time,' he said to the potboy who stood shaking his head gloomily.

'Been too many women,' said the potboy. 'Don't say I didn't warn you.'

To Jamie's surprise the taller of his captors, who had taken the oars, turned the boat's head upriver.

'I suppose I am not important enough.'

'How do you mean, sir?' asked the man sitting in the stern.

'I mean to go to the Tower of London,' said Jamie.

The two men laughed quietly together in the superior, insufferable manner of those in any country who know official secrets.

'All in good time, sir. All in good time.'

Meeting with a Gnome

At the end of a gallery, lit by tall windows on one side and lined by dark portraits on the other – among which Jamie saw one of his royal grandfather, a copy of a picture he had seen in Copenhagen – they arrived at a small oak door beside which stood a liveried porter armed with a partizan. Jamie's guides whispered inaudibly. The porter disappeared inside and after a few minutes appeared again, beckoning. Jamie bowed his farewell to the two men who had escorted him from the Rose of York. 'It may not be the Tower,' he said, 'but it's very handsome.'

Now he found himself in a small, overcrowded chamber hung with faded tapestries. On either side, three men, who were apparently clerks, sat writing.

In the middle, farther off and facing the door on the far side of a spacious oak table, sat a small man who seemed to have some malformation of the spine. An accident in childhood? A congenital deformity? It might be one or the other. This man, too, was writing busily.

A profound silence reigned, in which could be heard the faint scratching of pens on parchment and the soft blurts of the logs burning in the fireplace.

The central figure of the group did not lift his head when Jamie entered but one of the six others pointed to a chair with his quill. Jamie ignored the suggestion. He was familiar with this kind of reception. It was a commonplace in the anterooms of power. Important officials thought it necessary

128

to impress a visitor with his own insignificance and the gravity of the work he was interrupting.

Not far from him was a globe, standing waist high from the ground. Jamie went over to it. He observed out of the corner of his eye that two of the clerks were watching him. He began to revolve the globe which, to his delight, emitted a faint squeaking noise. After that the silence lasted another three minutes.

When Jamie was examining the coast of Greenland, someone spoke:

'Well?'

Jamie smiled into the brilliant dark eyes of the little gnome at the centre table. He said nothing.

'Your business, sir?' The voice was calm on the surface but it had a lot of tension in it.

'Do you mean what brings me here, or what is my occupation? The latter I can tell you. Ex-convict. As for the former –' He shrugged.

'Why don't you sit down?'

'For one thing, because you haven't asked me to.'

Jamie was aware that one of the clerks had raised his eyebrows and then had put down his pen. It was the nearest thing this room had ever seen to emotion.

The gnome frowned and motioned to a chair.

'Your globe,' said Jamie, sitting down. 'It's out of date. Look at the coast of Greenland. Pure imagination. Ortelius is making better globes than that nowadays.'

'I don't think I asked you to give me a lesson in geography,' said the little man sharply.

It did not seem to Jamie that he was called on to make any comment. After a minute the gnome spoke to one of the clerks –

'Wilson. Have this' – a sheet of parchment covered with his handwriting – 'copied for the lords lieutenant, one to each. Now go, all of you. I'll ring for you when I want you.'

The six clerks picked up their papers, pens and inkhorns and moved swiftly and quietly towards the door. When they had vanished, the gnome turned his extraordinarily luminous gaze on Jamie. Suddenly his expression was more relaxed.

'Many people think it is hard to govern a country,' he said. He shook his head sadly. 'Quite mistaken. All you need is six secretaries, and forty-six lords lieutenant. By the way, the name is Cecil, Robert Cecil.'

Jamie nodded.

'James Stuart,' he said. But Cecil seemed not to have heard.

'One thing I forgot,' he said. 'If you are going to govern, you should be able to count. Reading? Unimportant. Many successful rulers have been illiterate. But government is arithmetic. Simple as that. Count heads, ships, cannon, tax money. Essential. It was the plague of my old father's life. He could read. He could even write. But arithmetic! That beat him.'

'Strange.'

Cecil shook his head emphatically.

'Not strange at all. The old man used Roman numerals all his life. Have you ever tried to multiply MCIX by XXVI! Don't. You'd go mad. But Father could do nothing else. Slowed the machine up terribly. But I interrupted you.' He smiled. 'You were saying something. That's the trouble with us politicians. After a bit we think it's more important to talk than to listen. A mistake. One day a man all in black comes along with an axe and shows us where we have gone wrong.' He smiled whimsically. 'But go on. What were you saying?'

'James Stuart,' said Jamie. 'It's still my name.'

'Ah, yes.' Cecil seemed to be recalled abruptly from some realm of pleasant fantasy to the harsh realities of life. 'Stuart. Any relation? Yes, of course. You spell it differently. I remember. Ex-galley slave. Etcetera. By the way, Stuart, on the globe somewhere south of Greenland is an island called Ireland. See if you can find Kinsale somewhere on its coast. Use your imagination if necessary.'

'You haven't called me here to give you a lesson in geography,' Jamie reminded him.

Cecil looked at him fixedly for a moment. Jamie had the impression that the man all in black was lurking somewhere nearby just then. But only for a moment. Then Cecil's expression softened.

130

He rose and Jamie noticed the ease and grace of his movements. This was no cripple. He pulled open the door of a corner cupboard. From it he produced two glasses and a bottle.

'Today,' he said, 'I have sworn three men to secrecy – a valet, a doctor and a spy. The valet should be too frightened to talk. The doctor can't talk – the professional code forbids. To make sure of their silence, I have set the spy to watch them. Now it will be interesting to see which of them betrays the secret. What do you think?'

'All three,' said Jamie.

Cecil, pouring wine into a glass, stopped, interested.

'Why do you think so?'

'It is a spy's business to tell secrets. The doctor will tell in order to impress patients with his importance. And the valet will be frightened into telling.'

Cecil gave him a penetrating glance.

'You would make an excellent Secretary of State,' he said, continuing to fill the glass. When it was full he held it out to Jamie.

'Sherry?' he said. 'As good as any in Spain. But perhaps you are prejudiced against everything Spanish. No? Good. Look at that colour. Like amber. I wish I could think of a more original expression! Not a poet, that's the trouble. Tell me what you think of it?'

Jamie drank.

'Magnificent,' he said.

If you liked sherry, it was.

Cecil pushed the bottle across the table. 'Help yourself,' he said. Jamie reached for it.

'It comes from the Duke of Medina Sidonia's private cellar,' said Cecil. 'When the late Earl of Essex captured Cadiz, this was part of the spoils. Usually I keep it for ambassadors.'

'You flatter me.'

Cecil nodded his agreement.

'As you see, victory has its blessings, provided you don't allow it to go to your head. However, we are not here to discuss wine or the dangers of spiritual pride. Listen to me

131

carefully, Stuart.' He leant over the table. His eyes seemed to have dilated.

'You and I share one distinction,' he said. 'Lord Henry Howard hates us both. Myself he hates with a pure and original passion. You he hates because you are an enemy of the King of Scots who is his lordship's protégé. He has tried to have you killed by judicial process. Then he set two assassins on you. You have survived. But don't think that is likely to be the end of the business. Be sure there will be a next time, and probably even more brutal than the last. In the meantime, you are at large.'

'You are not afraid that I may leave London and the country, too?'

'Not in the least,' said Cecil with a gentle smile. 'You are a sensible man, although you pretend not to be. You have enough intelligence to suspect we are keeping an eye on you. Also,' the smile broadened on his pale, subtle face, 'you have reasons of your own for wishing to stay in London. I don't know what all of them are, but I think that one of them, at least, is charming. Maybe there are two of them.'

James, reflecting, thought that there might be even more.

'London,' he said, 'is a big city.'

'The queen thinks it's too big. But she can't think of any way of making it smaller. How you manage two women – that I must leave to you. Carey has every confidence that you can do it. As I have said, Stuart, you are at large. But it's conditional. Conditional!'

'Most things in life are, Mr Secretary,' said Jamie.

'Quite so. But in this case, the condition is more precise than it usually is. You have a piece of parchment hidden away somewhere which purports to show that your grandfather had the good manners to marry your grandmother before your father was born. As evidence, worthless. No doubt. But we are not in a court of law, you and I. We are in the arena of political power.' Cecil's voice rose and grew more emphatic. 'That parchment of yours frightens the King of Scots. It might lead credulous people to believe that *you* were the rightful King of Scots. People can sometimes be foolish. Now it happens that it suits me to have His Majesty

132

frightened. It does not matter why. So – but you can see where this argument is leading us . . . Hand over the parchment, Stuart.'

With a charming smile he held out across the table a small, white and shapely hand. Jamie gave a good impersonation of a man overwhelmed by bewilderment.

'I don't follow you. As long as the parchment is in my hand, will not King James go on being frightened?'

Cecil smiled pleasantly.

'True enough. But I want him to know that I can stop him from being frightened at any moment I choose to do so.'

'In other words, Your Excellency proposes to blackmail the King of Scots.'

Cecil looked pained.

'An ugly word, Stuart. The product of a limited philosophy. In politics, we learn to rise above such petty prejudices. We are dealing not with the finer issues of moral theology, but with cruder matters – with the future of kingdoms, with the peace of nations, with the balance of power among the sovereigns! If he behaves, your kinsman will become King of England one day. For reasons of my own, I mean to see that he behaves. For instance, I want to make sure that he does not fall under the influence of Lord Henry Howard who is a pensioner of the King of Spain and, between ourselves, very much of a fool. A vicious, dangerous fool.

'Now, suppose I were to whisper to King James's agent here that I have your piece of parchment locked in my strong-box – I could even let him see it – don't you think the king might take the hint? I should hope he would. He has more brains than most members of your family, if you will forgive me for saying so. But if, by any chance, that did not prove to be enough, I could strengthen my case. I could spread the rumour that you were about to marry a lady with as good a claim to the English throne as James of Scotland has. Imagine the emotion that news would raise in Edinburgh!'

At the thought, Cecil rubbed his hands together in elfin glee.

'Tell me,' said Jamie. 'What is her name?'

'Whose name?'

133

'I thought I should know my future wife's name.'

'But of course. Lady Arabella Stuart. She is a cousin of the king's, and, come to think of it, a cousin of yours, too. Very distant, it is true. Yes. You would make a splendid couple. She is only about six years older than you are. A mere nothing where so much is at stake. Yes, the more I think about – '

'How much are you prepared to give?' James broke in coldly.

'For the parchment? My impression is that I had paid for it when I kept you out of prison.'

'That would be a mistake, Mr Secretary,' said Jamie.

'In that case, what is your idea of a fair price?' asked the Secretary of State.

'That depends, doesn't it. For instance, on how interested I am in selling when the time comes to sell.'

Cecil sighed.

'Perhaps I can encourage your interest. The penalty for supplying arms to the queen's rebellious subjects is what you would expect it to be.' He brought the side of his hand sharply down on the table. 'Or would you rather we handed you over to the Spanish authorities as an escaped criminal? It's a delicate choice. Have another glass of sherry, Stuart.'

Jamie shook his head.

'Have I time to think this over?' he asked.

'Were it in my hands,' said Cecil, 'I would say all the time you need, provided we can pull you in when we want to. But the queen is sixty-eight. The life of a lady in her sixty-ninth year is good for – how long do you think?'

'In the case of that lady, there are no rules,' said Jamie.

Cecil laughed softly.

'No, by God, there are times when I think she will live to dance on my grave! But the odds are in my favour. I told you that politicians must be able to count. They must be able to guess, too. And guess right more often than not. Then they are called statesmen. Nearly seventy years ago, a certain clock was wound up. It is still ticking. For how much longer? That is the question. Before it stops, Stuart, there is a great deal to do. So don't keep me waiting too long.'

The silence in the room was more intense than ever. The Secretary of State kept his eyes on Jamie's while he filled a glass to the brim. The gentle sound of the wine as it flowed reached every corner of the room.

'Give me three days.'

'Three days! You need a long time to make up your mind, Mr Stuart.'

'I have a great deal to do, Your Excellency.'

'And at least two people to see,' said Cecil with a pleasant smile. 'Of course I shall have you watched. I shall tell them to behave with discretion.'

'Three days,' Jamie said.

'Very well. Three days from now I shall be at Greenwich in attendance. See me then. It will be quite interesting for you. People you will be glad to meet. Come in the evening and wear your most splendid clothes. One lady may have the eccentric notion she wants to see you. She is a strange woman.'

'An exceptional woman.'

'Among women,' said Cecil, 'there are no exceptions to being a woman.'

Jamie bowed. 'Three days,' he said.

'I hope I can give them to you,' said Cecil, 'it would be a pity if you were late.' He lifted the glass to his lips.

A log in the fireplace broke softly and threw a shower of sparks into the chimney. Cecil put the glass down and rang a small bell on his table.

Hanging Sword Alley

Stuart woke late and with a vague uneasiness in his mind. He rang repeatedly. No answer. He went out to the top of the stair and shouted. Silence. He ran downstairs barefoot in his shirt. The stone flags were cold. There was nobody about. When he went to explore the back premises of the Rose of York tavern which opened on a little courtyard, he found not a living soul. The fire was alight in the chimney. That was all. By bad luck, he must have stumbled unawares on some day of fast or repentance. Somebody ought to have warned him. In the end he boiled the kettle himself and, nursing a sense of grievance, took it up to his room.

After he had dressed, he went out into the alley. It was deserted. Either everybody was staying indoors or had gone to church. As if to strengthen this supposition, a bell began to ring in a church nearby. It had an exceptionally solemn sound. It was, perhaps, slower than usual.

He went down to the river's edge and looked along that stretch of the Thames. Although, in the distance, he could see some movement of vessels, there was not the customary bustle on the water. He was about to turn away, puzzled, when his eye fell on an object floating slowly past on the yellow tide. A body. No doubt about it. Some poor devil who had been set upon by footpads or, perhaps, had given up the struggle of existence in despair, and had thrown himself into the river.

While Jamie was pondering the mutability of fortune, the brevity of life and the fickleness of human happiness, he saw, farther out in the water, a second floating object very like the first. Jamie shuddered and told himself that he was turning

135

morbid. Full of profound and appropriate thoughts, he began to make his way towards the centre of the City.

For a time he passed nobody. From a church somewhere near came mournful music. When he arrived at his favourite cook shop, he found its door closed, its windows shuttered. At that point, a simple explanation of the whole mysterious paralysis occurred to him. He broke into a cold sweat of apprehension. *The queen was dead!*

That would account for it all. The silence. The solitude. The brooding oppression which could not only be the product of his imagination. The queen dead? After all, she was nearly seventy. He remembered Cecil's remark. 'Seventy years ago, a clock was wound up.' It would be the end of an era of greatness, which had spanned the age like a vast shining arch. After which...

After which, James, he told himself grimly, a man who has your name will be well advised to quit England as fast as possible. No time for farewells! A quick ride to the coast. Then the first packet to Calais or Flushing.

For James, King of Scots, would become King of England. Cecil had made that plain enough. And one of the new king's first acts would be to put his namesake and disowned relation, Jamie Stuart, in some safe place. Jamie thought he knew just the place that would seem most secure to His Majesty. Unless, of course, Cecil acted first, which very likely he would.

Suddenly, Jamie found that there was one fact in life more clamorous than an empty stomach. He acted quickly. At the jeweller's, where his money and his precious, perilous parchment were hidden, he knocked loudly and repeatedly on the door. There was no answer. Like the rest of London, the jeweller had apparently gone into retreat to mourn the great queen. Not far away was the astrologer's booth. But no! This was not a day to risk a brush with fate. Besides, on this of all mornings, the astrologer was sure to be overwhelmed with business.

He thought, however, that he knew where he might find Alan Beaton. Near the cathedral was a warren of little streets in which there were many print-sellers' and map-makers' booths. These shops were favourite haunts of Alan's.

In this part of the City there were more people to be seen in the streets. Even so, there seemed to be something different about them today, as if they were weighed down by some vast despondency. It was, no doubt, the weather that had changed, producing that famous English melancholy of which he had heard so much when he lived in Paris. It was the most cheerful explanation he could think of.

A haggard and woebegone individual passed him, walking with a white stick. Jamie had the impression that this person was being given a wide berth by those who met him in the street. Strange. In the open space in front of the west door of the old cathedral, a preacher occupied the open-air pulpit. He had a fair-sized audience, listening gravely.

Jamie went near enough to hear what he was saying. From his words he might pick up some hint of what all this meant. The preacher wore a long black gown which, when he raised his arms in a gesture of supplication or menace, produced an impressive and sinister effect.

'Sin ... Sin ... Sin ... '

The word was ominous but not unexpected. Hearing it, Jamie quickened his pace. Just as he passed out of earshot, he fancied that the sombre prophet announced 'The cause of plague is sin. And the cause of sin is the theatre.'

Plague!

With that word everything was explained – the silence, the empty streets, the penitential music in the churches. The man with the white stick, who was probably somebody who had come from an infected house.

At a map-maker's shop, Jamie knocked and called. When a man put his head out of a window above, he asked for Mr Beaton. The map-maker shook his head and pointed south towards the river. Then, without another word, the head disappeared.

Not far below the surface of this talented and energetic nation, Jamie decided, there is a vein of gloomy superstition. It was possible that this gloom provided the fuel for the intellectual brilliance of the English in much the same way as a similar brand of sombre philosophy had been transferred into the irresistible fury of Henry of Navarre's Huguenot

138

cavalry – according to his father who had fought alongside them. This was the theme of Jamie's speculations as he made his way downhill towards the river.

A coach drawn by four horses passed him. Inside it, he caught sight of serious women's faces. On top of the rear axle was strapped a variety of trunks. Evidently, it was hurrying to one of the north gates of the City. It did not go unobserved. The preacher saw it from his pulpit; his voice rang out:

'Lot's wife is trying to escape from the judgement of Almighty God. In vain! In vain! God's eyes sees all. His vengeance overtakes all. The judgement of sin follows wheresoever Lot's wife goes.'

The occupants of the coach cowered back into the shadows. The drivers whipped up their horses in a panic.

Some time after this, Jamie was visited by a sobering notion, stronger than any instinct and more elusive than a conviction. He was being followed, and not by the 'shadow' whom Cecil had appointed to supervise his movements – a surveillance which seemed in any case to have slackened lately. No. This was something different.

A man had passed him and looked into his eyes. Five minutes later – as he thought – the same man passed again walking in the opposite direction. There could be no doubt. He was being followed and, beyond question, would be attacked when it was convenient to the pursuers.

Jamie turned into the first side alley he came to. In a few minutes he was lost. He kept on, taking one turning and then another – no one pattern at all, plunging all the time more deeply into a quarter of the City which was filled with little traders and shabby houses, and smelled of decay and drains.

An iron sign hung above the entry to a narrow close. A sword hung by a chain from an iron rod. He read the words written on the wall: 'Hanging Sword Alley'. Somehow, he thought, it might bring him luck. He entered. And it seemed at first that he had been right. He walked straight into Endymion Jones, the man who could tell him something important about Lord Henry Howard.

The little thief turned when he caught sight of Jamie.

139

Another instant and he would have fled. Jamie, seeing the look of pure panic in his face, took him firmly by the shoulder.

'Endymion!' he said. 'The very man I want.'

'You let me alone, mister.'

'Don't talk like that, Endymion. Not when I'm going to put some business your way. Money, Endymion, beautiful money! Can you use it?'

Jones looked at him, with his eyes roving nervously about Jamie's face. He said nothing.

'Listen carefully,' said Jamie. 'I have seen Lord Southampton in the Tower.'

The little man's face lit up. 'Lord Southampton. How is he, sir?'

'He could be worse.'

'Good. Oh, that's good, sir.'

'He told me to ask you a question. He thought you would answer it.'

'Anything his lordship asks. Seeing what he did for me . . . What is it?'

'Lord Henry Howard – ever heard of him?'

Endymion might have nodded. It is impossible to be certain.

'Lord Henry is doing some business. Something he shouldn't be doing. What is it, Endymion?'

'Don't ask me that, sir.' The little man was trembling. 'Much as my life is worth. '

'Just one word. A clue. No more.'

Endymion shook his head. Jamie watched the feelings chase one another over his face and heard the words that finally came out in a rush and a whisper:

'Get me anyway . . . No use . . .' Then, as if it required great force to expel them: 'Spinola . . . the river.'

Like a flash he had torn his shoulder free and vanished, round a twist in the alley. Jamie stood in the alley for a few minutes, thinking over what he had heard, waiting. Waiting until he was startled by a blood-curdling scream coming from the direction in which Endymion had disappeared. It was certainly the little thief's voice, raised in pain or terror.

140

He broke into a run, towards the sounds, snatching out his sword as he ran.

What he saw as he turned the corner was no ordinary brawl but a deadly fight. Two men against one. Knives were flashing in the half-light of the alley. Jones was calling out for help, crying for mercy, screaming in pain. Then his voice died into a piteous moan. The shutters of houses looking into the alley were opened cautiously. Then they were slammed shut with force.

Alonzo Porter was kneeling on Endymion's chest with one bare hand, bent on throttling him. Porter's accomplice scrambled to his feet and, after a horrified glance at Jamie's naked blade, shouted a warning and took to his heels.

Porter rose with a snarl and lifted a knife from the cobbles. Jamie fumbled in his doublet and pulled a black object out. He threw it into Porter's face. 'You left your glove behind you, Mr Porter. Here it is!' Then he closed with Alonzo.

It was no moment for the finer points of sword play. Using the flat of his sword, and keeping out of reach of the knife, Jamie struck Porter repeatedly on the hand. After a few seconds of this punishment, Alonzo staggered away, cursing. Jamie made a spring towards him. Porter, with a backward look of white fury, disappeared in the labyrinth of alleys ahead.

There was no time to lose. Jamie knew that he would be back soon, accompanied. He looked down at the man on the ground. 'Endymion,' he said, 'you need a surgeon.'

Jones put one hand out feebly. His lips moved piteously. By leaning forward, Jamie could hear.

'No use. Wouldn't come. They've got me this time . . . Scream,' said Endymion. 'Listen. Message for the queen. True-born Englishman!' – his hand fluttered towards his chest – 'What are you? A Frog? Promise, before God.'

His will was wavering between doubt and trust, but his mind was steady enough.

'I promise,' said Jamie.

'Listen. Spinola's galleys. No moon. Quiet sea. When the signal goes – ' He stopped, smiled weakly, shrugged. 'Follow me?' he said.

'You tell it,' said Jamie, encouragingly. 'I'll listen.'

But Endymion's hold on consciousness was weakening fast. His eyebrows fluttered, his lips trembled. His hand pulled something from the neck of his doublet.

He was breathing noisily; struggling to get a phrase out. But it was too much. A clouded light came into his eyes. Jamie thought he heard a word.

Endymion held out a hand. The fingers opened. Something fell out and dropped lightly to the cobbles. A piece of paper.

Then Endymion's head fell back on the cobbles with a crash. God, he has hurt himself! But Endymion was past being hurt.

Somebody had arrived.

'If I were you, friend, I'd leave him to the men on duty. They will bring the death cart for him. Above all, don't touch him.'

Jamie looked up. A tall, grave-looking individual was standing beside him, hat in hand.

'Plague,' said the newcomer. 'The visitation of God on sinners.'

Jamie would have like to tell him he was wrong. Instead, he stooped and picked up the crumpled piece of paper that had fallen from Endymion's grasp. At the corner of the alley he stopped to read.

It was a letter addressed to His Excellency, the Lord Henry Howard. It was written in Italian, but Jamie, brought up in Paris where he had mixed with students of the Latin Quarter, had no difficulty in understanding it. It said that the writer's servant, 'whom your lordship will know', was in London for the purpose of gathering a crew 'for the purpose of which we have spoken before'. After many setbacks, this task was now, *Deo Gratias*, completed. On the first moonless night, or the second, depending on the state of wind and water, the enterprise against the guardship at Gravesend would be carried out. This would act as a signal to 'my ships' which would be lying between Gravesend and the mouth of the river. 'After that with the help of God and the Saints', etc., etc. The letter was signed 'F. Spinola'.

This then was the reason why Porter, employed by Lord

Henry, had pursued Endymion Jones with such murderous determination. The little thief had stolen from Lord Henry's purse or his lodgings a letter which showed that Howard, a member of the first English ducal house, was conspiring with the queen's enemies to bring about a disaster which would open the way to an attack on the Thames. Jamie remembered hearing from someone that Spinola meant to burn all the shipping between the Tower and the sea. With eight galleys on a dark night, it was not impossible.

Meanwhile – Jamie's eyes sparkled with pleasure – here was a piece of evidence which, were it once in Miranda's hands, would save her from any threat of blackmail by Lord Henry Howard!

Jamie looked back along the alley in the direction of poor, dead Endymion Jones. Men had clustered round the body – and they were not, he thought, the sanitary men employed to remove dead victims of the plague. No. From the look of them they were confederates of Porter's who had come to look for the document which Endymion Jones had stolen. After all, this was a part of the City that Porter regarded as his own.

It was time for Jamie to leave it.

He found a cook shop that was open and settled down for a long leisurely meal. When the sullen, wintry light was beginning to fade in the streets, he thought that it would be safe to go out. In a few minutes, he thought he was wrong.

An odd sensation had returned. He felt it at the back of his neck. That, and an irrational desire to turn on his heel and walk in a different direction, an impulse to become conspicuous for no reason at all, sudden fits of incomprehensible lethargy. Were these illusions?

He stopped a passer-by. 'A lot of strange people about today!' he said.

The man looked startled.

'You ought to see a doctor,' he said, and walked on, quickening his pace.

Soon afterwards, Jamie thought he had identified his pursuers; two of them, men who might have been chosen because of their ability to melt into a crowd. They were taking

143

the work in relays, one loitering while the other hurried purposefully forward.

It was a game that had several possible variations; for instance – when one man passed him, Jamie followed him, close at his heels. When the man quickened his steps, he did the same, keeping pace. In a minute or two, the hunter-turned-quarry showed symptoms of discomfort. Jamie decided to change the play. Behind him, following closely, would be the second man. Jamie turned suddenly on his heel and caught the second man's wrist before he could pull out his dagger. At the same instant, he stepped in and lifted his knee smartly. He heard a grunt of pain as he swung through an arch and began to run along a narrow alley which sloped steeply downhill. Jamie guessed that it would lead to the river bank. Wrong! He had come into a court from which there was no way out.

He saw a door on which somebody had painted a rough cross in red and the words, 'Lord have mercy upon us!'

A plague house! He shook the door. It was shut and bolted. But at his feet was a pot of red paint and a brush. A few yards away was another door. It opened when he pushed.

Jamie had just time to write the words 'Lord have mercy' and draw a cross on the door when he heard voices and the sound of running men. He threw down the brush and stepped inside, shutting the door quietly behind him.

In the gloom of an empty hallway, he plucked out his sword and waited. There was a noise of footsteps outside, quick first, then slowing down.

Somebody said angrily, 'You're sure it was here?'

Somebody answered sulkily, 'How can a man be sure with the light fading like this!'

A man shouted, 'Bring out your dead.'

No answer came.

The talk outside the door waned. After a bit, the footsteps moved away. Men grumbled as they left the yard.

Jamie allowed the silence to last a quarter of an hour, measured by the clock of a nearby church, before he stole out with infinite caution. London was immersed in a blue evening haze from a clear sky.

144

He found his way towards the river bank, meaning to take the first boat that came along.

After a little, he was able to attract the attention of a passing waterman.

'Where do you want to go, friend? . . . There? The bad quarter, eh? Jump in. Less sickness over there among the sinners than here among the saints. The devil looks after his own.' Rowing still, the boatman spat into the river. 'Maybe,' he went on, 'they are not such saints, after all. What do you think, sir?'

'Or maybe,' Jamie suggested, 'they are so good that the Lord can't wait to snatch them into heaven. Ever thought of that?'

The rower rested on his oars for a moment, while he surveyed Jamie with suspicion. 'No,' he said. 'But I notice that He has been in no hurry, touch wood, to take you or me.'

Jamie handed him a coin and stepped out on to the jetty.

'Not surprising,' he said. 'I'm a Leo myself.'

The boatman looked at him in bewilderment.

Jamie walked towards the Swan Theatre. No flag was flying. The doors were shut and barred. He went round to the stage door. It was open but when he looked in nobody was in sight. He went farther in. A voice he knew rumbled through the flimsy wooden corridors of the theatre.

'Who's there? . . . Oh, it's you. What have you come for, Stuart? To mock poor Lear upon the blasted heath? The theatre is shut, I tell you, Stuart! Finished! No more! The sun of art has sunk beneath the waves. The bright day is done and we are for the night. The night, Stuart, the night!'

Fletcher was sitting on an upturned box, a bottle in his hand. His voice fell to a tragic rumble. His chin sank towards his chest. He had not shaved lately.

'I have work for you,' said Jamie.

Keeping one ferocious eye fixed on him, Fletcher put the bottle to his lips. Then he wiped it with his sleeve.

'Are you insulting me, young man?' he said, dangerously. Jamie made haste to explain.

'When I said work,' he said, 'I meant fighting. If you are

no longer interested in bloody deeds, of course there is no more to be said.'

Fletcher put the bottle carefully on the floor and rose slowly to his feet.

'Do they pay soldiers in your war?' he asked.

'Let us go over to that drinking den of yours nearby and talk about the business. Incidentally, if you know of any out-of-work actors who are not paralysed, you might think of recruiting them.'

Fletcher shot him a sharp glance.

'First things first,' he said. 'Does your purse run to a bite of food, friend? The regiment fights better after the rations have come up.'

'Can you swim?' asked Jamie.

Fletcher frowned. 'What kind of war is this? Where do we fight? On land or on water?'

'On both,' said Jamie. 'Listen, Sergeant Fletcher.'

'Continue,' said the actor, majestically.

'It is a question of an attack on a craft on the river – one crammed with the riff-raff of London bent on doing an ill-service to the queen. Can you raise a company of likely fellows, men who don't shrink from a little rough work in a good cause?'

'Don't ask foolish questions, young man. I have only to whistle. But when is this feat to take place?'

'Tonight, Sergeant.'

Fletcher's eyebrows shot up.

'By God, we shall have to hurry, you and I. Meanwhile a rumbling in the belly warns me that the hour to eat has arrived.'

After ordering Fletcher an ample dinner, and leaving money to pay, Jamie left him. He had a great deal to do.

The Three Kings in Cheapside was no more than half an hour's walk from the Swan, over the Bridge and up the hill. Jamie went into the stableyard and shouted 'Tom!' When the groom limped into sight, Jamie said, 'Game for another trip, Tom? Like the last one, only more so. How's that leg, by the way?'

146

With toothless mouth and staring eyes, Tom said yes. His thigh wound was no more than a scratch.

'Two good horses,' said Jamie. 'We'll visit the Rose of York first.'

Jamie's baggage filled a little sack tied to the saddle. The old potboy shook his head despondently.

'Don't worry,' said Jamie. 'I've sworn off the women. Tie that piece of board up, will you. Jack Scream wants his name-plate.'

The next place he visited was the jeweller's. This time the door was opened, cautiously.

'So many of the wrong sort about today, my lord,' said the jeweller. 'Have to be careful. You'll want money, I think.'

'All of it,' said Jamie.

The jeweller filled his purse and handed over a small packet that Jamie had left there on the day he arrived in London. Jamie and Tom rode down to the river bank to look for Jabez Walker.

'Tell me, Jabez,' he said, when the waterman at last appeared 'What kind of weather can we expect tonight?'

Walker peered up at the sky, through a hedge of eyebrows. 'Be all right, I reckon. Depends what kind of weather interests you, sir.'

'State of the light. State of the water.'

The waterman fetched a long, noisy sigh.

'Sea should be quiet enough, though there's no saying this time of year. Water can build up fast on the Dutch coast. Then, before you know where you are, you're in real trouble down in the reaches below Greenwich.'

'H'm. Doubtful, eh?' said Jamie.

Jabez Walker shrugged his enormous shoulders.

'Ought to be all right, sir. Given the luck a gentleman is entitled to.'

'Gentleman?' said Jamie, haughtily. 'I'm a Leo!'

The waterman wrinkled his brow.

'Maybe you are and all, sir. But luck is what you'll need. French or Espingo or whatever you are. A bit of extra luck, see.'

'Will there be mist?' asked Jamie.

147

'Mist! Of course. Haze lying thick on the water. What do you expect. Be a night to watch what you're doing and listen most particular to what the leadsman cries. Else you'll be fast on a mudbank, and then God help poor sailors, what with the water falling and all.'

Jamie smiled.

'This river,' he said, waving his hand generously. 'It interests me.'

Walker's eyes grew round. He was shocked.

'You mean this – *London* river? Make no mistake, sir. There ain't another river like it in the world.'

'You are probably right. I don't deny it. But what interests me at the moment is this. What happens below the Bridge?'

'What you'd expect. The river goes twisting on until it comes to the sea. Ships by the hundred. Yards where the warships are lying up. The Queen's Palace. Fifteen miles farther down at Tilbury there's the boom they built when the Spanish were coming – the boom or what's left of it.'

'Meaning it might not be much of an obstacle?'

'It depends on what tries to break through. Besides, there's the guardship, between ourselves a bit of an old hulk, but with cannon and gunners aboard her.'

'The guardship,' said Jamie.

Walker nodded. 'Supposing somebody took a fancy to come where he has no business. Understand?'

Jamie understood. The guardship would be there to block a raider's path with its guns . . . If the guardship was there!

'Jabez,' he said. 'Can you gather some men for a rough night on the river?' He held up his purse and shook it.

Jabez Walker's eyes glittered. 'Go on, Your Excellency,' he said. 'You were saying?'

After Jamie had spoken for a few minutes, Jabez nodded. 'Should be easy, sir, and nice work, too, if I may say so.'

'One thing more, Jabez. There is an actor named Fletcher at the Swan Theatre. Once he was a sergeant fighting the queen's enemies in the Low Countries . . .'

It was dusk when, at last, Jamie and Tom set out by boat for Greenwich.

148

A Galliard with the Queen

The palace at Greenwich was brilliantly illuminated. At every window lights glimmered. At the entrance great flambeaux shook their rags of fire into the night. Landing from the river, Jamie could see the whole fantastic shape of the building, turreted, fretted – a preposterous, yet imposing, outline, dark against a sombre red glow on the landward side. He was greeted by armed sentries who, after a word or two, waved him on to the door. He asked a chamberlain for Carey and waited.

'By God,' he said when he caught sight of the Englishman's costume, 'what splendour! All these ribbons!'

Carey stroked his beard. 'What a sense of timing, Stuart! You arrive on the greatest night of the year – one of the high moments of the reign . . . Lord Mountjoy has won a victory at Kinsale. The rebels are broken. The Spaniards will leave the country.'

Jamie murmured his congratulations. It did not seem that this was a moment to brood over the arms which Alan Beaton and he had taken from Hamburg to the Spanish garrison, now, presumably, disarmed.

'So,' Carey went on, 'you find us here *en fête*! Get rid of your hat and cloak and come and help us to rejoice.'

In a vast, lavishly painted hall, Jamie caught a pair of intent and glowing eyes. Cecil.

'Tick, tick, tick, Mr Stuart,' said the secretary in his silky voice.

'I have until midnight, Sir Robert.'

'I advise you not to assume that, because Her Majesty has

won the battle in Ireland, we are ready to forgive.'

Jamie smiled and passed on. He had seen Miranda Vane.

'Could we talk for a few minutes?' he asked.

'Impossible! . . . No. If we are very quick, we can stroll along this gallery.'

He was delighted to see that it was empty. Taking a folded piece of paper from his pocket, he handed it to her.

'If Lord Henry knows you have that, Miranda, you can laugh at threats from his lordship. He will not wish to follow his brother to the scaffold.'

She read feverishly and, blushing deeply, kissed him on the lips. Although it was the palace of the Virgin Queen, Jamie thought there was passion in the kiss. He drew her into an alcove and took her in his arms. After a silence, her voice became a broken murmur which he quenched with his lips . . .

'Now I must fly,' she said at last. 'I am due to serve the queen's supper in the private apartments. Later, she will make an entrance. But you will see!'

A blaze of trumpets, sweet-sounding and insolent. A stamping of weapons on the floor. A hush. Then a sudden invasion of gold and scarlet liveries, of very tall men walking with a swagger. And in the midst of it all, a woman, old, over-dressed, crooked, and somehow wonderful.

Impressions chased one another through his head. Such a flashing wealth of jewels! A display which in anyone but a monarch would be thought vulgar! And, to come to the woman herself, such a nose, as if all the emperors since Charlemagne had contributed to this facial emblem of command! Such a glance, peremptory and exact as a signal on a battlefield!

The hair, a wig. The skin, shrivelled under all its layers of paint. In the end, however, it was not the senses but the mind which felt the impact. A unique personality was here. An old woman, playing a part, but greater than the part and, slyly, aware of it. And wonderful because she was victory over heavy odds; survival through countless perils; a name stamped on an era, at first in defiance and, then, in triumph.

150

The shouts of loyalty and rejoicing rose higher and higher under the painted rafters as the queen advanced in procession behind her gentlemen.

Jamie caught sight of someone behind her: a beautiful, clever little face, copper-coloured hair, cheeks delicately flushed, downcast eyes that contrived to suggest mutiny as well as devotion. Miranda Vane was on duty.

Jamie did like the rest. Summoning up the whole resources of his education among the nobles of Paris, he swept to the floor in one harmonious movement. Every limb, every finger, played its part in the superb obeisance which subtly suggested the varying ideas of abasement, adoration and virility. He heard a rustle behind him and someone saying, 'What a popinjay!' it is hard to please all the public.

When at last he turned his eyes upwards again, he found that he was looking into a wizened, heavily painted face out of which two grey eyes glared as hard and as bright as diamonds.

'You may kiss our hand.' The voice was a deep contralto, as clear as a bell and with a power all its own to thrill. Jamie had been determined not to be abashed, but this practised old woman just for a moment gave him the novel experience of awe. His lips touched jewels.

'This is the – ' Somebody hidden behind the queen had begun to explain. Jamie thought it might be Edward Carey. He was roughly interrupted.

'Let the boy talk for himself. I suppose he has a tongue. Your name, young man?'

'James Stuart, Majesty.'

'You bow very prettily, James. But why do you speak like a Frenchman?'

'Because I am half a Frenchman by birth, ma'am. And all a Frenchman by education.'

He heard a noise which, if it had been uttered by anyone but a queen, he would have called a grunt.

'I knew a Frenchman once,' she said. 'It was long ago and he was not at all like you, James, except, perhaps, in his impudence.'

'God forbid, ma'am! No.'

151

Her thin lips twisted into a satirical smile.

'Yes, James. When you reach my age, you can smell the truth without having it put under your nose. Rise, young man. Talking to you from this height will give me a crick in the neck.'

'To tell you the truth, it is rather hard on the knee, too.'

'God! You are tall!'

'It's a family weakness, ma'am.'

'If you were English, I might make you Captain of the Guard.'

'I doubt if the King of Scots will make me captain of *his* guard. If he has one!'

The queen smiled a lopsided smile.

'Oh, he has one. I pay for it. Don't you think he needs it? But you are right. With your name, and your reputation, more bad than good –'

'Could I defend myself to Your Majesty?'

'No doubt the stories are much exaggerated. You probably invented some of them yourself.'

'Ma'am!' he protested.

'Yes. You have certainly enough intelligence to know that the bad that people do is much more interesting than the good. The wisdom of this world, James! So far as you are concerned, the good may not be much and it is too obvious to need mentioning. You are tall, strong, handsome in a coarse kind of way – were I thirty years younger, I should probably have flirted with you. My taste was never too refined.'

'You overrate me, ma'am. I am too serious-minded to flirt.'

'Then your eyes and your tongue are deceivers. I don't think they are. Don't interrupt, sir! Queens must not be interrupted. You are said to be brave, which probably means you are stupid. You are said to be unusually clever with the rapier. Are there, by chance, any other qualities you are proud of?'

'By chance there is, ma'am. I am told that I dance well. Where I went to school, they paid a lot of attention to that.'

She smiled ruefully. 'Once, I was a good dancer, too,' she said.

152

'In Europe the report is that Your Majesty still dances beautifully and often.'

'Then report is as false as it usually is.'

'I believed it. In fact, if it is not over-bold to say so, I have had one ambition since I was at school. To dance the galliard with the great Queen of England.'

Her voice harshened. 'Then you have come to England too late, James Stuart.'

'With profound respect, Your Majesty, I think not. You have the carriage and the figure of a dancer. Your foot is as light as a leaf –'

'Leaves are lighter in autumn, young man.'

'This is not autumn. It is not even spring. It is the night on which Your Majesty has heard of the second great victory of your reign.'

Her face grew rigid. He thought that it would be white under the paint.

'And the hardest. And the one that cost the most,' she said harshly.

'And one to be celebrated ma'am.' He was carried away by his theme. 'The moment is right. The music is here. The lights are bright. The court is waiting. Tonight, of all nights in her life, the Queen of England should dance.'

Her hands clenched and unclenched as the diamonds flashed. For a moment he thought she would strike him or, worse, turn her back and leave him. But slowly her face softened. A spark of almost girlish mischief was kindled in her sharp grey eyes. It was as if she said, 'Why not?'

She clapped her hands once. Silence fell on the hall, silence threaded by a hundred whispers.

'Send for the master of my music,' said the queen aloud.

My God, thought Jamie, what have I done? What a show-off! What a buffoon I am!

A tall man, splendid in scarlet and gold, struck the floor with a partizan and spoke at Jamie's elbow. 'If anything untoward happens to Her Majesty,' he said quietly, 'your body will be found in the river off Gravesend tomorrow morning.' Jamie nodded.

What had Cecil said about the life of a woman of sixty-nine?

Tick, tick, tick. He turned to Miranda Vane. Her eyes were wide and glowing. 'You have done something no Englishman would dare to do. It seems that really you *are* French.'

'It is almost a year since I danced the galliard,' he murmured, with a grimace.

'Don't worry, James. She will show you the steps. Afterwards, if you like, you may dance with me.'

The music began to play. He did not know the air but he recognized the time. It was three-four – six steps of which the fifth was a leap. The galliard! He walked into the open space which had been cleared on the floor and, turning to the queen, made the profound obeisance which at the Louvre was reserved for princesses of the blood royal. So, at least, he had been told at the academy he attended in Paris.

Rising, he stepped forward and touched the tips of the fingers she offered. They were heavily ringed but nothing could hide their slim, white elegance. She seemed to have grown taller. She stood more erectly. At that moment, Jamie was sure that everything was going to be all right. 'Not too fast,' he told himself. 'Remember, the lady is in her sixty-ninth year.'

But from the first steps it was clear that the tempo and brisk-ness of the dance would be at the discretion of the queen. There would be no question of sparing an aged woman the more strenuous exertions of the galliard. Jamie was dancing with one whose body seemed to be composed of air caught somehow in a web of steel wires.

When it came to the fifth step, it was the high upward leap she performed, which usually only young girls and professional dancers attempted. When his eyebrows showed his amazement, a smile touched one corner of her mouth. She murmured something which he could not catch. It seemed to be in Italian. Probably she had said something about the need for constant practice. But with this lady one never knew.

At the end, a pulse was beating in her hollow temple.

But steadily and not too fast.

She frowned suddenly. 'I commit too many follies,' she said. 'Go and find a girl. The one! – ' She pointed to Miranda Vane. 'If you have not found her already!'

She sat down abruptly. She was an old woman again.

'The dance is over,' said Cecil, in a silky voice. 'Now to business, Stuart.'

'I must dance, Mr Secretary. Order of the queen!'

He bowed before Miranda.

'We must not dance too well,' she whispered. 'Or too long. I am on duty.'

At the end, Carey appeared. 'Somebody has arrived who wants to see you,' he said.

'To see *me*?'

Carey nodded. 'Somebody who says you will be expecting him. You can slip out and meet the man.'

At the palace entrance, beside the sentry box, Jamie found Jabez Walker, with a guard who looked as if nothing would please him better than to use the partizan he carried.

'What is it, Jabez?'

'Begging Your Excellency's pardon, but it seemed I ought to speak to you!'

'If it's a matter of life or death, Jabez.'

'That's for you to say, sir. Just tell this man to stop shaking his spear at me. It gives me the horrors.'

'Never mind him. Go on.'

'A boat filled with men – men of the wrong sort, if you follow me – has passed along the shore opposite, going to the east.'

'Did they have a good send-off from Old Mother Brown's?'

Jabez frowned and went on with his story.

'They shipped a keg of powder before they left the pier at Southwark. What's more, they have on board plenty of fancy stuff as well, tar and lint waste and such. Stuff to make a lovely blaze. No use you looking now, sir. Reckon they'll be round the bend of the river by this time.'

'Is there a moon tonight?'

Walker's eyes grew round.

'Moon? Tonight, sir? No, that there certainly ain't. Not after two of the morning. Won't be a moon now for three nights.'

'Have you a boat out there yourself?'

'Yes, sir. After what you said, sir. We followed 'em down river. They don't know they were being watched.'

'Stay where you are, Jabez.'

Jamie went back to the privy apartments where he found a guard blocking the way. A few minutes were needed before Edward Carey could be summoned to vouch for him.

'May I see the queen to take my farewell?'

'Already? Come along.'

The queen rose from the table where she had begun a hand of patience. 'Well, young man. I can see you have news.'

Jamie, speaking quickly, told his story in a few minutes. The queen listened closely. When he had finished, she walked slowly to the end of the room and mounted the steps to the dais. Then she sat on the chair of state. Cecil and others stood round, listening, deferential, alert to follow a train of thought or reinforce a doubt.

'At times princes should be content with part of the truth.' Her voice had the ominous ring of power. 'So I shall not ask what you were doing, James, when you met Spinola's galleys at sea.' Then, after a minute, 'Where is the Channel Guard, Mr Carey?'

'Somewhere off the Goodwin Sands, ma'am.' Carey was about to leave the room when she stopped him.

'No need to fetch a chart, Edward. I remember where the Goodwins are. My admirals are too far south to help us. And all these merchant ships lying between here and London Bridge. How many are there of them?'

'Twice as many as usual, ma'am,' said Carey. 'Stayed from unloading on account of the plague.'

'And the weather in the estuary?'

'No sea,' said Jamie. 'A light wind. The weather is likely to trouble nobody.'

The queen's mouth tightened.

'We could row down the estuary in that boat your friends have brought,' Carey suggested.

Jamie shrugged his shoulders. 'In that tub! We could never catch her!'

'We could ride by Dartford on the coast road,' Carey suggested.

Another courtier broke in. 'Ride! Twenty miles on a night as dark as this! And all the delays of signalling the ship at the end of the journey. Don't be a damned fool, man – saving Your Grace's presence.'

There was silence for a moment as everybody turned, abashed, to the terrible old woman huddled on the chair of state. Up there, on the dais with one thin shoulder pressed against the cushion behind her and her eyes, as bright as her jewels, glittering fiercely over the other shoulder. They had, for a moment, appeared to forget her and the deference they owed to the sovereign.

It was she who broke the pause. Suddenly, she leaned forward and her laugh crackled, raucous and commanding, so that they all jumped with surprise.

'God's wounds!' cried Elizabeth, scornfully. 'Call yourselves men of war. This impudent Genoese moneylender plans to raid the river, England's river, *our* river! – and all of you are bereft of an answer! What kind of war council is this! You, Sir Robert. What do you propose?'

The Secretary of State made a cautious gesture.

'Your Majesty, we are not all as clever as you are.'

'I think not. By God! I think not! What is to be done is clear and must be done at once.' She paused for a second and something like a grin – but a queen does not grin – curled her painted lips. She pointed towards the window where outside the river was flowing darkly to the sea.

'Come, let us go out.' She rose to her feet.

'Out, ma'am?'

'Yes. Out,' she said, sharply. 'Why? To think, of course. Don't you know that it is one of the few things that are better done in the open air. Go, ask that girl Miranda to bring me a coat.' Carey disappeared.

'There is not even a moon,' Cecil groaned.

The queen chuckled.

'Not even a moon! God! this is a degenerate age. There are not even flatterers left at my court! Nobody who has the wit to say' – here she began to mimic a grovelling voice – 'there is no need of a moon when Cynthia herself walks out!'

Jamie broke in on the laughter.

'We can do better than that, ma'am,' he said. 'When you walk out, the moon is ashamed to shine.'

'Say it in French, young man,' she said. 'Say in in the native tongue of flattery.'

Miranda came with a fur cloak. The queen led the way out on to the terrace that faced the river, a brilliant ebony plane sliding through the night.

A single light shone at the nearer bank. She pointed to it.

'Out there at the landing stage is our barge. Our watermen are in the palace. Twenty of them. If they are sober, they will do the business. If they are drunk, I will have them flogged by the master-at-arms.'

'Ma'am, ma'am – ' A man's voice broke out in shrill protest. Jamie thought he was probably the Captain of the Guard, all in scarlet and gold with a staff of office.

'Silence, Sir Kit! You can stay at home with the women.'

'Ma'am, I swear – ' Sir Kit's voice was indignant as well as shrill.

The queen made an impatient gesture.

'I said silence, man. Nobody doubts your valour but it is your duty to stay at your sovereign's side. Carey, send me the master of my barge.'

'Yes, ma'am – but – '

'Don't loiter, Edward. Do you want this Italian to burn every ship between here and the Tower? As Drake did in Cadiz Bay! Remember! No! That was when you were a little boy! Run, boy, run!'

'The barge will have to move fast, Your Majesty,' said Sir Robert. 'I reckon those villains will have half an hour's start of it.'

'If the queen's barge loses the race,' snapped the old woman on the terrace, 'I'll have every waterman of my crew keel-hauled by noon tomorrow. You know what that English word means, Monsieur Stuart?'

Jamie could guess.

'Ma'am,' he said. 'If I have your permission to muster the assault party – '

'Bring them here, sir.'

'With respect, I think it would be better if Your Majesty did not clap eyes on them.'

'Oh, I would recognize them, would I?'

158

'No. But Your Majesty's gaolers might.'

'I can believe it! That is the kind you are likely to recruit, Stuart! Like to like!' She began to chuckle. 'Go now. Waste no time . . . By God, I haven't enjoyed anything so much since the day we beat the Armada!'

She struck the terrace balustrade with a be-ringed, elegant claw that had become a fist.

Jamie bowed and hurried towards the landing stage.

At the waterside, a wind was blowing off-shore, light but cold. Under a lantern, Jabez Walker stood talking to the sentry.

'Where is the queen's barge?' asked Jamie.

Jabez looked surprised but pointed to a long dark shape moored under the landing stage. Jamie saw the elaborate outline of a carved cabin. The lantern light was reflected dully back from gilding. A row of small round windows ran along its length. He thought he could see silk hangings. Tassels. In the open woodwork of the hull, about the cabin, he reckoned that there were benches for twenty oarsmen – ten oars a side.

Carey came into the light, followed by a disorderly train of men donning their livery coats.

'We'll be one man short,' said Carey, frowning. 'You can guess why. For God's sake, say nothing to the queen.'

'Jabez,' said Jamie. 'Put your friends aboard that barge.'

The waterman's eyebrows rose in alarm.

'But it's the queen's, sir. We daren't – '

'Do what I tell you, Jabez. But don't let any of these rascals go into the cabin. We want no lice there.'

'By God, sir,' said Jabez. 'It will need more than me to keep that actor out of the cabin. Maybe you can.'

'Fletcher? He's a law to himself.'

'All the way down from London he has been singing fit to wake the dead. He was a soldier once.'

'He was,' said Jamie, 'and nobody is going to forget it.'

Jabez went to the edge of the jetty. He put something to his lips. A whistle. In a minute, Jamie heard a boat splash towards them. Oars were shipped noisily and wood crashed and jarred against the fenders that protected the queen's landing stage.

159

Lawrence Fletcher climbed ashore.

'Show me the enemy!' he said. 'Lead me into the cannon's mouth. What craft is that, Stuart?'

'That is the queen's barge. We'll travel in it to the scene of action.'

'Gloriana's own! You do things in style, young man.' Fletcher's voice was resonant with approval. 'These fellows – ' with a wave of his hand he indicated his companions in the boat – 'insist that I should lead the storming party. I have consented.'

'Good,' said Jamie.

'Is this the face that launched a thousand ships?' Fletcher came forward, arms outstretched.

He is drunk, Jamie decided, and took a step backwards.

Then he went quickly back to the palace to make his farewells. This time, he had no trouble about being admitted to the privy apartments.

Jamie threw himself on his knees on the soft carpet in front of the queen's chair.

'Majesty, have I your permission to leave?'

She looked at him stonily for a moment.

'Yes, you may go now. And don't come back until I send for you. Carey must answer for our barge. Do you hear that, Edward?'

Carey was on his knees beside Jamie.

'Ma'am,' he said.

'And don't get into mischief or I'll never look your mother in the face again. You, Stuart, at your peril, see that he behaves with discretion. You may not be a subject of mine, but I have a long arm. I can reach you anywhere in Christendom.'

He thought she was right.

The contralto sounded again. What a marvellous voice for a theatre!

'Did I tell you, you are not to come back? These are my orders. You cause trouble of one kind or another. I think you mean to make trouble. And don't look at me with those penitent eyes. I don't believe them. No. You are a good dancer, but you embarrass me with the King of Scots.'

'Speaking of that, ma'am – '

'Go on. Go on. My days are numbered but 1 suppose I can save one of them for you.'

Jamie fumbled at the neck of his shirt and from a small leather bag which hung round his neck pulled a small folded parchment on which a green seal had been broken. He held it out to the queen.

'What is it, boy?'

'My grandmother's marriage lines, Majesty.'

She leaned forward, snatched it, and looked at him hard.

'What is the price?' she asked. 'If I wanted to buy.'

'Gifts have no price.'

'Be serious, boy.' Her voice was suddenly harsher. 'Queens do not take gifts from commmoners. How much?'

Even at that moment, Jamie could not help admiring her effrontery. *She* did not take presents! He found himself uttering thoughts that he did not know existed.

'I want my rights,' he said. 'No more than that. My grandmother's estate in Scotland, at present in the hands of a robber called Lord Orkney. And besides that, if you please, a letter from the King of Scots to the King of France recommending me for the lieutenancy of the Scottish Archers. I think he owes me no less.'

Until that moment it had not occured to him. But the longer he thought of it, the more brilliant the idea seemed. The possibilities it held for a young man were dazzling. The resolution stiffened in Jamie's face.

The queen's painted eyebrows rose. Her mouth became a circle of astonishment.

'By God! she said, 'you know how to do business after all, young man! If only I could do what you wish!'

'Your Majesty can do it if she cares to be benevolent.'

'Lieutenancy of the Scottish Archers? What's that?'

Carey spoke: 'The second place in the first corps in the French king's service, ma'am. Like Your Majesty's gentlemen pensioners – except that they are Scots and pensioners of the King of France. The post is in the gift of King James.'

'Is it, by God?' she said. 'I think King James will want to give it to a different kind of candidate from this one.'

'Very likely, ma'am.'

161

'But kings don't get always what they would like, eh.' Her eyes were like two grey arrows fixed on Jamie's. 'So you are willing to give up your chance to be a king,' she said. 'Well, every man to his taste. A king . . . It's a dangerous trade, boy. One day, the throne, the next the dungeon, the scaffold or exile. The important thing is to have something to fall back on if things go badly. Now I always knew that if I were turned out in only my petticoat I could always make a living. Now what about you, James? Is there any art you could turn a hand to apart from making eyes at young girls?'

'Ma'am,' said Jamie. 'I made my living once.'

'Doing what? Don't tell me if it was discreditable.'

'Teaching the noble art of self-defence. Fencing, in short.'

'Did you have any success?'

'It led to other things,' said Jamie with a faint grin.

Her eyes rested on his for a moment, half in annoyance, half in amusement.

'I can believe that,' she said in a voice that was almost a growl.

'Next time,' said Jamie, 'I think I shall teach dancing.'

The queen clapped her hands together. She began to laugh and stopped abruptly.

'Go! Go!' she cried irritably. 'Go, before I change my mind.'

She held out her long, white, be-ringed fingers to be kissed. As Jamie, rising from his knees, hurried from the chamber, he thought he heard the sound of an old woman's laughter breaking out again.

Cecil stood at the door. As Jamie went past, 'Clever,' he said. 'But you should have asked for a peerage. A Scots peerage of course.'

'With my grandmother's lands – unnecessary – they carry the right to a barony!' said Jamie.

'Cecil was right,' he said to Carey as they walked briskly to the door that led to the water. He had remembered a snatch of conversation from their first meeting.

'Cecil is always right. That's why he is still Secretary of State. What did he say, James?'

Jamie was not sure that he remembered the exact words but

162

it was something like – 'Even an exceptional woman is no exception to being a woman.'

It made Carey grunt in appreciation.

'But here is my cousin,' said Carey, and moved away.

It was Miranda Vane, looking just as she had been when Jamie first set eyes on her. Her eyes were sparkling, her lips were trembling. She was quivering with anger, and very beautiful. 'I could kill the little bitch,' she said.

What had happened? He gathered that one of the queen's jewels had been mislaid and she had been blamed. Wrongly, wrongly! That traitress, Patricia Cobbold, was responsible.

Then, quite suddenly, the storm was over. She took both Jamie's hands in hers and looked into his eyes with an expression full of malice and good nature.

'James,' she said, 'I hear you are leaving on some expedition which sounds mad and dangerous. You will come back soon, won't you?' She kissed him.

'If the queen allows me to.'

'She will. I know that. You are the kind of man she likes.' She kissed him again.

'But the secretary does not approve of me.'

'Oh, the secretary! And Lord Henry hates you. Oh, James, how do I thank you?' Her eyes danced.

'You can write a sonnet for me.'

She frowned. 'A sonnet. No! That man – the one you have not met – has written a string of sonnets which, he says, are about me. They are not. I shall not write a sonnet for you, James.'

'Well, now you are free again, Miranda. I need not tell you how to use your freedom – prudently, of course, but well – until I see you!'

'We are the same kind, Jamie,' she said.

Their kiss was too long and passionate for the palace of a Virgin Queen.

'Just one thing. Liz gave me a message for you,' she said. 'She is buying a wax image of the girl you marry so that she can stick pins in it.'

'Tell her she may be committing suicide,' he said. 'Oh, and will you give me one of your hairs, Miranda?'

She smiled slowly, blushed and pulled a hair from her head. He curled it round a finger and put it beside the one he already had in his purse.

'A rhymed couplet,' he said. Then he kissed her hand and left her.

'What Ship Are You?'

On the cold jetty, the queen's bargemaster was stamping about in a fury within the sea-coat he was struggling into.

'What is all this damned nonsense, gentlemen? What do you think I have here, a queen's galleon of forty guns? Nothing of the sort! Only the queen's barge, a top-heavy old rowing boat that will overturn in the first gale.'

Jamie understood the man's feelings. In all likelihood he had been snatched away from a cosy game of hazard in the royal kitchen. He left Carey to do the explaining.

'We have a fight on our hands, bargemaster, and nobody need come who doesn't want to.'

'That isn't what I mean, Mr Carey.'

'You have cutlasses aboard? And pistols?'

Jamie looked down at the barge. Fletcher was lolling at his ease in the queen's cabin. His eyes were shining. He was in excellent voice, declaiming verse, then:

'Stuart, I am ready to sail!'

'In a minute we cast off,' said Jamie.

'Who is that fellow?' said Carey. 'I know the voice.'

'A soldier fallen on evil times.'

'The town is full of them,' said Carey.

The watermen were settling into place on the benches. He saw that one man was sitting apart from the others in the stern.

'You have a man to spare, bargemaster,' he said.

'I am a man short. It's the same thing, more or less. Accidents will happen, sir. I'll keep him in reserve, like.'

'But you can find a sweep for him, I suppose. Yes? In that

165

case, would you think of giving a sweep to me, just to even things up?'

'To you, sir?' The master looked Jamie up and down. He was going to laugh, but did not. Jamie threw off his cloak and began to unbutton his doublet.

'If I were you, master, I'd take him,' said Carey.

Jamie was standing there in his shirt. The bargemaster surveyed his shoulders critically.

'You done this before, sir?'

'You'll find that he can row,' said Carey.

Jamie nodded, grinning.

'He's had plenty of practice,' said Carey.

'Come on!' shouted the bargemaster, and jumped into the big craft.

From the cabin came Fletcher's voice robust and urgent: 'Marvellous! What splendour I lend to the simple fancy of the playwright.'

After an hour of rowing, teased by the wind and nagged at by contrary currents, they rested, while someone passed round a jug of beer. Can I hold out? Jamie wondered. Already his heart was pounding. There was no sign, however, of uneasiness in the men rowing between him and the stern; they were not suffering from the stiff pace set by the stroke.

They looked like old navy hands to Jamie. Probably this sort of thing meant nothing to them. They did it every day, ferrying the queen between Whitehall and Greenwich. They were so many rowing machines made out of some dark polished wood and moved by steel rods . . . they smelt, the smell of healthy sweat on unwashed bodies. The rowers Jamie had known before had a stronger odour. It would never do to show any signs of discomfort. They bent once more to the oars.

Jamie noticed one good thing: the tide was beginning to turn, although an uncertain wind still hovered above the barge, tugging the bow first to one side and then to the other. The two banks were no more than dark accompanying presences, punctured now and then by weak points of light.

After a minute, Jamie felt more confident. He was getting his wind back. And the oar he was pulling was little more than half the weight of a sweep on the Spanish galley he had toiled

166

in. Here the rowing style was more elegant, the strokes longer and more powerful, ending in a smooth withdrawal from the water.

During the short rest, Jamie had slipped off his shirt. His neighbour on the bench looked at the brand on his shoulder. GAL. It could just be seen in the light of the cabin lantern behind them.

'What's that, mate?'

'That's a prize the Spaniards give you for rowing.'

The man laughed derisively. 'Here,' he shouted to his friends, 'we got somebody's prize bull calf aboard.' The barge rumbled with mirth.

There is a clown like this aboard every ship, thought Jamie.

Fletcher was reciting poetry in the cabin.

At that moment a whistle sounded, thin as a silver thread. Men bent to the oars. The stroke was longer now. The barge sprang forward in the water. A smell of salt was beginning to invade the sad odours of the mudflats. Somewhere ahead was the guardship. Somewhere nearer was the boat that was carrying the guardship's furtive enemies on their way to the attack.

Jabez Walker, flat on his stomach in the barge's prow, would see it – the old water rat would see it if any man on the seven seas could. And then – Jamie looked at the sword he had unbuckled and laid between his feet. There you are, old friend. Very soon now! The excitement that he could feel tingling in him – he had never known it to be at fault as a presage of battle.

After a time – an inordinate time – somebody blew a whistle softly and Jamie knew that it was Jabez. With his extraordinary eyesight he had picked up something in the darkness of the river. The movement of a boat that he had seen before.

The lights in the barge's cabin were extinguished. Fletcher was not declaiming now. The pace of the rowing slowed down. The rustling sounds in the water alongside grew fainter. Now the queen's barge was moving over silk.

Back in the stern, weapons were being passed round, to judge by the dull sounds as steel met steel. Swords, pistols, and pikes – all useful arms for an assault on a crew that

167

would have its mind elsewhere, that would be thinking of a simple operation of war, an attack by petard and fireworks on an unsuspecting victim.

In imagination, Jamie could picture the tension in the boat ahead of them. Its occupants would have their minds fixed on the sky out to the east where, very soon, the black bulk of the guardship would take shape out of the grey vagueness . . . if they were all on course! The absurd idea had occurred to him that the boat and the barge had perhaps both missed their mark and, at morning light, would find themselves somewhere off the French coast. That would be an interesting situation.

While he was pondering the question, the bargemaster growled a command and the movement of the oars slowed down still more. Jamie stole a glance over his shoulder. They were creeping up on a boat which did not seem to be aware of their presence. No! He had spoken too soon. Somewhere ahead a man had given what sounded like a warning, something between a shout and a groan.

Then, resounding over the water, came the bargemaster's voice, through a speaking trumpet: 'Heave to!'

For an instant, silence, then someone shouting back, 'Who says?'

Again the trumpet: 'In the queen's name!'

In response to a signal Jamie did not hear, stroke began to increase the speed at which the oars in the barge were plied. Jamie fell into the rhythm with the others. The water gulped and gurgled along the side of the big, clumsy, ornate craft. Jamie felt the moisture running over his ribs. Behind him, he sensed the assault party crouching low, tense, motionless, weapons at the ready. Pray God they did not, by some imprudence, set off the keg of powder and blow everybody to smithereens.

The trouble is, Stuart, he told himself, straining at his oar, you are essentially a coward. In the heat of a skirmish you choke back your timidity. But when you have to trust to another man's judgement, when you have to wait and see in what form death may be coming, then you show a streak of –

The sudden babble of voices was astonishingly close. The

helmsman had put the rudder over abruptly. There was a crash that almost snatched the oar from his grasp. Then a rasping shudder along the sacred timbers of the royal barge. There would be work for the carpenters in the navy yard at Deptford and a tongue-lashing from the queen for Edward Carey! Jamie let his oar hang into the water – the rest of the rowers had shipped their sweeps as regulation decreed. He stooped for his sword and pulled it up.

Somebody cried, 'What ship are you?' from the other boat.

A nearer voice – it might be the bargemaster's – 'You'll find out bloody soon!'

Somebody fired a pistol. In the darkness there was a sudden brief core of yellow light.

Jamie, balanced on a rowing bench, at the side of the barge, found himself faced by a long jump over inky water. He remembered he was an indifferent swimmer. But it was too late to improve. As he jumped he was aware that the two boats were pulled together by grapnels. All round him men were shouting. He would not be jumping alone.

Facing him was the crouched figure of a burly man wearing a boat-cloak. He had a scarf tied round his head. Or was it a bandage? Through his mind there was a flash of something like recognition. Was this not the man with the ear-ring?

Just as he jumped, somebody gave him a prod from behind so that he landed badly on the other boat. His foot slipped and, as he pitched forward, staggering, a hand gripped him by the throat, a thumb was on his larynx, pressing brutally.

Jamie felt himself swaying backwards. The next thing would be the water. While he struggled, he heard someone make choking noises. But the noises faded quickly. Everything faded. Then, somewhere at the back of it all, before it vanished into nothing, there was a brief, angry incursion of voices. And a hard pain in his throat, which became more important than anything else . . .

Darkness was a field sown with sparks which steadied and became stars, and then, just as quickly, sank into a vast, soft cushion, deep blue in colour, very beautiful, something to wonder at, to struggle feebly against . . .

Abruptly Jamie was aware of a world that was a good deal

less beautiful and not at all comfortable. Above him two men were locked in a mysterious but apparently deadly struggle.

If only he had his sword, but someone had taken it away. The tears of annoyance started to his eyes; he lifted his hand in protest against the injustice of life.

In God's name! The hand was grasping his sword! A mystery, a miracle!

Without hesitating, without knowing why, action moving ahead of thought, as it ought to do, he thrust upwards at one of the struggling bodies above him, the one he knew – but how? – on what evidence? It did not belong to a friend.

Somebody had been about to give a scream of pain and then had thought better of it. Jamie smiled secretly. He turned over and slowly climbed up a steep hard slope. It was as high as a man's knees and it had the shape of a boat's hull.

More slowly still, one of the wrestlers above him buckled at the knees and slid downwards. For a second of time, the man he had been struggling with supported him under the arms. Then he let go and the first man crumpled up. Something hit the gunwale noisily. A man's head!

'You caught him where it hurt most, sir,' said Jabez Walker. In the bottom of the boat a man was lying still. Jamie noticed two things about him. His breeches were soaked in blood. And he had a bandage round his head. Strange. Jamie had see the man before.

'Dead?' he asked, pointing to him.

Jabez Walker stooped over the man and put a hand to his wrist. 'No,' he said. 'But he didn't like that stab you gave him from below. Look at that ear-ring, sir. Pretty, ain't it.' He held it out for Jamie to admire. 'Pity he hasn't got the twin. I'll ask him about it when he comes to.'

The fight was still going on farther for'ard, but Jamie thought it would be finished soon. A voice sounded across the water, asking a question. Jamie turned towards it. With a shock he saw the mass of a big warship very near. It would be the guardship, very tall, very black, very imposing. Lanterns were moving along its decks. A rumbling came from it. Cannon were being run out.

'They're ready now, sir. Guns out. Gun ports open,' said

Jabez Walker, with derision in his voice. 'Just ten minutes late. Good old navy! Lucky they had us to help them.'

'We'll be lucky if they don't blow us out of the water,' gasped Jamie. His throat hurt and he did not like the row of gun muzzles a musket shot away. He did not trust their expression.

'Don't worry about that. Couldn't hit the steeple of St Paul's. How's your head, sir? It made a noise like the crack of doom hitting the ship's timbers like that.'

'It's all right. It's my throat that worries me.'

The fighting for'ard had died away. The clang of steel on steel had ceased. Somebody was groaning. Somebody else launched into a lecture on the tactics of fighting in boats – 'In those damnable Dutch canals,' said Fletcher, 'we had plenty of it.'

From the guardship, someone wanted blasphemously to know who they were. It would give him the greatest pleasure in the world to blow them off the face of the water.

'Don't shoot,' Jamie shouted. 'We have half a last of powder on board.'

Silence weighed briefly on the water.

'Then keep your distance. I'm sending a dinghy over for your leader.'

'That means you, Jamie,' said Carey, smugly.

Jamie climbed on to a high deck and found himself looking into a suspicious face. He talked quickly. The guardship captain lifted the lantern once and stared into his face.

'You can believe him. Never mind the accent,' said Carey. 'Look over the side and you'll see the queen's barge.'

The captain took the lantern with him and looked. His eyebrows rose a fraction of an inch.

'Now what do we do?' he said.

Jamie told him what was in his mind.

'There won't be a moon tomorrow night,' he said at the end of it. 'Meanwhile, Mr Carey can alert the navy in the Medway.'

The captain snorted.

'There's no navy in the Medway able to do a quick job. Parsimony!' he said. 'That's the ruin of the English navy.'

171

'Maybe I can convince the admiral that he should put something on to the water,' said Carey with a shrug.

'In any case, I can find a ship,' said Jamie. 'All I need is a day to make things ready before the signal is given.'

'It's a question of timing,' said Carey. 'After we are sure that this Italian, Spinola, has not changed his mind . . .'

'If the weather remains right for the galleys, he won't change his mind.' Jamie was sure. 'For him, it's the chance of a century. Revenge for Cadiz! Drake himself eclipsed! And all those merchant ships to plunder! No. He will lead the galleys into the estuary as soon as he sees the fire – the fire you are going to light to deceive him, Captain.'

'Yes. But when?'

'We have to guess what will be the best time. But perhaps twenty-four hours from now.'

'You will be ready then yourself, James?' asked Carey.

'Find me a good horse on the north shore and I can do it.'

Carey pondered for a moment. 'I know a place where there's a waterside inn.' he said. 'I'll take you there now. After that, you must look after yourself. Come along. Good night, Captain. I'll be back by morning. Meanwhile, let none of your prisoners put a foot ashore.'

Rowed over in the barge, the two, Jamie and Edward Carey, talked about the plans for the following night. While they did so, Lawrence Fletcher addressed the rowers in sonorous blank verse.

'These ruffians you brought down from London,' said Carey 'Dregs! Combing of the gutters. Where the devil did you find them?'

'They fought well. Admit that they fought well.'

'They might have been worse. How many of them do you need for the job tomorrow?'

'I should like the actor to come, Edward. More if they want to.'

'There is my inn.' Carey pointed to a grey, oblong shape, shimmering in the darkness ahead of the barge, low down, near the water's edge.

When the time came, Fletcher and Tom the groom elected to

go with Jamie. Fletcher spoke of the diabolical fascination of war. The blood had coursed more swiftly through his veins. Etc. Tom smiled vacantly and washed his knife in the Thames water. The rest thought it was time to go home to their wives with the story of England's latest naval victory.

'To think that they have wives,' said Jamie.

'I'll see that they are paid,' said Carey. 'Good luck, Jamie.'

When the distance between the barge and the shore was widening, Jamie remembered something.

'One galley will be named *The Trinidad*,' he shouted. 'Save it for me.'

He saw Carey's arm lifted in acknowledgement.

'With luck, we'll be able to hire horses here,' Jamie said.

'What we can't hire, we'll take,' said Fletcher. 'For the queen's service.'

Tom frowned and shambled off towards the inn.

Daylight Robbery

Like a shining curtain, the morning mists were lifting fast when the three riders pulled up on the brow of a hill. Below them was a complex pattern of land and water, flat as a map and gleaming with the lights of dawn – silver on the creeks and river mouths, gold on sand and mud. A touching and innocent spectacle at that moment in the life of the morning. A few fisher boats were coming back to harbour with the night's catch – slow work, for there was barely a breath of wind. Apart from those, the only vessel in sight was *The Dark Lady*.

She looked small and harmless enough. Smoke was rising blue and vertical from her galley stack, as simple and domestic a sight as was likely to be seen in a cove frequented by all manner of unlawful craft and prudently ignored by searchers of Her Majesty's Customs.

Jamie kicked his horse forward to slither down the slope. He knew that, in a second, Fletcher, inspired by the view, would begin to recite appropriate verse. Half an hour later, when they had covered some distance on the damp flat plain below, Tom was dispatched to Sir Ferdinand Vane's house with a message that Jamie had scribbled. And, in due course, Jamie and Fletcher were rowed across to the deck of *The Dark Lady*.

'See that black girl,' said Jamie. 'Isn't she lovely! Painted her myself.'

'I am black but comely, o ye daughters of Jerusalem, as the tents of Kedar,' Fletcher intoned. 'Wonderful.'

They climbed aboard.

Alan Beaton, his teeth chattering with the cold air, blue-white in the cheeks, scowled at them. Jamie pointed at Fletcher, and gave his name. 'An Englishman', he said. Alan nodded without enthusiasm.

'I've more bad news for you,' he said. 'That Highland thief, Alistair MacIan, is here.'

James's eyes opened wide with delight. Never could the arrival of the outlaw of the Scottish glens have been more timely.

'Magnificent!' he said.

'Terrible! What is more, he has brought with him three of the most desperate of his kind that I ever clapped eyes on. Real terrors.'

'But I thought he planned to stay in Ireland.'

Alan shook his head.

'He saw the way the war was going and left in time. Alistair is not such a fool as you might think. Only what evil spirit made him pick this craft from all the ships in the North Sea? Of all the devilish pieces of bad luck.'

'Does he have a girl with him?'

'He has not, man. That's the only good thing about it. It seems they had words, that Irish girl and he. Alistair has a hasty temper but evidently she had a worse. A real hell-cat.' Alan's eyebrows rose at the horror of it.

'So?'

'Would you believe it, he and these Gaelic ne'er-do-wells are on their way to join Sinclair in Russia. Captain George Sinclair who is going to capture Moscow. If they can find him! In any case, Ireland is well rid of them, in my opinion. And so, please God, will this ship be before very long.'

'They'll make good settlers for you in Virginia,' said Jamie, smoothly.

He thought he could hear someone crooning a melancholy song.

'That's one of them!' said Alan. 'They're sobering up at last, but, by God, the trouble they've given us! Now tell us your news, Jamie.'

'It couldn't be better, boy. There's going to be a battle and

175

we're going to be in it. Against heavy odds but with the hope of a big profit at the end of it. Just the kind of battle you and Alistair like best.'

Alan Beaton looked at him suspiciously.

'I don't like the sound of it, James. What are the odds would you say?'

'Six to one.'

'Six to one *against*!' Alan's mouth had opened. Jamie went on softly.

'I'm talking about a battle. Alan, not about a massacre. A battle against Spanish galleys – '

'Like that time off the Dutch coast?' Alan's blue eyes grew big with alarm.

'Not like it at all!' said Jamie. 'Utterly different. This time, the English navy is on our side.'

Lawrence Fletcher, who had been listening impatiently to this conversation, cleared his throat impressively.

'What's more, Mr Beaton, *I* am on your side. The name is Fletcher, sir. Sergeant Fletcher, late of Her Majesty's forces in the Low Countries. Now, alas, fallen on evil times.' He made a gesture, florid, full of pathos. 'Would there, by chance, be something to drink on board this ship? I suffer from an affection of the vocal cords – '

'There might be beer, if those thirsty devils of Highland-men have left any.'

'Beer will do very well,' said Fletcher, graciously. 'After all, at this time of the morning I am not thinking of drink as a social custom. Merely as an analgesic device, if you understand me. Afterwards, we can discuss tactics. I shall of course lead the storming party.'

'Listen – ' Alan began. But Fletcher waved him down imperiously.

'Later,' he said. 'Later. First, the throat must be soothed and the mind lubricated. We must all be our best for the council of war.'

Beer was found. Fletcher's trained nose led him to cheese and bread. While he was occupied, Alan Beaton turned angrily on Jamie: 'What the devil is this about? Who is he?'

Jamie's hand waved soothingly.

176

'You haven't heard it all,' he said. 'We are likely to be joined in this business by Sir Ferdinand Vane, a friend of mine, a distinguished English pirate and enormously rich. My impression is, Alan, that he could be persuaded to put up some money for your Virginian adventure.'

Alan's expression eased.

'He lives not far from here,' Jamie went on. 'A house like a palace, a vast estate near the sea. Ships by the dozen! An army of seamen. And, incidentally, he has five young daughters. Or did I mention that before?'

Alan gave him a sharp look. 'You don't waste your time James,' he said. 'Now, about Virginia – '

'Later, later,' said Jamie.

Overcome by sleep, he found a corner where one of the seamen had been sleeping until he was routed out by the skipper to make the ship ready to sail. When Jamie woke up, Alistair and his Gaelic trio, pale and subdued after their revels, were lurching morosely about the deck. The Highlander contemplated Jamie with a cold eye.

'What's all this about more fighting?' he asked. 'Is there to be no peace any more in this world? Has man not yet had his fill of bloodshed?'

'This time,' said Jamie, 'you'll be on the other side. You'll be fighting against the Spaniards.'

'Indeed,' said Alistair, cheering up a little. 'I never liked those people very much anyway. That certainly makes a difference. I will explain it to my children.'

A few minutes later, Jamie heard the high pitch of a grindstone. The Highlandmen were sharpening their claymores.

Lawrence Fletcher approached, thunder on his brow, lightning in his gaze. He frowned in the direction of the sound of sharpening, and threw out a declamatory arm:

> 'The multiplying villainies of Nature
> Do swarm upon me from the western isles
> Of Kern and gallowglasses – '

'Lines from a play being written now. Even as I speak, a team of poets is at work on it. You see what the writer means, don't you!' His eyebrows rose, tremendous, arresting.

177

Jamie waited for him to go on. After a minute, he did.

'Tell me, do these savages understand that I am a sergeant?' he demanded.

'Have no fear,' said Jamie. 'When the trumpet sounds, they will follow their leader.'

'M'm, yes,' said Fletcher. 'But will the headstrong cattle know their leader when they see him?'

'Without a doubt. They have the instinct of the warrior.'

At that moment a hail came from the water. Sir Ferdinand Vane approached in a heavily laden boat. Cursing his gout, he pulled himself aboard and darted a critical eye around, the eye of a shipowner, the eye of a pirate.

'And with this lot you are going to take on the galleys of Spain!' he said. 'Boy, good luck to you! You'll need it. Meanwhile –'

He wagged his beard at a clattering heap of metal that his boatmen were heaving on board – 'Here are a few tools of the trade. Old armour that has been rusting in the parish church since the Armada year. Shot for your culverins. Fireworks – our English contribution to the art of war. Do you know how to use them? It's a knack . . . Now, lead me to the young man who wants to make a settlement in Virginia . . . At least his hair is the right colour! . . . Have you money, young sir? And a ship? I hear that you've been talking to Lord Southampton. In the Tower! Maybe his stay there will teach him some sense. Better birds than he have been housed in that cage. Now about this battle –'

Sir Ferdinand spoke as one who had fought many actions against Spanish galleys. 'It's a question of artillery tactics, mainly. You hold them off with your culverins. That can be done if you have good gunners. The trouble is that English gunnery is not as good as it should be.'

'In this ship the gunners are German,' said Jamie.

Sir Ferdinand obviously did not know quite how to take this unexpected news.

'Germans, eh! . . . Well, we'll see. The point is that, if the weather favours the galleys, you need two ships, yes, two ships – one lying east to west, the other north to south, lashed together by a cable through the hawser holes – if you

178

see what I mean? That way, no matter how the galleys come at you, you can give 'em a broadside. It's more than they can stand.'

'The trouble is,' said Alan Beaton, 'we have only one ship. This one.'

Sir Ferdinand tugged at his beard. His expression suggested that he was thinking that, whatever you did, there would always be somebody dissatisfied. His sharp blue eyes darted this way and that.

'Suppose I make you an offer,' he said, at last. 'I have a snug little craft not many miles from here, called *Rosebud*. And let me tell you at once that this little rose of mine has a thorn. I would be willing to bet that she is better armed than this one of yours. With good gunners, too, English though they are. Now, say I were to bring her along before nightfall – she could be lying off the entrance to this cove? Then, together, the two ships – we could practise that lashing together business. What do you say?' He threw up his arms.

'Good. Very good,' said Alan.

'Wait till I've finished. You've heard only half the story. In return for which inestimable service, I'll want two-thirds of the spoils, if any. In all the circumstances, reasonable. I'd even call it generous ...'

Alan Beaton said, 'Well ...'

'If you don't think it's fair, just say so,' said Sir Ferdinand. 'Don't hesitate ...'

When he was out of earshot, Alan Beaton grumbled to Jamie . . . 'It's sheer daylight robbery,' he said. 'Of all the old bandits I ever met! You said he is a pirate? You're right. By God, you're right.'

'You needn't agree to his terms if you don't want to.'

'Of course I must agree! I want him to fit out a ship for the Virginia venture. But believe me, boy, once I'm in the Indies, I'll see that Sir Ferdinand Vane pays a reasonable price for his spoils!'

'H'sh,' said Jamie.

Sir Ferdinand came over to them. 'If you would like to talk business,' he said, 'why don't you come over to my house? I have charts there – plenty of them! The Indies. The Ameri-

179

can coast. Everything. And you, Stuart, can amuse the girls
– if they amuse you.'

'I'll do what I can,' said Jamie, politely.

'Will your friends, the savages, be coming?' Sir Ferdinand
nodded coolly in the direction of Alistair and the Highlanders.

'I think not,' said Jamie. 'They are tired. They have had a
hard time these last few days.'

He could see that there might be trouble if the Highlanders
were allowed to meet the Vane sisters.

Vain Jane Surrenders

Riding over to the house, Sir Ferdinand said, casually, 'Do you remember that ruffian who called himself Captain Chandler, the friend of Lord Henry? Strange friend, I'd say. Some people think he is still lurking about in the neighbourhood somewhere. What do you think he would be up to, Stuart?'

Jamie's eyes opened wide.

'Don't ask me,' he said. 'All I know about Chandler is that he was going to burn my –'

'And he would have too,' Vane said. 'Nothing would have pleased him more! I've tried to run him to earth so that we could string him up. But no luck so far.'

He shrugged.

'In these seaward parts, Stuart, people don't ask too many questions. There are no lack of houses where a man can hide. Houses where they are used to finding queer fish in the net. All he needs is the right kind of friends.'

'What kind would that be?' Jamie asked, politely.

'Thieves,' said Sir Ferdinand, cheerfully. 'Smugglers, spies passing messages to and fro across to France and the Low Countries. Pirates.'

Pirates . . . Jamie thought it very likely. Sir Ferdinand would not be the only man on this coast doing that kind of business.

'I wonder why Chandler is still haunting this part of the country?' he said.

'He was hurt, remember. One of my girls hurt him. By mistake, I expect. She is not the kind to hurt a fly. Then I

181

think he may have picked up some word about that ship of yours. Some news the Spaniards would be interested to hear. He is probably taking their ducats. Just the kind to do it. Anyhow, people think he is somewhere not too far away.'

Sir Ferdinand nodded solemnly, and pointed ahead.

'Here we are, then,' he said.

Ahead, through trees, Jamie could see a wing of the house, rosy-red brick walls, mullioned windows, thin white smoke rising from the chimneys.

He turned to Alan Beaton who was riding alongside him.

'That's it,' he said.

Alan's blue eyes grew round with wonder.

'A palace,' he said, reverently.

'Didn't I tell you.'

Dogs barking in the stableyard, women calling in the house; standing in the hall, a slim young girl with blonde hair, who gave a squeal when she caught sight of Jamie. A second later, he found himself tightly clasped in the arms of Liz Vane.

'This is Alan Beaton,' he said, a minute later. 'He comes from Scotland. Treat him gently, Liz.'

She curtseyed and, taking a step forward, kissed Alan on the cheek.

'It's an old English custom,' Jamie explained.

Alan looked as if he wanted very much to say something but could not find words because of the turmoil of emotions which was making him blush so deeply.

Sir Ferdinand, who had entered the house by a door leading in from the stables, now appeared. 'Mr Beaton,' he said, 'I keep the charts in this room here' – he threw open a door – 'Let us have a talk about the voyage to Virginia. How rich are you, Beaton?'

Alan muttered something, looked round wildly and, frowning deeply, accepted the invitation.

When he had vanished, 'What marvellous hair!' said Liz in ecstasy.

Jamie looked at her in amazement. Women's taste was extraordinary. How wise he had been not to bring Alistair MacIan to the house.

'That colour!' he said with a grimace.

182

'Is he rich? Is he of good family?'

'Even richer than I am. As for the family, it is respectable enough, although not, of course, as good as mine,' he said. 'In any case, I will not allow you to marry him.'

'Thank you, Jamie. But I thought of him for –' She paused, with a finger on her lips as if she was trying to decide which of her sisters to name.

'Where are the others?' he said.

'Kate is changing her frock. Molly is in the stables. Her horse has gone lame. As soon as she heard you were in sight, Jane went to tint her cheeks so as to captivate Your Highness. At present, I am the only Vane available,' she said.

'It is the moment I have waited for,' he said.

'Liar! ... James, let me go ! ... If you come into this room you will find it quieter. And the furniture is more comfortable. Then you can tell me about your meeting with the queen. Edward Carey sent a note this morning. It did not tell us much, but it made it clear there was a lot to tell ...'

The light was already beginning to fade and Jamie was nearing the end of his account of his meeting with the queen when:

'Do you mean she really can dance the galliard – impossible.'

'Liz,' he told her solemnly, 'if she took it into her head she could dance the volta.'

'Impossible ... I love the volta.'

'Let us try.'

'We have no music.'

'I shall sing,' he said.

Then the door opened and Molly came in.

'I thought you would be here,' she said. 'Oh, so you have one to spare!' as Jamie rose and kissed her.

'I have plenty to spare,' said Jamie, kissing her again.

'I have just heard strange news in the stables,' she said. 'Hutton, the groom, thinks that he saw Captain Chandler making his way through the woods to the shore. Already there was a story that a boat has been hired to take somebody out to sea. No name has been given.'

'Chandler! said Liz, with sparkling eyes.

'The man you pinned to his saddle,' said Jamie.

183

'Don't say that,' said Molly. 'It will only make her faint all over again!'

'Let us go and find Chandler before he gets into that boat,' said Jamie.

'Hutton can probably help,' said Molly. In a moment, she was leading the way to the stableyard.

'Where are you going?' said Kate, who had suddenly appeared. Liz told her in some breathless words and they pressed on. At the last moment, two things happened, simultaneously. Alan Beaton emerged from the study where he had been closeted with Sir Ferdinand, and Jane, exquisitely dressed, coiffed and painted – a vision of cool and calculated loveliness – appeared at the foot of the stairs.

Jamie was conscious that, in a flash as it were, something had happened between his friend, the red-haired, ambitious young business adventurer from Scotland, and the coolest, the most remote, the most consciously beautiful of the Vane sisters. But he had no time just then to work out the implications of the encounter.

Molly was calling out for Hutton. Kate was picking up a cloak and slipping it round her shoulders. And Liz, with dancing eyes, was pulling him into the cold evening air.

Hutton's news turned out to be more doubtful than Molly had reported. 'Might have been he, miss,' he said, scratching his head. 'Dunno about that. But somebody thought so. Could have been all of a mistake, see what I mean.'

He spoke of a cove that anybody might use who wanted to leave the country, quiet-like – 'Maybe I shouldn't say it, miss.' They saddled horses and made off at the trot, two by two, in the direction he indicated. 'But what makes you think it will be tonight he wants to leave the country?' asked Hutton.

They had no idea, until Liz said, 'Jamie is sure it will be tonight and Jamie is a gypsy.'

'He is no more of a gypsy than I am,' said Alan Beaton, indignantly. But nobody listened to him. At the last minute, Lady Vane appeared in the doorway.

'Mad,' she said, throwing up her hands. 'All mad! And that young Frenchman – he always makes them worse.'

'This is a wild-goose chase,' said Alan, as they rode along.

'But the geese are swans,' said Jamie. 'Tell me, have you and Sir Ferdinand decided anything?'

Alan nodded. 'He is going into the City to see if he can find enough money. Then he will found a company of Virginia, with a charter from the Queen, the *Queen*, no less!! Lord Southampton will venture a thousand pounds, plus a ship he has down at Plymouth. I and the skipper of *The Dark Lady* will be in for a hundred each. How about you, James?'

'Me?'

'Yes. Don't you want a slice of the New World?'

Without waiting for an answer, Alan cantered ahead. At that moment, Jamie saw that Jane, frowning and more haughty than usual, was uttering some words out of the side of her mouth to Liz.

In a few minutes the youngest of the Vane girls slipped back. Her fat little pony was bounding alongside Jamie's horse.

'What did she say just now?' he asked.

'Jane? My beautiful sister?'

'Yes.'

'She thinks that your friend Alan has a very inelegant seat on a horse.'

Jamie looked. Jane was right. And she herself rode like a goddess.

'You will see. He will improve very quickly,' he said. 'Like to bet?'

'Isn't love wonderful,' sighed Liz.

She gave her pony a touch of the whip and, in a second, had overtaken the other three girls up in front.

Alan dropped back beside Jamie.

'About the New World,' Jamie said.

'Yes,' said Alan.

Just then Jamie's eye registered the fact that the four girls riding in front had shaken their mounts into a canter.

'They've spotted something,' he said, excitedly. 'Aren't these Vane girls marvellous, Alan? I'd like to marry them all.'

'There's one of them you won't marry, my lad,' said Alan, in a hard, flat voice that made Jamie look round sharply. He was about to say something when he decided not to. Alan was looking back at him out of a face of granite.

185

'Yes,' said Alan, 'and see that you remember it.' Never had his hair looked so red.

Jamie kicked his horse into a hard gallop. So it was serious! Alan Beaton and – of all the wonders – Jane Vane! Jane for a thousand crowns! That look which he had surprised passing between them in the hall of Vane House! It had been the summons to surrender and, at the same time, the submission of the garrison! Of all the remarkable things, that this money-grabbing Scotsman, with the cold, blue eyes and the hot, red hair, and a mind like an abacus – that he should be swept off his feet by the haughty, self-sufficient Jane and – more extraordinary still – that he should evoke a response from her! How puzzling, how unexpected, and how wonderful life was! As if one needed the New World!

Before him a stretch of open country sloped gently down to the sea. There were green flecks of meadow and tawny patches of bogland. One of the girls – Liz – waved her whip. Jamie thought she was pointing at two figures on a spit of sand in the distance.

'Virginia,' he said, 'and Jane Vane as well! You grasping devil!'

Alan nodded and grinned back at him. For the first time, Jamie thought that he saw something appealing in his friend's face, a softness about the mouth, a warmth in those blue eyes. At that moment there was something about Alan that reminded him of his sister, Mary Beaton.

'Those two on the sands,' said Alan. 'They are running for cover to the trees. You can be sure they have horses hidden there. But we'll be too late to catch them.'

'We'll see about that,' said Jamie, who had seen a bridle-way snaking through the meadow which offered a chance of heading off the fugitives. But after cantering for a hundred yards he pulled up. Something else had occurred to him. Something he wanted to say, although this was hardly the moment to say it.

On the right the four Vane girls were riding on a course parallel to him heading for the trees.

'Anyhow, it will be years before you can marry her,' he said.

186

'Who says that?' Alan's mount was blowing hard.

'I do, for one,' said Jamie.

'Why?'

'Because she won't be allowed to marry before Miranda marries. Simple as that. You haven't seen Miranda, have you? Then, she'll have to wait for Molly and Kate. They are all older than Jane. Have some sense, boy. These things go by seniority.'

'Not in my life,' said Alan.

Jamie shook his head.

'Take my advice. Wait until you've seen Miranda. She will be the first leaf to fall from the tree. Incidentally, she is the most beautiful of all the Vanes.'

'Do you want to fight, Stuart?' said Alan coldly.

It was time to change the subject.

'I don't think we are going to catch Chandler,' he said. 'What does it matter? If we put that boat out of his reach, we'll have done all that matters.'

Alan was still too angry to speak. But Jamie noticed that he had eased over to the right, nearer to the girls.

They broke into the outlying trees about ten yards apart, their horses stepping high among broken twigs and heaps of dry leaves.

A moment later, Jamie was riding blindly forward, brushing the branches out of his face. The chilling gloom of a winter afternoon brooded over the thicket.

Somewhere to the side, invisible among the trees, he could hear Alan's horse crashing about. And somewhere beyond him, out of sight and audible only as a succession of rustling noises at varying depths of sound, were the Vane girls and Hutton, the groom. And somewhere ahead, God alone knew where, were Chandler and his unknown companion.

He pulled up. He did not know why. Something about the sounds he heard had suggested an abrupt change in the situation. And, a few seconds later, came the sound of a shot deadened by the trees and the dry leaves underfoot. Jamie turned his horse's head towards it and put in his heels hard. His ears told him where to aim for. Instinct made him ride somewhat to the left of that. He knew that none of the Vane

187

girls was carrying a pistol. Did Hutton have one? It was possible, although in the haste of departure he did not think that the groom picked up a firearm.

Suddenly alarmed, Jamie cursed himself for having brought only his dagger with him.

He pulled the blade an inch out of the sheath. The easy movement of the steel reassured him. Ahead of him were cries and answering cries. His horse shied and plunged as another horse went past it, riderless. He thought he had seen it before.

Jamie dismounted. He threw the reins over his horse's head and tied them to the stump of an oak. Then he went forward on foot, dagger at the ready. A few steps farther on he stopped. Someone was coming towards him, breaking through the branches in a hurry. There he was. A man holding a pistol and a naked sword. A man limping badly. A man whose face was convulsed with some wild passion, of fear or rage. Who could say? The thin, disdainful mouth twisted the long yellow cheeks paler than they were when he had seen them before.

'Good evening, Captain Chandler,' said Jamie.

For a second Chandler did not recognize him. Then he snarled. He threw his pistol away and came in fast with his sword-point held low.

'You!' he said. 'You!'

There are moments in life, thought Jamie, when pride is not only a sin but a mistake. This is one of them. He jumped quickly to one side, putting the thorns of a bramble bush between him and Chandler's rush. He reckoned that he only needed to gain a few seconds of time and that Chandler would be in a hurry and might make a mistake. An instant later, he realized how optimistic he had been. A professional killer of Chandler's experience did not make mistakes in a situation of this kind.

A murderous glint appeared in his pale eyes when he grasped the fact that Jamie had nothing to defend himself with but his little dagger and his agility.

The blade came, in fact, aimed as was to be expected at the area just below the breast bone. Chandler meant to finish the job then and there. Jamie moved an inch to the side and parried, thanking God his dagger had a steel guard. The point

188

touched the cloth of his doublet as it passed. Once was luck.

Chandler came on again, fast. Jamie did not like the jerky look in his eye. It would be nice to think that it meant Chandler was not yet better of the wound Liz had given him. But it was not a moment for hope. Jamie saved himself from the second thrust by an ungainly movement of the dagger across his body. Twice was the act of God. Thrice would be – ?

Don't deceive yourself, James. There will be no thrice. Already he could feel the cold damp breaking out on his brow. There was only one thing to do – go on, dancing on one foot and the other, hoping that help would come in time.

'Why are you bleeding, Captain?' he said. 'Look at your leg.' He jerked a thumb towards the thigh that had felt Liz's little knife.

Chandler sneered but for a flash his glance went down. For a flash, but it was long enough. Jamie was inside the captain's guard and his dagger was at the captain's belly.

'Drop the blade, Chandler,' he said, 'or have six inches of this in your guts.'

Chandler looked at him, his face working.

'Clever bastard,' he said.

Jamie pressed the dagger point harder against Chandler's body.

'Drop it, Chandler. And let me hear it fall.'

He heard the sword hit the ground. 'Now take a step back, Chandler. And another.' Keeping his eyes on Chandler's face, Jamie stooped. He had underrated the speed with which the captain's boot could move. Jamie's hand went up to shield his face. His dagger fell. Chandler clawed for it but did not get it. Jamie's fist caught him on the side of the neck hard, but not hard enough. Chandler reached for his knees in a diving tackle.

Then he got his feet under him so that he could use his hands on Jamie where it would hurt most. Jamie's fingers closed round his neck, but could not reach the windpipe. The two men writhed savagely together and fell sideways. In falling, Chandler twisted round and got on top. There was a shot from somewhere. Jamie felt Chandler scramble to his feet. A moment later, Jamie was looking up at Alan with a smoking pistol in his hand.

189

'I'll kill him. I'll kill the swine.' Alan was white and his voice shook with indignation. His eyes blazed with murder. 'Do you know what he's done? Startled the horses. One of the girls fell off and hurt herself. By God, he is a cowardly dog.'

It did not seem too dastardly but he knew that special allowance must be made for Alan's feelings.

'Which one?' said Jamie.

But by that time Alan was some yards away, running through the trees.

'Look out,' said Jamie. 'He has a sword.'

'So have I.'

Yes, thought Jamie, but he is a professional. But he said nothing. After all, that blue glare in Alan's eyes might be worth something in a fight. Somewhere ahead, he could hear Chandler crashing through the dead branches underfoot. There was a horse loose in the wood. The fugitive might mount it. At that time, Jamie thought of his own horse lightly tethered not far away. He hurried towards it. The Vane girls crowded forward leading their horses. 'It's Jane,' said Kate. 'She was thrown when her horse reared.'

'And hurt – how badly?'

'Not badly, I think. Her shoulder struck a tree as she fell. We'll take her to the surgeon now.'

Jamie heard the sound of a horse galloping through the soft ground not far away.

'I think Chandler has stolen her horse,' he said.

Alan appeared. 'He has gone. Take your horse, James. Go after him. And don't fail to bring him back alive.'

'No. Jane will need the horse to go to the surgeon.'

'She will take my horse,' said Alan flatly.

And there was Jane, pale but quite composed, not a strand of her hair out of place. She was holding one arm to her side.

'It is nothing at all,' she said.

Jamie noticed that she did not look once at Alan, who went to fetch his horse.

'Poor man,' said Liz pathetically. 'And he can't marry her.'

Jamie looked at her in amazement.

190

'He's going to marry her, darling,' he said.

'One strange thing, sir,' It was Hutton, the groom, who was talking.

'Go on.'

'We've come on a house in the forest, well-hidden by the trees. Looks nothing at all from the outside. A charcoal burner's hut, thinks I. But no. I looked inside.'

'What did you find?'

'Better come over and look for yourself, sir.'

The hut was not far off. Inside, it was well-stocked: weapons, some sea clothes, a larder in which there was enough food to keep several men for weeks, half a dozen bunks with bedding.

'What do you think Hutton?' said Jamie, after he had glanced round.

The groom shrugged. 'Dunno, sir. Be a nice place to hide, if anybody wanted to hide.'

'Somebody's been hiding lately,' said Jamie. 'Look at this.' From under one of the mattresses he pulled out a bundle of papers covered with writing. They were in neither English nor French. They might have been in Spanish. Every now and then the calligraphy was interrupted by figures.

Letters in cypher.

'Looks like you've stumbled on something, Hutton.'

'That's not all, sir. Have you seen this?'

He led the way out to a clearing on a patch of rising ground. Somebody had built a bonfire there all ready for kindling. They climbed up to it and Jamie found that, when he stood beside the heap of dry wood, he was looking over a wide stretch of sea.

'A beacon,' he said.

'As you might say,' said Hutton. 'Used to be something of that kind hereabouts, that year the Spanish were going to come.'

'We'll ride back and have a word with Sir Ferdinand.'

'That captain, sir. He's gone off with Miss Jane's horse, one of the best in the stable,' said Hutton bitterly.

When they told Sir Ferdinand, he raised his white eyebrows and rubbed his chubby freckled hands together. After a minute he took his eyes from Jamie's and looked into the

191

distance. It seemed that he had heard a story of this kind many times before. Perhaps he had.

At last, 'Spies,' he said, 'slipping in and out of the country. Goes on all the time. They were using that hut as a port of call. I'll send a man to take the letters up to Greenwich. Sir Robert should be able to put names to those figures you see. That's his job, ain't it. Our job, my boy is to deal with Spinola's galleys.'

'Yes,' said Jamie.

Sir Ferdinand nodded. 'I'll have a guard put on this bonfire tonight so there will be nobody signalling to the Spaniards from hereabouts. Lucky that we came over from the ship when we did. And now – time we were on our way.' He looked up at the sky already dusted with faint stars. 'Should be good weather for a fight. Not much wind. No moon. Reckon it's time we were at the ships, boy. Where's that Scots fellow, Beaton?'

'He has been taking Miss Jane to the surgeon, sir.'

'Has he, by God! What on earth for?'

They rode quickly to the water's edge where, at the last minute, a courier appeared, wearing a livery which everyone treated with respect. The rider dismounted and muttered something to one of the grooms. Jamie found that people were looking at him:

'Stuart. Stuart.'

A sealed packet was put into his hand.

'I'll follow in a minute, Sir Ferdinand.'

He tore open the seals and read with difficulty, for by that time the light was feeble. Also, the writing was unfamiliar.

Dear James Stuart,

Edward Carey tells me that I may hope to reach you at this ship which is lying somewhere off our coast – somewhere it has no right to be, I am sure. Long ago you said we were like one another, 'of the same tribe' was that not it? And we are. But something else divides us, dear James. We belong to different ages. You are a barbarian. I am not. What I am – that is another matter. In the ocean of history, two fish are swimming. They are very far apart. And it was only chance that they met . . .

The queen has fallen in love with you. I know this is so

192

because she spends so much time telling us girls how awful you are. There is no rogue so bad as a Scots rogue, it seems. And all the time she is laughing. What it means is that it would be high treason for anyone to fall in love with you. So do not tempt me. You know how weak I am.

By the way, I have decided to marry. Don't you think it is time? He will be rich, handsome, a peer of the realm, or, better still, the eldest son of a peer. Most important of all, he will admire my poems. You never showed the slightest interest in them.

When I am a married woman, I shall be allowed to see you again. Then Her Majesty cannot object and nobody else will.

You may ask what is the purpose of this letter? Simple. Treason. It is to tell you that, whatever the queen may have said, she is willing for you to come back. But will Mr Secretary agree?

That, dear James, is *your* problem.

M.V.

I cannot tell you with what impatience I look forward to being married.

Jamie put the letter in his pocket and walked quickly to the quayside where the boat was waiting to row him across to *The Dark Lady*. He looked more thoughtful than usual.

Crisis in The Trinidad

Vane had dispatched two fisher boats which he owned with orders to lie out in the estuary and signal if any strange naval craft were seen approaching the Thames. In addition, they were to intercept any suspicious boat seen leaving the shore. A look-out was posted in the crow's nest of the *Rosebud* which, with *The Dark Lady* beside her, lay behind a sandbank. From the estuary, the two ships would be scarcely visible. Lawrence Fletcher threw himself with enthusiasm into the work of planning the forthcoming action.

When he came on board, Jamie was puzzled to see that the actor was arranging a white scarf so that it hung down his back. 'They must see their leader,' Fletcher explained. A long experience of night actions in the wars of Flanders was adduced to support the costume. As for weapons, he had chosen for himself a pike of medium length. 'Very convenient for this kind of work.'

Alistair MacIan was still brooding in wonder over a handful of fire arrows which Vane had brought on board. The Highlander had never seen such instruments of destruction.

'Diabolical,' he said in delight. 'Fiendish! The last word in modern science!'

Jamie found a rusty breastplate and steel cap among Sir Ferdinand's armoury which fitted him perfectly. He looked forward to the coming fight with a fairly easy mind. He heard someone speaking from far above, from heaven maybe.

'A light at sea.'

'Acknowledge it, man,' said a voice which seemed to come from lower down.

'Aye, aye, sir.'

'After that, count the flashes...'

'One ... two ... three ... four ... five ... six.'

'Six, by God! Spinola has brought his whole fleet with him, said Sir Ferdinand Vane.

Jamie was impelled to take part in the conversation. He said, 'I knew he would try it. This is the last moonless night for a month. And no sea worth talking about.'

By this time *The Dark Lady* was in a hubbub. A whistle was blowing; bare feet were scampering about her deck, ropes were being pulled. Very soon she was nosing her way cautiously into the open water of the estuary close behind *Rosebud*. They were going to take up position in the estuary so that the galleys, which had passed westwards towards the inner river, could not return to the open sea without dealing with the two ships. There was a small wind, just enough to keep the two ships moving. After half an hour, *Rosebud* let an anchor down. *The Dark Lady* followed suit.

By that time the two were in the middle of the fairway which runs out to sea close to the Essex coast.

There followed hours of watchfulness, during which men nodded off where they lay on the decks. It ended when a whistle was blown. Everybody talked at once.

'There it is! Look at that!'

Somewhere to the east a red fire blew up. A distant explosion shook over the water. The anchors were brought up.

Jamie, asleep on deck like others, rubbed his eyelids apart, and peered into the darkness. After this came a long and chilly wait. Sometimes they thought they heard the sound of gunfire. Far off, a small eye of flame opened and shut which might have been the burst of a cannon. Nobody could be sure. After a time they settled down, chilly and stiff, to wait. There was always the disagreeable chance that the galleys would take the southern route to the open sea and avoid an encounter.

The water stayed calm. The wind was no more than a cold

breath above the deck. Jamie thought that he could imagine a faint lightening in the sky to the east. About then, a whistle blew.

Men stumbled to their feet, shaking themselves like bears. A hush fell. 'Listen!' After a bit, he could hear the steady beat of oars, growing louder. Spinola's galleys had failed to surprise the guardship. Now, without too much haste, in good order, they were making for the sea. From somewhere below, a rumbling noise. The guns were being run out.

Looking out, he could see that the two ships were lying, a cable length apart, across the central channel of the fairway.

A shout echoed across the water. *Rosebud*'s guns spoke first. It was no more than a sharp warning. They were still out of range of the enemy. He could hear deep splashes in the water. A pause during which Jamie guessed that the admiral of the galleys was sizing up this new adversary.

Peering into the darkness he saw the winking of lights – coloured sparks – signal rockets, in all likelihood. The attack followed within minutes. The galleys had an advantage which they meant to use. At that hour of the morning they would see their enemies silhouetted against the first, ghostly light of morning. The oars, surging more and more loudly, were driven at the high speed of imminent attack.

Any minute now, Jamie knew, the slaves would clash their chains, warning that the collision was imminent. The cannon in the bow of the foremost galley – for he was sure that in this narrow seaway they would attack in line – would discharge their fivefold load of iron.

Ah! there it was! The rough music of the brandished fetters came across the water, thin and sinister. The deck under Jamie's feet heaved as *The Dark Lady* loosed her first broadside. Somewhere sailors were cheering. Somewhere out there, between him and the dark English coast, other cannon were barking into action.

Alistair came up, cursing in a sad voice.

'I can see nothing, James. For God's sake – give me a target for my beautiful little bow.'

'Brother, it will come soon enough. You'll see five nasty little red eyes out there. Fire somewhere between them.'

196

If Alistair meant to go on with the discussion, he thought better of it. The first galley fired a salvo. Jamie felt one thud after another on the timbers of *The Dark Lady*. With a high-pitched exultant shout, Alistair launched one of his fire arrows at the looming shadow of the galley. A minute later, there was a splash of flame in the heart of the shadow. 'Did you see that, boy? What science can do! Marvellous. Now watch this.' He fitted another fire arrow.

Under their feet, the culverins belched again. The galleys drew off. Spinola was changing his plan. Jamie could see the signal lights flaring. Now they would gather round the two ships and come into the attack like a swarm of wasps from every side.

Seamen ran past him, handling a coil of rope. The time had come to lash the ships together. The fight was moving to its crisis. There was now enough light to add shadowy and inexplicable movements to the confusions of the night.

Black shapes swept past for a second, and then were swallowed up in the darkness. The curved arc of a lateen sail startled Jamie. It was caught in outline by a flash of spectral light in the sky and vanished again. At a masthead lamps winked in neat formations of red and green. For a moment the gunfire hesitated and the rumble of gun trucks slackened and then ceased.

Hoarse and desperate shouts came from the teams at work lashing the two ships together. From the deck of the *Rosebud* came a torrent of instructions, plentifully interspersed with curses, on how the *Lady* should be handled so that the L-formation vital for this kind of action should be achieved.

'Bring her to the wind on the port tack.' He thought that he recognized Sir Ferdinand's voice from the deck of the *Rosebud*. 'Port a little.'

He wondered vaguely how a ship could be brought to the wind when there was hardly enough wind to move a dead leaf. Somebody, who seemed to be of much the same mind, shouted back in German something that was either a curse or a protest. The unreason born of fear or hatred, in which battles are fought, sounded in men's voices.

All of a sudden the ship jarred from repeated shocks as

197

the culverins on the gundeck prodded the night in anger. Overhead, missiles passed in quick intakes of air. Jamie, kneeling behind a stout balk of timber, crouched still lower. Soon the collision must come which would give him and his comrades, most of them flat beside him on the deck, their opportunity.

The gunners, who would be able to see better than he could, had lowered the muzzles of their culverins. They were reaping a harvest of oars to judge by the clatter of broken wood. Meanwhile, the cables groaned for'ard as they held the lurching shuddering ships together.

Beside him Alistair MacIan, crooning to himself, was aiming smouldering shafts with cool exactness. That's a man who finds pleasure in his work, Jamie thought with envy, as he noted the rapt smile on the Highlander's face. At that moment Alistair gave a warning cry and ducked.

An instant later, a shuddering crash tilted the ship and seemed to throw her backwards. One of the galleys had broken through the curtain of gunfire. The *Lady* staggered. Her culverins were silent. Jamie could guess why. It did not need much imagination to picture the chaos on the gundeck. He waited for a torrent of armed men, clad in steel, holding the black menace of the long Spanish pikes, to pour on to the deck beside him. Pulling his cap further down over his brows, he rose to his feet.

Alistair had laid his bow on the deck and had drawn his claymore. He was folding his plaid carefully over one forearm. Close beside him, three other tall Highlanders stood ready. Further along, Lawrence Fletcher, with a pike poised in his grasp, arranged the white scarf at his back.

'You have never met those Spaniards before, I believe,' he remarked. 'They are good enough soldiers, but deliberate – slow in their thinking! All that we need to repel them is speed.'

Jamie noticed that, while he uttered the word 'speed', Fletcher's pace had slowed down. What a mixture of good sense and bravado! The good sense, Jamie thought, was more likely to prevail if the bravado was allowed its fling.

Time passed. It seemed that the galley had lurched away

198

into the darkness. Jamie waited, listening to the culverins which for a minute were firing more slowly.

'What is that you are singing?' asked Alistair MacIan irritably. After a moment, Jamie realized that the question was being put to him.

'Singing?' he said in amazement.

'Just a minute ago, when the ship hit us.'

'Yes,' said one of the Highlanders. 'Yes. There was certainly a song.'

'In French,' said Alistair, severely.

'French?'

'A thing like that might put a man off!' Alistair complained. 'You might have put *me* off! In a battle I must have all my faculties concentrated.'

Jamie was as much irritated by his companion's egotism as by his delusions. However, before he could retort, the Highlander had picked up his bow and sent another shaft into the darkness. Bullets were passing in quick rushes of wind.

It could not be denied that Alistair was one of those natural optimists who hide the conviction that no harm can come to him behind a mask of fatalistic philosophy! It would be a waste of time to duck a bullet which destiny intended for you. Besides, it would be undignified, and MacIan had extravagant ideas about how a gentleman of family should behave under fire.

'There you are again!' exclaimed Alistair bitterly.

'Again what?'

'Singing! Sounds to me like a song for children.'

Jamie was about to retort in annoyance when all voices were drowned by a shattering noise like a high-pitched clap of thunder. On the far side of the ship a concussion followed that threw them to the deck. The *Lady* had collided with another vessel. Jamie found himself looking from close up at the sternworks of a galley. Amid a mass of carving he read a name. By this time there was enough light for that. It was glimmering in golden letters: *Trinidad*.

'It's mine!' he cried, and balanced on the poop rail before throwing himself recklessly forward. At that moment the two

199

ships worked uneasily against one another with the movement of the sea. The moment had come to act.

He caught the woodwork of the stern gallery and pulled himself aboard the Spaniard. For a moment he thought the gallery would give way under his weight. But it held fast. After him, shouting Gaelic protests or curses, came Alistair.

'What the devil are you doing?' he demanded.

'Taking this ship, that's what,' said Jamie.

'You're mad. I always knew it.'

'We're going to make you fast with a grapnel,' came a voice from the *Lady*. Jamie thought it was Alan talking. The iron prongs were swung and thrown. At the second throw, they caught on a carved piece of the galley's sternworks.

For a second or two Jamie and Alistair stood alone on the galley. It seemed that the Spaniards had not observed them so far.

One after another, Alistair's Highlanders climbed to join them.

'Where might we be going, Alistair MacIan,' one of them asked, standing precariously on the gallery.

'Ask his lordship,' said Alistair sourly, nodding at Jamie.

The two Highlanders stood grinning at one another like cats. A third man was on the deck below ready to climb. But Jamie felt the gallery crack ominously below them.

'Time for shelter,' he said, and smashed in a cabin window with the hilt of his sword. Head first, they dived inside, one after another. Jamie heard noise below which told him that the rest of the storming party was following in the darkness. A moment after, Lawrence Fletcher put a head in at the window.

'Who do you think is the leader of this assault?' he demanded indignantly.

'You are,' said Jamie. 'Go ahead, Sergeant.'

At that moment trumpets sounded on the galley and drums beat the call to arms. The cabin door opened and an arm holding a lantern appeared. A claymore flashed. The lantern pitched forward. Blackness returned and a smell of oil. An unseen man screamed with pain.

'No time to lose!' said Jamie, moving to the door. 'After you, Sergeant.'

200

Outside, there was a loud crack followed by shouts which grew fainter rapidly. The grapnel rope had parted. The two ships swayed apart. Jamie remembered something. He swung round and put his head out of the window. He shouted between his hands, 'Alan! Look after my signboard. Remember? Jacques, Escrime.'

But at his elbow somebody was trying to tell him something. It was the groom, holding up an oblong parcel. Jamie guessed that it was the signboard which Tom was going to use as a buckler. Jamie laughed. The groom was good. Through the smashed window he could see that the lights of *The Dark Lady* were growing smaller second by second.

A clamour of voices, a clash of steel. He turned to meet the crisis in *The Trinidad*.

Haste! Haste! Post Haste!

One sealed missive was enclosed within the other. The outer was superscribed 'Haste! Haste! Post Haste. Haste! For life. For life,' and addressed to The Secretary, Greenwich Palace. It ran:

To the Right Honourable and my very good friend, Sir Robert Cecil Kt. Her Majesty's Principal Secretary of State.
Sir, The enclosed is for the eyes of Her Blessed Majesty alone.
Your obedient servant, F. Vane.
At sea.

The inner letter:

To the Queen's Most Excellent Majesty.
Madam. In the early morning of the 10th inst. I was in my vessel the *Rosebud* about one league S.S.E. of the Essex coast in the company of an Easterling, *The Dark Lady*; the sea was slight, a breeze blowing almost due W. No moon. We were thinking ill of no man and expecting none when, without warning or provocation, we were attacked by 6 (six) galleys wearing the Spanish colours and commanded, as I believe, by one Frederico Spinola, bearing the commission of the King of Spain. The attack of this malicious enemy seemed to come from all sides at once but, the alarm being given, the drums beat to quarters and the two ships delivered a prompt and lively fire.

Thanks to the interposition of Divine Providence, they were disposed in such a manner as to maintain a continuous defence no matter from what direction the attack of those miscreants might come. After some hours' exchange of gunfire, I am happy to report that the assault was beaten off. One galley was sunk with all hands, another captured and the rest fled in the direction of the Flemish coast pursued by vessels of Your Majesty's Channel Guard which had, in the meantime, arrived on the scene. Casualties in the *Rosebud* and the Easterling were slight, with the following serious exception.

James Stuart, a foolhardy young man of French or Scottish origin, with some equally rash companions boarded one of the galleys. What their purpose was Heaven alone knows. Perhaps to capture the ship. They were mad enough! If so, their design was certainly frustrated and they were carried away when the ships parted. It must be assumed we shall never see them again. Either they are dead or they will suffer the short and cruel life of the galley slave.

Alongside this passage was a marginal note in another hand: 'If this be found true then, at all costs, let it be kept from the K. of Scots. E.'

The letter continued:

In the captured galley, the *San Matthew*, little was found in the way of pillage. An iron chest was opened but contained no bullion.

Marginal note heavily underlined: '*Secretary. Have this matter strictly examined forthwith. E.*'

A small jewel case containing trinkets is being sent to Y.M. by another hand. With humble duty I am

> Your Majesty's loving servant and subject,
> Ferdinand Vane.

'You are Going to Die, Don Alfonso!'

In the small companionway immediately outside the cabin, the stench of the galley struck them in the face like a blow from a dirty sponge. It was as if a hundred polecats were out there; as if they had stepped into a menagerie from which the keepers had fled. All that, with a little whiff of the pest house thrown in. Lawrence Fletcher, who was in the lead, swore and pinched his nose between his fingers.

'Make poetry out of this if you can!' said Jamie.

But it was no moment for talk.

Spaniards crowded in from the open deck outside. In a space not much bigger than two coffins, as Jamie thought, a muddled, horrible, body-to-body fight came into sudden and furious life. It was something between a scuffle and a skirmish, a hurried brutal thing in which fists and knives were handier weapons than swords and pikes.

While he was using his rapier as a dagger, gripping the blade hard, Jamie cut his palm. The blood flowed, warm and copious. A Spaniard lifted a small axe above him. Jamie would have been too late to ward off the blow. But a broad knife flashed into the Spaniard's ribs. Jamie turned. 'It's you!' he said.

It was Tom, the groom, gaping vacantly and gleefully. A butcher's knife. A butcher's cut.

Trampling and pushing, Jamie reached the opening that led from the companionway to the open deck. He found himself looking along the hundred feet coursier of the galley, at a sky

204

studded with dying stars. Here there was cleaner air to breathe and more room to fight in.

He could even begin to fence until he was jostled by someone who came alongside him wielding a pike. Fletcher, grim-faced, silent. Suddenly the Spaniard in front of Jamie was staggering, was gripping his belly with his hands. Then he dropped on his knees. Fletcher's pike had struck him.

Another of the defenders came forward and then, after a minute, vanished. He had lost his foothold and taken a wild leap into the swarming mass of men on the rowing benches below, the gleaming bodies of the slaves who had been keeping the galley in movement through the quiet black waters towards the distant, unseen shores of Spanish Flanders, or neutral France.

The Spaniard was pulled down by vengeful hands lifted from the oars. Fetters clinked. A man's shout was choked into a groan.

Jamie took a deep breath of the strong-smelling air. Behind him, pandemonium had broken out – the fight for the key point of the galley – the cabin from which the craft was steered. If the storming party could win that position, and if he and a handful of men could hold the coursier against the counter-attack that was sure to be launched from the fo'c's'le, then the rest would be all right. But the chances were not good.

At the distant end of the coursier, little sparks of flame appeared. Dull sounds were carried away by the wind. Prudently, he dropped on one knee to await the attack. For a moment the galley seemed to veer helplessly from one side to another. Then it steadied, as if the battle for the helm had been won. It was a moment for hope.

Jamie rose and grabbed the rail of the coursier. He made a funnel of his hands and spoke in all the Spanish he could muster. A shot puffed past his cheek. He bawled into the night and the breeze.

'Brothers, comrades of the slave benches, freedom is at hand! I am one of you. I have the same brand as yours on my shoulder.'

He could sense that already the motion of the ship had

slackened. The oars were coming to stillness as the oarsmen – those driven, straining convicts packed below – listened to him.

'Members of the brotherhood, row on! Before the light of day arrives we shall be on the coast of France. There this galley will be beached, by my orders. And there, by the laws of God and France, you will be free men. Free!'

How much of this oration was understood by his audience he could not tell. The expression on the dull, brutalized faces below him did not alter perceptibly. A minute afterwards, he thought that the stroke of the oars was faster, that more energy had been put into the rhythm of the galley. But he could not be sure. What was more important, just then, was that Alistair MacIan, breathing hard, arrived at his shoulder.

'We have captured the helm,' he said. 'That groom of yours, Tom – what a boy with a knife! Horrible.'

Jamie asked no questions about the struggle which must have taken place in the cabin from which the craft was steered. He kept his eyes fixed on the fo'c's'le, at the other end of the long, empty coursier. From there trouble was going to come.

'Where do we make for?' Alistair asked.

'Make for the French coast. Eastwards. Eastwards.'

There was an outbreak of heavy firing somewhere in the distance across the water. Bright flashes were reflected on the sea. What it meant, he could not guess. Perhaps the ships of the Channel Guard had, at last, wakened up to what was happening and were moving in now that the worst danger to the Thames was past.

He had no opportunity to look more closely into the business. 'Tell them eastwards,' he said to Alistair. 'Then come back.'

Two shots thudded from the fo'c's'le. A blow on his steel-cap made him stagger. But at that range, the metal of the cap he was wearing blunted the force of the bullet. Two men were advancing along the coursier.

Jamie threw off his cloak. The moment had arrived when he needed all the freedom of movement he could get.

The two were running towards him, waving the long whips they carried, the instruments of discipline. They were a muscular and, as far as he could see, an ugly pair. But if they had possessed the beauty of archangels, he would still have thought them a hateful blot upon the fair earth. They were overseers, members of the evil company of torturers and flagellants, and once he had been in their power.

He felt a rush of exultation. He knew he could deal with one adversary at a time on the narrow gangway. And armed only with whips and daggers, they would be no match for his sword. And Alistair would be back at his side at any moment. Probably Lawrence Fletcher as well.

I may not be the best swordsman in Europe he said – Modesty! false modesty! There were moments, and this was one of them, when Jamie thought that he *was*. It seemed that the two men with the whips had much the same idea. They stopped; one edged behind the other, out of reach of his blade. Then the scene changed abruptly. The two overseers were brushed roughly aside. Jamie found himself facing an adversary of a different calibre.

He was a tall, sparely built man in a breastplate of gleaming black steel, inlaid with gold, wearing on his head an Italian morion of the best pattern, product of some workshop in Ferrara. Hard black eyes, drawn together under a frown.

Jamie's heart swelled with pleasure. He looked forward to the combat, although he knew that he would fight better in his shirt. The pity was that he could not take off breastplate, doublet – and shirt as well.

'I know you,' he said in French. 'I know you, Don Alfonso Saavedra. Have you said your prayers? If not, do so now. You are going to die, Don Alfonso!'

Vulgar, Jamie reproached himself. Vulgar, and not at all your style. Boastful and, perhaps, untrue. He may be a better fighter than you are.

But Jamie could not argue against the sublime conviction that he was an executioner sent to exact the penalty for – how much suffering, how many deaths?

The swords crossed with the tremulous notes of steel for which the opening bars of a duel are scored. In a moment, he knew that he was facing a master of the classical style of fencing, a fighter cold, precise and murderous. His blind assurance left him.

James, he said to himself, this is the one occasion in your life when you must make no mistakes. So put aside any idea that you are going to avenge hundreds of poor devils, dead or alive. You are not God's assassin. This is not a crusade, or an artistic display. This is a moment for the hard, exact science of the sword: the timing, the pace, the measuring eye, the mind drained of everything but the imminent crisis, the danger, the *now*!

In the first exchanges, when each was estimating the skill of the other, forming an opinion of his style – and trying to fathom his temperament in search of a clue to what might be expected, Jamie was aware of the gravity with which the Spaniard – for this was certainly a Spaniard and not an Italian – approached the business of killing.

His own first idea was to make it a long fight – he was the younger of the two, and he would last the longer. But in a moment a different thought came into his mind. The sky was growing paler, already the stars were fading. And as the light grew, it would be in his eyes. An argument for quickening the pace!

As it turned out, though, it was Don Alfonso who launched the first attack. After a sudden, furious interchange of strokes which Jamie parried, first easily and then more awkwardly, the Spaniard thrust for his thigh. The point gashed past within a finger's breadth of the flesh, deflected by a lightning flick of his blade. Jamie bounded forward at once with relish in a counter-attack. There was a crescendo of shrill noise before, at last, Don Alfonso extricated himself.

The antagonists withdrew and, for a moment, lowered their points, staring at one another, breathing hard. A silence had fallen which Jamie for a moment could not account for. Then he understood. The oarsmen had stopped rowing to watch the conflict that was going on just over their heads.

Behind the Spaniard and – as Jamie knew without looking round – behind him, men were poised, sword in hand, neither daring nor wishing to interfere while the two champions fought it out. At this moment, something happened that altered the temper of the battle.

Overseers with whips appeared among the slaves. Crack,

crack, crack – 'Get to your duty, carrion' – Jamie remembered enough Spanish to understand. The oars began to move, forward and back, half-heartedly, and then with more vigour.

The churning sound of a war galley moving through the water gained strength. Crack, crack, crack! the long whips hissed and fell. A man groaned.

And James Stuart, with the brand of the slave on his shoulder leapt forward in a white, re-kindled rage, to kill the man in black armour who had once been his gaoler. He was the image of justice, a grim, pale-jawed angel of resolve with a sword which he used as if it were as light as a wand.

One, two, three times the Spaniard parried, twice with ease, the third time with difficulty, before Jamie saw an opening, no wider than a finger. It lasted only a minute fraction of time. He thrust with all the force of his shoulder an inch below the black armour. Don Alfonso staggered. A sigh ran round the ship. The oars had come to a pause once more.

James waited a second, his sword lowered.

'Finish him, man,' he heard Alistair, a foot from his shoulder. Jamie waited. Don Alfonso began to raise his point slowly and then more slowly. He swayed for a moment and fell headlong on to the rowing benches below.

Can dumb cattle turn in a flash into raging beasts? From that moment onwards through life, Jamie believed it. He began to go forward, hesitated. He could hear grim sounds as the slaves trampled their tormentor.

'Stop them,' he said helplessly to the Highlander behind him.

Alistair gave a savage laugh. 'Who are you to deny the slaves their moment of justice?' he asked. 'You don't have to look, Jamie. Here, drink this. It's only Irish, but it's just the medicine for a cold morning.'

'That's no way for a gentleman to die.'

'Maybe not, but it is good enough for a torturer.'

Jamie went to the edge of the coursier and shouted in what he hoped was Spanish.

'Don't touch him, any of you! Or we'll shoot. Keep him alive until we land. Let the French handle him.'

'Drink,' said Alistair. 'This is not the age of chivalry.'

Jamie wiped his lips and took a pull at the deerskin flask that Alistair held out. Immediately afterwards, he had the impression that, somewhere in the lower levels of his brain, he had been given a smart shock.

Alistair nodded. 'Yes? Good stuff, boy!'

'By God, Stuart' – it was Fletcher speaking – 'there was a moment when I thought he had you. I was about to rush to the rescue, but then I thought, the boy is good and will be all the better for experience. You have a pretty style, Stuart – not that style is everything.'

Jamie smiled at him weakly. He jerked his head in the direction of the after quarters of the galley.

'How is it below, Lawrence?'

'How do you think? The ship is all ours. This end of it is all ours. And what can they do?' He nodded at the group of Spaniards on the fo'c's'le.

At that moment there was a loud explosion for'ard and a blow on the timbers behind them. The soldiers in the galley had brought a heavy arquebus into action.

Jamie and Fletcher crouched for cover. Alistair went within and appeared again with his bow. He fired three shafts before scoring a hit on one of the men who were serving the arquebus forward.

'This wind,' he said, with a grimace of apology. 'It disturbs a person's aim.'

The slaves, who had seen the arrow go home, jangled their fetters hideously.

'We had better find cover,' said Jamie.

'We need a map,' said Fletcher. 'A chart. An image of the perils of navigation – shoals, submerged rocks, headlands and havens of refuge, if any. Without something of the kind, we are as good as dead men. But where is it, I ask?'

'Either it's down below in the steering room,' said Jamie, 'or we must trust to luck to lead us to France.'

Alistair, his bow ready, watched the men at the distant end of the coursier.

At sea, the firing was growing fainter. The fight between the other galleys and the English navy was passing into the distance. It was moving farther north. It seemed that the Italian admiral was making an effort to reach Dunkirk before the English galleons overtook him. He would need more than his share of luck, for by this time the wind was freshening.

Jamie could hear its thin whistle sounding at the galley's cabin windows. Nor'-nor'-west. Giving the fleeing ships an extra turn of speed, but causing the most damnable discomfort on the rowing benches when those big smooth green waves came mounting inwards. Discomfort – wet – cold – windy. It would soon be translated into a fading effort by the men who pulled the forty-foot-long sweeps.

When Jamie went out on the deck again, the light had changed. Ahead he could see a dark coastline which grew more distinct every minute. France. He thought that he recognized the windmills above Calais. They would soon have arrived, unless there was trouble from the remnants of *The Trinidad*'s crew. On the whole, he thought not.

The downfall of Don Alfonso, lying unconscious and white-faced under the feet of the slaves, had taken the heart out of his men. And Alistair was always present, wrapped in his plaid, consulting his flask from time to time, with his bow close at hand, a reminder that the desperadoes who had boarded the galley might have something more to say.

'We shall run her ashore on some French beach,' said Jamie. 'The slaves will then be free men –'

'An ill-bred lot they are, James!'

Alistair's lip curled with aristocratic disdain.

'Don't go by their looks. Remember, I was one of them myself a couple of years ago. What I was going to say was that when we beach the ship, the French will take possession of her. Yes, there is no justice in this world, Alistair! No loot for you and me! They will condemn her as a French prize, very likely. So, take my advice and look around for anything that could be hidden and sold to the Calais merchants before any interfering French searchers arrive. There might be wine, jewellery, clothes – this Don Alfonso is rich.'

Alistair looked solemn. After a minute he said, jerking his head towards the fo'c's'le:

'Just take this bow of mine, Jamie, for a few minutes. If

you see any movement from these cattle along there, touch them up with a shot. Don't worry about taking human life. You will probably miss.'

Drifting away to the north across a sea like a well polished pewter plate was the last of the naval fight. The galleys, elegant and nervous were by this time barely visible in the glistening smudge of morning light on the horizon. The English ships, swelling importantly out of a smoky smear, wore the curved breasts of birds. Now and then one of their guns spoke. Jamie thought that, after all, the Spaniards might reach the cover of their home batteries.

Someone behind him gave what sounded like a warning call. The steering of *The Trinidad* was being altered abruptly. A patrol ship – French? – came up from nowhere and slammed a shot across their bows. Indignant words spoken into a trumpet came vaguely across. *The Trinidad* paid no need.

On the deck above him, somebody was jiggling the galley on a tortuous course towards a target which Jamie did not see for a little. A mysterious wave of hope, spreading through the minds of a hundred slaves, lent a new impetus to the ship.

When the land struck them, the impact was a long, grinding crunch which threw him to his knees.

A hundred men rose from the benches shouting one word over and over again. The shout of that mob, resonant with menace, grew in volume every second.

'They want something,' said Alistair. 'What the devil do they want?'

At that moment Jamie understood the strident music of clanking fetters.

'The keys – the keys! They want the keys that will unlock their chains.'

One of the ship's officers would have them – probably one of the group there on the fo'c's'le. He held up a hand and shouted: 'The keys. Hand them over and we'll give you ten minutes to get clear.'

He pointed to the beach.

'Is that France?' asked Alistair.

'It had better be,' he replied.

Somebody was shouting in Spanish. Jamie gathered that the

212

keys for the fetters were somewhere in their part of the ship. Minutes later, he was holding up a huge iron ring loaded with keys before a pack of wild animals, as they seemed to be, yelling ferociously and reaching up with their claws. 'Go down and bring out Don Alfonso,' he shouted in Spanish on the fo'c's'le. 'Hurry, I am going to set the slaves free.' He threw the keys to the wolves.

'They had better hurry if they want to reach Don Alfonso alive,' said Alistair.

'We had better hurry ourselves,' said Jamie. 'Come on, boys.' He jumped into two feet of a cold salt water and floundered up on to the firm, dry sand of France.

To Find a Girl

'The French are a civil kind of people,' said Alistair next morning.

Jamie Stuart snorted. 'They were damned glad to be rid of us,' he said.

The two, along with Alistair's train of Highlanders, had been riding south all morning, after the gates of Calais had opened to them and they had left the town. After thinking Jamie's remarks over, Alistair allowed an aggrieved look to come into his face.

'After all, as Scotsmen, we are their allies. I had an uncle who fought in one of their wars. Uncle Roderick – he had only one weakness, poor man.'

'Still, they think that Scotsmen should pay for their drink like other people,' said Jamie. 'I thought last night you were going to be thrown into the Calais gaol.'

There had been trouble in the town before Lawrence Fletcher was at last given a passage back to England on a Dover packet.

When Jamie had suggested that he, too, might go to Paris, Fletcher's eyebrows were like a declaration of war. 'Paris! They don't even speak English there. One day, I shall go with my touring company. On a civilizing mission!'

'I shall arrange it,' said Jamie. 'I'll write to you.'

Young Tom, the groom, decided that, after all, he would resist Jamie's offer of a trip to Paris, all found. The truth was, he was scared of being among foreigners.

Jamie paid the groom handsomely and received from him the signboard that said, 'Monsieur Jacques. Escrime.'

214

The farewells had gone on well into the night. Sometimes they were friendly, sometimes on the verge of war, with French officers of the law hovering in the background. But the officers had orders, Jamie discovered, to see that all those foreigners who had been involved in the fight with the Spanish galleys were safely out of the town by daybreak.

'How long will it take us to reach there?' asked Alistair, meaning Paris.

'About two days,' said Jamie, meaning three.

'And then, what happens?'

'Then we see if the French army is interested in giving employment to its old allies, the Scots. You could remind them of your Uncle Roderick. They will probably remember him. But you can't be sure. Some people have damned unreliable memories.'

They rode on in silence. Alistair and his friends grew steadily gloomier, and more restless in the saddle. Highlanders are bad horsemen. Jamie had noticed it before. The weather became colder. The wind had swung round to the east and ranged over the bleak landscape with the questing fury of a wolf-pack. From time to time, there was what Alistair called a smirr of rain – a fine icy drizzle which made their chins seek the shelter of fur or plaid. That night they ate well and slept miserably.

It was the following afternoon, when they passed through a countryside broken up with hills and forest land, that the event occurred which took all of them by surprise.

Bunched together and keeping their eyes open on all sides, they had plunged into a dense forest of splendid trees. Here they were out of the wind but snow fell out of a heavy sky in big leisurely flakes. Only by watching the open space between the trees overhead could they hope to stay on the road to the south.

After a time, Alistair pulled his horse up sharply. He held up one hand.

'Riders,' he announced, in a low voice, 'ahead and on either side of the track. Scores of them.'

Listening, Jamie could hear nothing. But the other Highlanders nodded their agreement with Alistair. The party rode

215

on warily, their spirits sinking until Jamie began to hum the tune which was his normal comfort in moments of boredom or anxiety.

'At least you might tell us the words,' Alistair grumbled.

'It has no words,' said Jamie, and sang them.

Other voices joined his. Men supplied grace notes; imitated drums or trumpets at moments that seemed suitable. With one hand gripping their throats, they mimicked the bagpipes; yelled, whistled and went boom-boom with all the cheerfulness imaginable.

'There is a second verse,' shouted Jamie, who had just made one up.

'Go on,' they shouted back. 'Sing it.'

Just as he was about to begin, he realized that the cavalcade had come to a sudden halt. A few yards ahead of them a group of riders had appeared out of the trees. In their midst was a bronzed man with a tremendous hooked nose, bushy eyebrows, glittering eyes and a bristling beard. His face was alive with intelligence and humour.

'*Ventre-saint-gris!*' he said. 'Where did you hear that song, young man?'

Peasant French, French of the far south, French spoken by some country squire, the French of a captain of horse – Good God! Jamie stared, recognized and plucked off his hat. He leapt down from the saddle and bowed in the snow to Henri Quatre, King of France and Navarre!

'From my father, sire,' he said.

'Did you, by God? I last heard it at Ivry. To this day I remember the tune.'

'My father sang it at Ivry,' said Jamie. 'At least, he always said he did.'

The king laughed.

'Old soldiers never lie – and don't always tell the truth, eh? Please be covered. Snow is uncommonly bad for the brain. Would you be kind enough to tell me your name?'

'James Stuart, sire. Scottish – and French.'

The eyebrows rose. The flakes of snow on the beard sparkled.

'James Stuart? Isn't there another man of that name somewhere?'

216

Jamie grinned.

'Perhaps an impostor, Majesty,' he suggested, meeting a luminous gaze under arched eyebrows.

'M'm ... And your companions?'

'They are Scotsmen. Gentlemen who follow the profession of arms.'

The king ran an appraising eye over them. Then, noting the rags, the rusty swords, the hostile blue eyes, he nodded:

'Even in this peaceful land,' he said, 'we can find use for that kind. Come and dine with us, Stuart.'

Alistair MacIan was presented by Jamie as *'le roi des montagnes'*.

'I understand,' said the king. 'I was once King of the Mountains myself.'

Happily, the three other Highlanders, MacDonell, Mac-Lean and MacLeod, were the sons of chiefs. They, too, could sit down at table with the king.

In a grey manor house used as a hunting lodge by some local nobleman, they sat round a crowded table. Jamie noted without surprise that a cluster of dazzling young women were present. He observed, too, that the fashion of displayed bosoms seemed to have spread to France. He had the prudence to address these beauties only in terms of the most distant respect. From one of them, a delicious little brunette, he discovered that the king was on his way to attend the blessing of a new foundling hospital he had endowed.

Jamie raised his hands in admiration.

'What generosity!'

'Yes,' she said, with a kittenish smile, 'more than usual. For the king has supplied not only the hospital but many of the foundlings as well.'

'He has all the virtues,' said James.

'Tell me, who is your friend, the fascinating one?'

'A brigand, madame,' said Jamie, frowning.

For it was, of course, of Alistair she spoke. This new proof that women's taste in some matters could not be relied on filled him with despondency for quite a few minutes.

After a time, MacLean brought out bagpipes and MacLeod danced a sword dance.

217

'The music is frightful,' said the king. 'But the dancing is superb.'

'*Quelles cuisses!*' sighed a young woman sitting near Jamie. Another young woman, sitting opposite her, made a remark in an undertone. Jamie could not catch what she said, but from the laughter that followed he thought that he could guess its general purport. MacLeod was, in fact, an exceptionally well-built young man.

While the conversation was on the subject of dancing, Jamie mentioned to the king that he had danced with the Queen of England. Henri's eyes grew larger. 'At her age – what is she?'

'Sixty-nine, sire.'

'*Incroyable!* The galliard! A dance for girls!'

'I am told that she dances it first thing every morning. For exercise.'

The king questioned Jamie closely about his family.

'So, were it not for one small piece of paper which you have imprudently given to Queen Elizabeth, you might be a king, James!'

'She has promised to pay for that piece of paper.'

Henri looked at him with compassion.

'My boy, that queen does not pay for something she has already got. Be reasonable.'

'Besides, if I had not given it to her, she would have sent me to the Tower – and I never wanted to be a king.'

'Strange,' said the king. 'I always did. And do you know why? Listen, James –'

He intoned. Jamie was reminded of Lawrence Fletcher.

'*Henri, roi de France et de Navarre.*'

The last R was like a roll of kettledrums.

'The rhythm. The vowel sounds! A poem in itself. How could I resist it! Have you no feeling for the power of words, James? So I entered Paris. I was master of a ruined country. But I was King of France!'

He paused. Jamie said nothing. The king leaned forward. He smelt strongly of garlic.

His eyes seemed to search Jamie's face. Looking for what? Once again he changed the course of the talk.

'So your father was one of us that day at Ivry?'

'At Coutras, too, sire.'

'Ah! At Coutras! Our first victory! I remember, there was a troop of Scottish horse under Lord Wemyss. They were there. My cousin Condé was here' – a knife and a salt cellar were placed on the table – 'I was here.' A wineglass marked the place. It reminded Jamie of evenings when his father had fought his battles over again with garrulous old comrades. 'Condé was unhorsed. Then a Scotsman dismounted and gave up his horse to my cousin.'

'That was my father, sire. He told the story often.'

'Your father!' Henri's eyes were round, his eyebrows mocking. 'Then I have been paying a pension all these years to the wrong man... Old soldiers!'

It seemed to Jamie that the king was finding, in his looks, some traces of those ancient days. His mind harked back to something he had said earlier.

'I was king,' said Henri. 'But king at a price? I had changed my church to win the crown. But was not the life of France worth more than my own personal opinion as a man? What do I believe? I am a good Catholic, of course. But – and what did all that matter anyway, compared with bringing this people back from the abyss?

'I have a friend who writes. He is called Montaigne. He said to me one day: "Henri, you are not quite a Protestant and the Guises are not quite Catholics." And what of France? Is she entirely Catholic? I think not. If I am a divided man, I am the best sovereign for a divided people. I am called not to judge but to reconcile . . . In those days, one had to forgive the unforgiveable. On the day I entered Paris, I sought out that virago, that murderess, the queen of the Guises, the Duchess of Montpensier. I wooed her. I charmed her. Was I wrong? . . .'

Jamie smiled and shook his head. He was oddly moved. He was a little drunk. 'Paris is worth a mass,' he said.

The king gave a start. 'Is that original?' he asked.

Jamie shrugged.

The king allowed his glistening eyes to rove over the delicious women at the table. He picked up the hand of the nearest and kissed it. Then he began again.

'So the Queen of England dances every morning? Amazing! As a boy, I had one piece of luck. My grandfather was a crank about exercise, diet, the upbringing of boys. So I grew up like the heather, rough and twisting, something between wire and wood – no beauty! My grandfather would have something in common with that queen . . . Like her, he danced like a madman . . .'

He paused for a moment, looking thoughtful.

'You know, James, there are times when I think I am the first of a new kind of men. Egotism? Maybe, but the thought comes over me – it did so only today. I forget why – men are anxious or angry about things that to me seem utterly trivial. Not simply that I would not go to war for them. I would not cross the street for them! People say that I am too frivolous, too cynical! No doubt. But the truth is I do not care a fig about the things most men alive around me care for passionately.

'That is why I say that I, Henri de Bourbon, am the first of a new race of man – or, at least, of princes. Always excepting that strange old woman in England.'

Something like awe came into his voice. 'God, what an artist!' he said, and emptied his wineglass at a gulp.

He clapped his hands. Silence was instant.

'Music,' he said. 'Monsieur Stuart will now dance the galliard. James, choose which of those ladies you wish to be your partner.'

'As I wish to dance with them all,' said James, 'will Your Majesty have the kindness to choose for me?'

'Before the night is over, I promise you will dance with them all,' said the king. 'Begin with the lady beside you. She is said to have the prettiest breasts in France.'

'Some things a man must find out for himself,' said James, rising from the table and bowing to his neighbour. Already he heard a young woman with flashing dark eyes asking Alistair to explain to her how his plaid was fastened.

'To begin with, it is best to lie on the floor,' Alistair was saying.

Music began.

*

James pulled up. Alistair, doing the same beside him, said something heartfelt in Gaelic. They had come to the summit of Montmartre, to the convents and the windmills that hung above the valley. Below, almost under their feet as it seemed, a shining river snaked away to the west. Islands divided it. Three bridges crossed it. The spires of churches and palaces rose out of a great smear of buildings. Beyond the river the land swept upwards, so as to encircle a vast, shallow, densely populated bowl. The light, at once soft and disturbing, hung over it all, shining through the faint, mauve haze of smoke vibrating.

'Paris,' said Jamie, making a polite gesture of proprietorship.

Alistair, humped ungracefully over his saddle, said something which could not be understood and might be either admiration or horror.

'Do we take it?' he asked with a shrewd sideways look, and a hand swung out, taking in the whole vista before them. 'Big enough,' he said.

Jamie shook his head.

'It's mine already,' he said.

'Selfish,' said Alistair, and turned to those innocent, wondering, unfrightened Highlanders who had come all the way from some lost glens, driven by the congenital madness of their kind to see the world.

It was time to ride on down the steep hill which, as Jamie remembered from reconnaissance exercises with his class at Antoine de Pluvinel's Academy, would grow steeper as it descended. Soon he would smell that special piercing smell made up of charcoal, herbs, dung and cheap wine which was Paris. It was the end of a long detour and the beginning of — what?

He thought of a letter he had written to that beautiful girl, Mary Beaton, who had, more than any girl he had known, more even than Miranda Vane, the power to allure and rebuff simultaneously — to allure without being aware of it, to rebuff by a cool cunning that was as far from coldness as you could imagine — how could one tell?

She was down there now, somewhere in that maze of roofs,

enticing French marquises, repelling princes of the blood royal, and probably being seduced by some charming penniless cad from Gascony with nothing to his name but a languishing eye and a gift for timely silences.

It would not be Jamie's fault if things went wrong. Reluctantly, he did not think they would. But how was he to be sure? The Beatons were full of surprises. Who would ever have thought that Alan Beaton would fall victim to that cool beauty, Jane Vane? No, there was more in the Beatons than appeared on the surface!

As for himself, he had realized in time that girls were no good to an ambitious, sagacious young man making his way in the world. They deflected his aim. They took up the time, thought, energy which he should be giving to more important matters. In short, he had been wise to give them up . . . Last night? . . . No, that did not count. The occasion was unique.

By an untimely coincidence, Jamie had a vivid picture of the King of France and Navarre as, with a predatory gleam in his eye, he had bent over the hand of a beautiful young woman. Girls – they had not kept Henri from a throne! There was suddenly a light in Jamie's eye. He pulled off his hat and shook his glistening curls in the wind. Then he startled his horse with the savagery of his spurs.

'Here!' cried Alistair in alarm. 'Where are you going to, Jamie?'

But they had pulled up in front of the Porte Montmartre and the sudden unleashing of noise from the city pent up behind it before he answered.

'To find a girl,' said Jamie, throwing his hat into the air.